the start
of me and
you

Books by Emery Lord

The Start of Me and You
When We Collided
The Names They Gave Us

the start of me and you

EMERY LORD

BLOOMSBURY

LONDON OXFORD NEW YORK NEW DELHI SYDNEY

Bloomsbury Publishing, London, Oxford, New York, New Delhi and Sydney

First published in Great Britain in August 2017 by Bloomsbury Publishing Plc
50 Bedford Square, London WC1B 3DP

First published in the USA in March 2015 by Bloomsbury Children's Books
1385 Broadway, New York, New York 10018

www.bloomsbury.com
www.emerylord.com

A CIP catalogue record for this book is available from the British Library

ISBN 978 1 4088 8837 7

Typeset by Westchester Publishing Services
Printed and bound in Great Britain by CPI Group (UK) Ltd, Croydon CR0 4YY

1 3 5 7 9 10 8 6 4 2

To J (for that year, for every year, for everything)

Chapter One

Of all the places to have something memorable happen to you, Oakhurst, Indiana, had to be one of the worst. Our town was too big for people to know everything about you, but just small enough for them to clench down on one defining moment like teeth clamped on prey. Won the spelling bee in fourth grade? You are Dictionary Girl forever. Laughed a little too hard in sixth grade? You will still be the Guy Who Peed His Pants as you walk across the stage to receive your diploma.

And I was the Girl Whose Boyfriend Drowned.

The day before our junior year began, Tessa sat across from me in our booth at Alcott's Books and Beans, reading while we hid from the August heat. I sucked down the last of my iced coffee and leaned back.

"I'm gonna look around before we have to go," I said.

"Okay." She didn't glance up. Her skin had soaked up the summer sun so that she glowed from the inside out, tan skin disguising the only feature we shared—our freckles. Mine were more pronounced than ever, scatters of pinpoints against my still-pale skin.

I glanced back over each shoulder as I scanned the shelves for *TV Writers' Boot Camp*. No one but my grandmother knew I'd been slowly but surely writing a script for my favorite show, *The Mission District*, about a plucky father-daughter duo running a diner in San Francisco. The script occupied the small, secret spaces of my days, though I'd never planned to *do* anything with it. At least I hadn't until I discovered a summer screen-writing program at New York University. There were a hundred reasons I shouldn't apply—too expensive, too improbable that I'd get in, and too impossible that my mom would agree to it before next summer. Still, I kept editing the script, almost compulsively.

Moments before flagging down an employee to help me find the book, I noticed a woman beelining toward me. I recognized her—the mom of someone in my grade, though I couldn't remember whom. By the time she made eye contact with me, it was too late to run off. And to make matters worse, I could sense someone on my other side, surveying the poetry and plays section—someone who would witness every awkward moment heading my way.

"Hello, Paige. How are you?" Adjusting the sensible purse on her shoulder, she gave me That Look, full of pity. You'd think, given the diversity of the human population, that we would have come up with multiple facial expressions for sympathy. But no. There's one: eyebrows and mouth downturned, head tilted like a curious bird.

That's all it took. Aaron's grinning face flashed in my mind, an expression that meant he was up to something. The ache of his absence throbbed in the center of my chest, as real as any physical pain I'd ever felt. Just as quickly, the guilt entered my bloodstream like a toxin. There I was, clinging to the scraps of happiness that I could finally feel again: coffee and books and an afternoon with my best friend. What right did I have, when he was gone?

"Fine, thank you," I said. I'd seen That Look on hundreds of faces in the year since Aaron died. People had no idea what it did to me, how it brought back feelings in sharp pangs.

The woman forged on with that grim-but-caring smile. "I heard the school built a garden to commemorate Aaron. That's so nice. I read an article in the paper that . . ."

She kept talking, but her voice fuzzed over as I fought off memories of the garden dedication ceremony, the smell of mulch and springtime. The whole sophomore class was herded outside for it last April. Tessa, Kayleigh, and Morgan stood tightly around me, like they could physically shield me from all the stares. Aaron's parents and brother shook hands with school-board members and dabbed at tears. The principal said a few words. He'd asked me to speak as well, but I said it should be Clark Driscoll, Aaron's best friend.

". . . a fitting tribute, I think," the woman concluded, finally.

"Yes," I said. "Very fitting."

"Well, tell your mom I said hello."

"Will do." This fib seemed more polite than asking her name. I forced a smile as she walked away.

As always, I felt like a fraud, accepting condolences from strangers. Aaron Rosenthal and I met after my fifteenth birthday, and we went out for two months. Compared to his parents and friends, I barely knew him. I knew the good things—how he did goofy stuff just to make me laugh. How he used to lace our fingers together as we walked, squeezing my hand when he was excited about something. And he was *always* excited about something—no tough-guy smoke screen like other guys in our grade. Of course, he probably got grumpy sometimes. I just didn't know him long enough or well enough to see it.

I mourned for his life, but I also mourned, selfishly, for myself. The first boy to really notice me drowned in a freak accident, and I would never know the whole of him. The idea of us still hung in the air, but we'd never be more than a few golden memories and a bundle of what-ifs. How do you find closure in that—especially when strangers treat you like a widow to a devoted husband? In post-mourning purgatory, I was stuck like the hardened gum under our booth's table.

And that's when I glanced to my left.

The person standing there—the guy who'd heard that whole exchange—was Ryan Chase. My ultimate, since-middle-school pipe dream of a crush. I hadn't seen him in months, and he'd since become a special brand of hot over the summer. Tan skin, light-brown hair lightened further by the sun. Standing this close, I realized we'd probably be the same height if I was wearing heels, but he didn't need to be tall—not with that blue-eyed, broad-shouldered thing happening.

I jerked my head away, mortified. I told myself he hadn't heard that woman talking, but he stepped closer to me and said quietly, "Hey. You all right?"

I didn't think Ryan Chase even knew who I was, but of course he did—Paige Hancock, the Girl Whose Boyfriend Drowned.

"Yeah." Heat pulsed in my cheeks like a heartbeat. If I turned all the way toward him, he'd think I had sunburn the color of raw chicken. "Fine. Thanks."

"It sucks," he said. "The sympathy, I mean. Because it's mostly for them—so they can pat themselves on the back for being caring."

"Yes!" I turned to him, accidentally baring my fluorescent face. "That's it exactly."

He nodded. It was such a serious topic, but he smiled as pleasantly as if we were talking about cupcakes. "My sister had cancer a few years back. She's okay now, but we became pros at talking to total strangers about it."

I knew this, of course. He was the Boy Whose Sister Had Cancer until he started going out with Leanne Woods freshman year. Then he was Ryan Chase: the Boy Everyone Wanted to Date. But my crush on him started way before that—when his sister was sick, in fact. It started in the cereal aisle, where he did the sweetest thing I'd ever seen a boy my age do.

A comment popped into my mind. I wasn't even sure if it made sense, but I'd been silent for too long already. So I deadpanned, "I guess I'm minor league in terms of pity acceptance. But I'm hoping to go pro this year. Hey, maybe that lady was a scout."

Ryan Chase laughed. I mentally thanked my dad for all his years of complaining that Indiana doesn't have a Major League Baseball team.

"So," Ryan said. "You picking up books for school tomorrow?"

"Yep," I said, suddenly glad that I hadn't found the screen-writing book.

"Me, too. There was a lot of summer reading for Honors

English, and I just realized there was one I didn't get to. Guess I'm cramming already."

"Do you have fourth period Honors?"

"Yeah! You, too?"

I nodded, now denying the urge to dance in little circles. *I share a class with Ryan Chase. Who laughed at something I said. Never mind that he has a girlfriend of two years.*

"Cool! Well . . . I should buy this and get started." He held up the play in his hands.

"Yeah, I should get back to my friend." This was code for: *I have friends, I swear.* "So . . . I guess I'll see you in class tomorrow."

"Yeah," he said, flashing the heartbreaker grin. "See you tomorrow. We'll make it a good year."

My heart tried to skip right after him.

And then, just like that, it came crashing down.

The guilt, as always, started low, rumbling in my feet and stomach. It rose like lava, hot across my chest until I felt sweaty. After a random woman reminded me how painfully gone Aaron was, I turned around and swooned over Ryan Chase?

No, I commanded myself. *You have to stop this.*

I'd done it for months now—the dizzying dance between grief and normalcy and the guilt I felt in moving between the two. I talked about that a lot during my year of therapy, though nothing the therapist said seemed, at the time, to help.

But I'd finished my last-ever session a week before and realized: I'm on my own now. I'd have to cope in the moment—not wait until my appointments. The therapist had encouraged me to address my feelings head-on. And the truth was, sometimes pretending to be brave eventually made me *feel* brave.

So I lengthened my spine, shoulders back. I summoned the flecks of courage in me—little zaps from somewhere in my bloodstream. Not many, but enough. Enough to stand up tall as I strode back to the corner booth. *We'll make it a good year.* Yes, Ryan Chase, we will.

But how? Is that something I could plan out? I mean, I planned my lunches and my outfits and even made study plans for tests, complete with extensive notes from class. Why not plan a great year? Last year, that seemed impossible—mapping a plan in the shadow lands of loss. Now, though, maybe I could fake my way through every step until things were truly good again. I could draw a path back to happiness, step by step.

I plopped into our booth, determination coursing in me like caffeine.

"Everything okay?" Tessa asked, looking up.

"Yes," I said, reaching into my bag. "Well, it will be. The whole . . . stranger talking to me about Aaron thing happened."

She snorted angrily. She'd stood beside me during so many uncomfortable interactions—near piles of apples at the farmers' market, while buying sodas at the gas station, in the allergy medicine section of the drug store.

"It's fine," I said. "Because I've realized I just need a *plan*."

I thumped my planner onto the table, as aggressive as I'd ever been with it.

When Tessa bought me the planner a few Christmases back, I knew she was kind of teasing me about what she called "type A tendencies." But I didn't care. It was love at first sight: lavender leather with my initials embossed in the corner and pages of clean white paper, segmented into weeks and months. Ever since, I'd unwrapped a refill calendar for each new year. My favorite holiday tradition became sliding the fresh pages into the soft purple binding.

"A plan for what?" Tessa asked. "Avoiding the pity brigade? I guess we could wear masks. Masquerade ones. With feathers."

I almost smiled, thinking of us in peacock plumes and gold sequins. "No. A plan to have a better year. Proactive things."

"Oh." Her magazine dropped to the table. "Great. Like what?"

The notes section in the back of my planner already had lists on it. But there, after my packing list from our summer family vacation and lines of school supplies I'd purchased and checked off, I found a new page.

"Well, technically, I've only thought of one thing so far," I said, and I wrote it in neatly at the top: 1. Parties/social events. "I'm going to Maggie Brennan's party next weekend."

Tessa pursed her lips—not quite a frown. "Are you sure you want to start so big? We could reintroduce you to high school society somewhere less overwhelming."

"I'm sure." Every year the class president throws a back-to-school party and invites everyone in our grade. I'd missed last year's, of course, since it was only two weeks after Aaron died. That period blurred like one dark shadow in my mind—the numb days holed up in my room and the jarring return to school. Morgan insisted on painting my nails every weekend while we marathoned TV shows. It seemed so silly, so pointless. Until I looked down at my mint-green or petal-pink nails in class: one beautiful, glossy thing in my life. My friends added the first colors to my black-and-white world.

Tessa nudged my arm. "I've got one. You could rejoin one of the groups you did freshman year. Chorus or French Club or something."

"Perfect. Yes." I couldn't handle my extracurricular activities last year, between the therapy appointments and everything else. "Although . . . that's ironic, coming from you."

"I'm *involved*. I go to yoga and the Carmichael."

Tessa was the only person in the history of the world with a fake ID and no interest in drinking. She had to be twenty-one to get into the Carmichael to see all the best indie bands perform. I think the staff knew she was in high school, but they also knew how serious she was about music. She rarely invited me or anyone else. Those shows weren't social events for Tessa. They were personal: between her and the band onstage.

"Exercise and concerts are not cocurriculars."

"They are if you want to work for a record label and teach yoga on the side," she said. "You know, what you're doing is kind of a yoga thing. Well, technically I think it's a Buddhist thing, but I learned it from a yogi: beginner's mind."

I made a face like she'd suggested a juice cleanse—which she had, for all I knew. Yoga wasn't for me. I'd tried a few sessions when she first discovered it, until my King Pigeon pose turned into Pretzel Who Fell Over onto a Nice Older Lady. "What does that mean?"

"It means trying to approach new experiences with no preexisting judgments. You always go in as a beginner, even if you're not. That way, you're open to anything that happens."

"Yes," I said. "Exactly."

Join a group at school and go to a big party—seemed

manageable enough. But two items made for a pretty anemic plan. I would need more.

"I should probably get home," I said, glancing at my phone. "My dad's picking us up at six."

My parents didn't compromise at all while they were married, but they somehow managed to be flexible with custody—arranged around our variable schedules. This week, Wednesday and Sunday were highlighted yellow in my planner, indicating dinner with my dad.

Tessa gathered her things. "What's he making?"

"Spinach and feta lasagna, I think." Since the divorce, my dad had developed a flair for creative cuisine, with his successes equaled by mighty failures. This delighted Tessa, never knowing what would be served or how. It was less funny to me, since those were my odds for two out of seven dinners a week.

"Cameron won't like that," Tessa said. There was nothing I knew about my own sister that Tessa didn't also know. My younger sister was infamous for her aversions—to green vegetables, dairy, and acting like a rational human being.

"Tell me about it. You could come over, if you want."

"Wish I could, but my parents are coming home," Tessa said, sliding her sunglasses on as we walked to her car. Her blond hair absorbed the sunlight into its white-gold waves. "For three whole days."

Tessa's parents, Norah and Roger McMahon, owned an international chain of boutique hotels called Maison. They moved to Oakhurst when Tessa was in elementary school, but they frequently traveled for business. Tessa had what I considered my dream life: limited parental supervision, fabulous vacations, and a massive house. Her grandmother lived with her, but now that Tessa was old enough to drive, Gran McMahon spent more than a few long weekends at Maison Boca Raton with her "manfriend." Even when she was home, Tessa's grandmother was always flitting off to the country club, meeting friends for bridge or attending fund-raisers.

We climbed into the car—Tessa's, as always, since I didn't have my own. I'd gotten my license earlier in the summer, on the exact day of my sixteenth birthday. Unfortunately for me, my mom's car broke down a mere week before my driver's test. Eight thousand dollars later, my hope of inheriting her car sat in the junkyard next to a blown piston, whatever that was.

After all that—six months of driving practice split between my mom splaying her hands in a panicky "stop" motion and my dad whistling while he watched out the window—no car or freedom for me.

"I know it's the last-day-of-summer nostalgia talking," Tessa said, opening the windows. "But it's kind of beautiful here, every once in a while."

Framed by the open car window, the tree-lined streets became a blur of deep greens and broad branches. These wide oaks announced every changing season, sprawling from the WELCOME TO OAKHURST sign to the oldest section of town. Along the main drag, new restaurants and shops popped up every few months, but the trees made the town feel charming and contained.

When I was younger, Oakhurst seemed like a nice enough place to live. I didn't remember much about Seattle, where Cameron and I were born, and nothing could have been worse than muggy Georgia, where we lived in a podunk town for my first-grade year. But when Aaron died, Oakhurst closed in around me, shrinking to the size of a snow globe. I was encased inside this tiny world, where pity flurried around me instead of snow.

"Tell your dad hi from me," Tessa said, as she pulled into the driveway. "Pick you up at seven tomorrow morning?"

"Great." I tried to sound casual, but the first-day-of-school nerves sparked inside me as I made my way to the door.

~

Dinner ran long, and my mind kept wandering toward my plan. My younger sister prattled to my dad about drama in her dance class while I searched for other ways I could make a better year for myself. I needed to brainstorm with someone I trusted—someone who would know what to do. And, fortunately, I had the perfect person.

At home, I said hello to my mom inside and hurried upstairs to call Grammy. My mom preferred that I only speak to my grandmother in person, since talking on the phone occasionally confused her. She lived only a few miles away, in an assisted-living facility. But it was too late to go over there, and I needed to talk now, so I shut my door firmly behind me.

My grandmother's memory started to stall about ten months ago, and it quickly worsened to almost no short-term memory. It was sad to watch, incurable and degenerative, so I wanted to keep telling her all my secrets before it was too late—before I faded in her mind.

I told her about my recurring drowning nightmare, about how I couldn't even submerge my head in bathtub water anymore. I told her how desperately I envied my friends. I complained about driving lessons with my mother and about my annoying sister. She knew every facet of my feelings about Aaron, every sorrow that lingered still.

"Hello?" Her voice sounded tired, and I almost regretted calling.

"Grammy?" I kept my voice quiet so my mother wouldn't hear me. "It's Paige."

"Oh, hello, sweet girl," she said, perking up. "How are you?"

"Okay . . . just making sure I'm all set for school tomorrow." My first-day outfit hung on my closet door, ironed and ready since I picked it out last week.

"Goodness me, a sophomore already," my grandmother mused. Wrong. A junior. This was where her short-term memory hovered—around a year ago. It wasn't worth making the correction and confusing her late at night. "Growing up so fast. Are you excited about your classes?"

"Yeah, I am." Some subjects bored me, of course, but I'd always felt comfortable with the structure of school, the schedule and syllabi and a notebook for every class. "Hey, Grammy?"

"Yes, honey?"

I leaned against the edge of my bed, pressing my feet into the carpet. My voice became a whisper. This was not a question I wanted overheard—not by my mother or sister or even the walls of my bedroom. "After Gramps died, what did . . . I mean . . . did anything make you feel better, eventually? Like, happy again?"

"Oh, sweet girl. I know it's so hard, everything with your friend, but it just happened. You can't expect to feel like yourself right away."

Wrong again. It happened 12.5 months ago; 54 weeks. "I know. I just . . . wondered."

"Well," she said, a bit of intrigue in her voice. "I dated a little after your grandfather, you know."

"You did?"

"Oh, sure. Never found that same magic again, but I didn't expect to. Had enough love for two lifetimes." I could hear her smile. My grandfather died before I was born, so her pain wasn't fresh. She missed my grandfather with fondness now. "Dating was nice. Usually. I met new people, and I learned a lot about myself. Kissed a few frogs."

I laughed, even though a part of me cringed at my grandmother kissing anyone. "What else did you do?"

"Well," she said. "I traveled. I took that trip to Paris the year I turned fifty."

"You were *fifty*?"

My grandmother and I had talked about her trip to Paris a hundred times, in the hours I spent getting her help with freshman and sophomore French homework. She'd tell me about the patisseries and the people, the museums and landmarks. I had no idea that was only twenty years ago.

"How old did you think I was, silly?"

"In your twenties," I admitted, and she laughed. On her mantel, there was a framed photograph of my grandmother twirling in a full skirt and tan trench coat in front of the Eiffel Tower. Her body and face were blurred, but her hair was brown and to her shoulders.

"Certainly not," she said. "It was my first time

traveling without your grandfather. Your mother was in college, and I stayed for six whole weeks. It was terrifying and liberating. One of my fondest memories."

"Wow," I said. Traveling solo. Like to Manhattan, for the screen-writing program.

"Wow, indeed," she said. "I hope it doesn't sound boastful to say that I admire my younger self. That gal had pluck. And you do, too, sweet girl. You just have to ask yourself what scares you most about moving forward."

My mind flashed with images that the recurring nightmare had imprinted—underwater thrashing, water in my nose and filling my lungs. Swimming. That's what scared me most.

Before I could respond to my grandmother, my mom knocked at my bedroom door, opening it simultaneously. This nettled me every time—knocking while already entering. She didn't actually respect my privacy, but she pretended to with that little knock.

"Hey," she said. "Who are you talking to?"

I covered up the phone's speaker. "Tessa."

Even if my grandmother heard me through the phone, lying to my mother, she wouldn't remember long enough to out me.

My mom sighed as she grasped the door handle. "Okay, well . . . you have to be up early. And you'll see Tessa in the morning, so I don't want you up talking all night . . ."

"I won't be," I said as she pulled the door closed. "Good night."

My mother had always been strict, but she reacted to Aaron's death with even more rules—as if by controlling my life, she could protect me from harm. She constantly encouraged me to be social, but she enforced a ridiculous curfew. She asked if I wanted to talk, but if I did, she wound up telling me what to do, when all I'd wanted was someone to listen.

"Hey, Grammy?" I said into the phone. "I'm here again. Sorry about that."

"No need to apologize. We should both be off to bed."

I sighed. "Yeah. I guess I have a big day ahead of me."

"You have a big *life* ahead of you, sweet girl. And beginning again gets easier with each step," she said. My throat ached with repressed tears. After conversations like this, I couldn't believe that she'd eventually forget my name, forget my face. Forget that she once saw me for who I really was.

After I hung up, I pulled my planner out of my bag and added the things my grandma did for herself: date and travel. If only Ryan Chase was single, we could fall in love and go to Paris: two birds with one stone.

I could barely bring myself to add the last task. The first four I actually wanted to do, on some level. But I had no interest in swimming or even going near water. I was,

however, interested in sleeping soundly again someday. So
I swallowed hard and wrote it in.

1. Parties/social events
2. New group
3. Date
4. Travel
5. Swim

There, I thought. A plan. At the top, I wrote:
How to Begin Again

Chapter Two

By the time Tessa picked me up, I had been ready for half an hour, even after reironing my skirt. I hoped the outfit would say: *Hey, Ryan Chase. I'm actually not a creepy bookstore loner. In fact, I have these legs.* I checked my schedule no less than twenty times, preoccupied with showing up to the right classes. I went to one wrong class on the first day of eighth grade, and that horrible moment— the sinking realization as the teacher never called my last name—scarred me for life.

"Happy first day of junior year," Tessa said flatly, cranking up the music as she backed out of the driveway. She wore beat-up jeans and a white linen shirt with colorful embroidery scrawled across the top, possibly from the trip to Mexico with her parents in July. Her hair was still damp at the roots, waves drying in the warm air through the open windows.

We pulled into the junior lot, and it hit me: we're half-way done. Some days, it felt as if we'd been in high school for our whole lives. Other days, freshman and sophomore year felt like the white lines on the highway—a passing blur along a much bigger journey. This time next year, we'd be seniors. The main high school building—outdated by at least twenty years—loomed in front of us like a behemoth, and I stared at it head-on.

"You ready?" Tessa removed her sunglasses. I glanced around, sizing up our classmates as they reunited after a whole summer. It was always the same first-day information—who started dating someone new, who changed their hair color, whose parents bought them a new car? Not me, on any count.

"I guess." My response was followed by the palm of someone's hand, slapping against the window of the passenger's seat. Morgan's grinning face followed.

"Hi!" she squealed, giving me a quick hug as we got out of the car. I'd seen Morgan almost every day of summer vacation, but her excitement made it seem like we'd been separated for years, by flood and famine. As usual, her red hair was parted with a scientific attention rivaled only by NASA and tucked behind her ears to reveal pearl earrings.

"Kayleigh," Morgan said over her shoulder. "They're here. Get off the phone."

Kayleigh, who was leaning on Morgan's car a few feet away, kept typing. I smiled at the sight of her bright-pink jeans. She'd been at camp most of the summer, and I'd missed her boldness—and not just in her outfits.

"Aren't you guys excited?!" Morgan asked, clutching my arm. I nodded to appease her, and Tessa shrugged. "It's going to be the most perfect year!"

I smiled, almost tempted to make the correction. "Perfect" is an absolute adjective and can't be modified. Something is or isn't perfect. It can't be more or less perfect.

"I know that look." Morgan narrowed her eyes at me. "Go ahead."

"I don't know what you're talking about," I lied.

"Yeah right, Grammar Girl." Morgan's head pivoted back around. "Kayleigh Renée! C'mon!"

"Sorry," Kayleigh said, pocketing her phone. She glanced around at us and smiled, her pink lip gloss catching the morning sun. "Hi, juniors."

We started toward the main building, where a red banner hung across the front doors: OHS—ANOTHER "SUPERIOR" YEAR. I wasn't sure why they were trying to sell us, since attendance was obligatory. Oakhurst High scored well in state rankings every year, mostly because of its location. Settled in our cushy suburb outside of Indianapolis, the school was full of kids whose parents worked downtown and expected excellence. Even the druggies and slackers made grades decent enough for technical school or junior college.

"Another superiorly boring year," Tessa grumbled, hiking up her jeans by the belt loops.

Morgan gave Tessa a sidelong glance. "Those jeans look like they're going to fall off you."

Tessa shot her a dark look. "It is not my fault that they don't make cute jeans in my size."

Kayleigh shifted her eyes toward Tessa. "Everyone hates you—you know that, right?"

"You missed me this summer," Tessa said, nudging Kayleigh with her elbow.

She grinned back. "I probably would have missed you more if you ever gained a pound from all that junk you eat."

Kayleigh had arrived home earlier that week with a shorter haircut and a senior boyfriend named Eric, who lived two towns over. They were together for the last few weeks of camp, and they'd even "fooled around." I wasn't fully clear on what that meant, details-wise, but Kayleigh's face was smug when she told us.

My friends had all had boyfriends before—only a few of whom lasted more than a month or two. Tessa lost interest in high school guys after her last date at the beginning of the summer. He had apparently listened to techno music in the car and then tried to kiss her in a way that could only be described, according to her, as reptilian.

Inside the doors, the familiar smell of school rushed over me, musty textbooks mingled with the scent of freshly painted walls, and I took a deep breath.

"Did you just intentionally inhale the scent of *high school*?" Kayleigh asked, laughing.

I shrugged. "I know it's not a *good* smell, but it smells like . . . possibility."

"Possibility has a smell?" Morgan asked, teasing me. "What else does? Happiness?"

"Sure," I said, giving her a defiant look. "Birthday candle smoke. Movie theater popcorn. A fresh Christmas tree."

"Warm pancakes," Tessa added. "Chlorine and sunscreen—like the pool."

Those last two things didn't hold any happiness for me these days, but I turned to Morgan and Kayleigh. "Exactly."

"Well, my locker's upstairs, so I'll see you guys at lunch," Kayleigh said as we passed the first staircase. She turned around and wiggled her eyebrows at me. "I hope you go to the right classes! And no huffing your new school supplies."

"Shut up," I muttered, but she just laughed.

As we turned down the junior hallway, there they were: all the faces we'd grown up with—the ones that Aaron belonged beside. I received That Look from at least ten people. Their eyes clouded over, faces suddenly marred by sadness and memory. When they saw my face, they also saw his. Tessa and Morgan, to their infinite credit, pretended not to notice.

"This is my locker," Morgan said, checking her planner. The locker combination was written at the top of the page, in handwriting so precise that it made Times New Roman look sloppy. "Stop here for a second."

She twisted the lock around, and Tessa leaned back against the wall, bored already. Tessa's GPA was almost as high as mine, but she never put in more effort than was absolutely necessary. I'd overheard people in our grade call Tessa intense, but she was just calm and thoughtful, detached from the standard drama.

Loud laughter echoed against the hallway, and we all looked in its direction. A group of girls surrounded Ryan Chase, who had his head thrown back.

I'd been looking at him the same way since sixth grade—smitten but glancing over casually, embarrassed that my crush would shine right through. That was the year his older sister went through chemotherapy, and I saw them in the grocery store together. I was there with my mom, half reading a book while I followed her around the store. In the cereal aisle, I spotted Ryan, who had recently shaved his head. His sister sat in a wheelchair, with a hat on and blankets wrapped around her.

The grocery store radio started playing "Dancing Queen" overhead, and Ryan spun her wheelchair around. I could tell she was smiling, even with her mouth hidden by a surgical mask. He danced in front of her wheelchair, unselfconscious and silly, and his sister shimmied a little under the blankets. When their dad noticed, I could tell he was scolding Ryan. But his sister reached up to hold his hand as their dad pushed her forward.

His sister went into remission soon after, but I thought of that day often—especially since I'd fully realized how much bravery it takes to create happy moments even when you don't feel happy.

"Ryan Chase," Morgan said. "Cuter than ever."

My mom called her "boy crazy" because Morgan developed a crush on every guy who was reasonably clean and polite. Morgan preferred to think of herself as a romantic, always ready for the possibility of true love.

Tessa tilted her head, examining him. "He looks like a golden retriever."

"What does *that* mean?" Morgan asked.

"You know. Cute but generic. Like you'd see him, or a golden retriever, in a J.Crew catalog, wearing a nice-but-forgettable sweater. Doesn't he have a girlfriend anyway? Leah something?"

"Leanne Woods. And no—not anymore. You didn't hear?" Morgan asked.

"Wait, what?" My head snapped toward her.

"They broke up," Morgan said, her voice hushed. "On the Fourth of July, at the fireworks downtown. Apparently, it was . . . quite an explosive fight."

She took a beat, waiting for us to appreciate her word-play, but Tessa just rolled her eyes. My pulse beat in my ears.

"Leanne dumped him for a college guy," Morgan said. "After two *years*, she just . . . dropped him like a knockoff purse."

"I'm surprised you kept that to yourself for a month," Tessa said, snorting.

Morgan shrugged. "I figured you heard—I mean, every-one did."

I so had not. I would have remembered, though Tessa wouldn't have. Gossip turned to white noise before enter-ing her ears. Her brain wasn't even programmed to acknowledge it. Morgan, on the other hand, had moral lim-itations that kicked in right after Shameless Gossip, which she was always thrilled to share.

"It's too bad," Morgan said. "Ryan is so cute and seems nice. I heard he's been, like . . . really depressed about it. Apparently he's barely hung out with anyone but his cousin since it happened."

I couldn't find it in my heart to consider this situation "too bad." Ryan Chase was finally single, and we'd bonded yesterday, with the promise of more time together in fourth period Honors English. The dating part of my begin-again plan suddenly seemed a lot more appealing.

"Well, I'm sorry that happened to him," Tessa said, "but I still think he seems conceited and annoying."

This was easy for her to say. Tessa's default mode was unimpressed. She had been so many places and met so many people that nothing particularly fazed her, for better or worse.

Morgan shut her locker. "You think everyone is annoying."

"Not everyone. Not you guys."

"Oh, *please*." Morgan laughed. "It totally annoys you when I share information—"

"*Gossip*," Tessa said.

"—and when Paige corrects our grammar."

I glared at Morgan, but Tessa smiled, peeling off toward her own locker.

"That," she said, "I am used to."

Morgan linked her arm through mine, not noticing my annoyance. She waited until Tessa was out of earshot. "We gotta talk birthday plans for her soon."

"Her parents are taking us to Barrett House for dinner," I said, still grumpy.

"Oh my God. That's like, *fancy* fancy." As we made our way down the hall, Morgan glanced over. She bumped her hip into mine. "Oh, don't be mad at me, Grammar Girl. You know we secretly love it."

I'd earned the super-creative nickname Grammar Girl from my evil ex-neighbor, Chrissie Cohen, and the rest of Bus 84. It was the kind of mortifying middle-school story that didn't become funny as you grew up. Those two words made me want to sink inside myself.

After three periods of syllabi explanation, I met up with Morgan to walk to Honors English. Our teacher was new to the district, so she wouldn't know me as the girl who was dating Aaron Rosenthal when he died. I found such relief in that fact—and such guilt in my relief.

We arrived in time to claim the perfect seats: far enough away from the teacher that we could pass notes, but not so far that it looked like we tried to sit far away. Ms. Pepper stood out in a sophisticated dress, with dark hair falling to her shoulders. Rectangular glasses perched smartly on her nose, like a superhero's cerebral alter ego.

But Ms. Pepper lost my attention as Ryan Chase sauntered in the door, so cute that it felt like slow motion. He passed by me, his red T-shirt drawing my eye to the V-shape of his back, from broad shoulders to slim waist.

He sat down next to a tall, dark-haired guy who looked familiar. It took me a moment to place him: Max Watson, Ryan's cousin. So he was back. He went to Oakhurst public with the rest of us until middle school, when he transferred to the Coventry School. I always figured he switched to private school because he got bullied. He was ganglier then, with the same dark-rimmed glasses and a hand that shot up to answer every question in class. Ryan leaned in to whisper something to Max, who laughed in response.

As the bell rang, everyone adjusted forward—diligent little students on the first day.

"As you all should know, I'm Ms. Pepper, and I'm responsible for your Honors English education this year. I like to think that I'm a pretty fun teacher, but my idea of fun includes learning, so take that as you will," she said, picking up a piece of chalk.

"Comedy that will not be well received is as follows: Sergeant Pepper, anything regarding sneezes, and telling me your name is Mr. Salt." She wrote each word on the board.

The whole class chuckled nervously. It was always hard to gauge the teacher's personality on the first day of school. Fortunately, although she kept a straight face, Ms. Pepper seemed to realize she was being funny.

"For those of you who are curious: yes, I did stop after my master's degree because the idea of being Dr. Pepper was unacceptable."

She swiped thick lines of chalk through the words she'd written on the board: SGT, SNEEZES, SALT, DR.

"Is there any other humor you'd like to get out of your systems?"

The class fell silent. She seemed to be holding back a smirk. "I know it's the first day and no one wants to talk, but speak now or forever hold your peace . . ."

Ryan Chase raised his hand from the front of the classroom.

"Excellent. Yes. What's your name?" she asked.

"Ryan Chase," he said. His voice—steady and deep—sent a shiver down my spine.

"And what would you like to contribute?" she asked gamely, poised to add more to the list.

"Do you ever make red-hot chili?" he asked. I could hear his grin. Laughter twittered across the room.

"Absolutely not," Ms. Pepper said, smiling before she added RED-HOT CHILI to the list and crossed it out. "Very nice, Mr. Chase. Anyone else?"

Everyone looked around the room, searching the couch cushions of their brains for any possible joke. I almost raised my hand and said, *You must hate the daily grind*, but I doubted that a ground pepper reference would dazzle any of my classmates.

"Okay, then. Moving on." She erased the five outlawed phrases. "I have two goals for you this year. The first is for you to learn about literature. The second is for you to learn about one another. So, to that point, I have decided to mix up your seating assignments."

I wrinkled my nose. Of course, after Morgan and I got the best seats.

"In this bowl, I have all your names. I will draw at random, and that's where you'll sit. Starting with the seat closest to my desk . . . Morgan Sullivan!" she said, reading off the first piece of paper.

Morgan moved to her new desk, displacing a girl I didn't recognize. Three rows later, my current seat was filled by Tyler Roberts, leaving me standing in the back. I waited for my name to be called as most of the classroom filled up. Finally, it was only me and Ryan Chase left standing at the back of the classroom.

"Hello again," he said to me.

"Hey." My voice sounded breathy, like I hadn't used enough air in my attempt to speak. I hoped it came off more like "flirty" and less like "bronchitis."

"Second to last seat by the door will be . . . ," Ms. Pepper said, plucking the final papers from the bowl. "Paige Hancock, making the last seat for Red-Hot Chili Chase."

I took my seat, feeling the sudden compulsion to smooth the back of my hair. My stomach fidgeted as I situated my things, clenching with the fear that I would somehow drop all my books or spontaneously fall out of my seat.

"Hey, man," Ryan Chase said, high-fiving Tyler Roberts one row across, in my old seat.

"*Lucky*," Morgan mouthed, making eye contact from across the room.

I stared directly ahead, already tuning out Ms. Pepper in favor of planning how my relationship with Ryan Chase would begin with this seating arrangement.

"Okay. Moving right along. As you'll see on the syllabus, the first piece we're studying this year is *Hamlet*. For those of you who plan to move on to AP English next year, you should know: the AP exam is obsessed with the Bard. And, therefore, we are also obsessed with the Bard. Aren't we?" she asked. "Repeat after me: I am obsessed with the Bard."

"I am obsessed with the Bard," everyone mumbled. Only Max Watson's voice rang out. Luckily for him, he was now too tall to be shoved in a locker, but that kind of enthusiastic participation might inspire people to try anyway.

"Sonnet Fourteen," Ms. Pepper continued, "which was part of your summer reading, culminates with these two lines: 'Or else of thee this I prognosticate: thy end is truth's and beauty's doom and date.'"

From behind me, Ryan Chase whispered something to Tyler that I couldn't quite make out.

"Mr. Chase, what does 'prognosticate' mean?"

"It's when . . . ," he began, seriously, "you procrastinate, but . . . the prognosis on your decision to procrastinate is good."

I laughed along with the rest of the class, and even Ms. Pepper fought a smile. "I assume that was your approach to the reading assignment. Let's try cousin door number two. Max?"

I wondered how she knew their relation to each other. I wouldn't put it past Max to introduce himself before class.

"To prophesize," Max said.

"Correct," Ms. Pepper said, turning to the board. "Now let's talk briefly about Shakespeare's choice to use 'truth' and 'beauty.' Those two words are tied together in another famous work by which English Romantic poet?"

Maggie Brennan raised her hand. So did Max. This kid had no public school survival skills. "Maggie?"

" 'Ode on a Grecian Urn,' " Maggie said. "Keats."

"Indeed. 'Beauty is truth and truth beauty.' " She wrote on the board: TRUTH = BEAUTY? BEAUTY = TRUTH? "This is one of the great questions of all art, including writing. What makes something beautiful? What makes it truthful? Beauty is subjective. Is truth? Are they really related? I want you to keep these questions in mind, as we'll be returning to them throughout the year."

"Now," she continued. "Back to your summer reading. The sonnet form: how many lines does it contain?"

"Fourteen!" Ryan Chase called from behind me. "Same number as the title of the Sonnet we were supposed to read: Fourteen."

"Very good," Ms. Pepper said.

Before I could stop myself, I smiled over my shoulder.

He winked at me. "I read it. I was just joking before."

His smile flustered me as I began to script the many, meaningful conversations we'd have in this class. Ryan Chase was right: we were going to make it a great year.

Chapter Three

Aaron was camping with his Boy Scout troop when he jumped off a rocky ledge into the river below. He was goofing around, showing off, but the river current picked him up with unexpected force. It wasn't anyone's fault, and no one could have stopped it. Still, I ached for the guys in his troop. They'd carry that day—those images, the panic— for the rest of their lives.

My drowning nightmares began the week after he died. Only it wasn't Aaron in the dream—it was me. In slumber, my foot would twitch, and in the next moment I was falling, falling, falling. The water stung as my skin hit the surface, wrapping around my body and filling my mouth as I sank, flailing.

At least twice a week I awoke breathless and teary in the darkness, trying to convince myself that I was okay. I'd throw my duvet off my body, overheated and terrified of feeling trapped. It always took at least one episode of *Friends* on my laptop, the familiar jokes and laugh track lulling me back to sleep.

Even thinking about the nightmare, I relived the uncontrollable thudding of my heart, the cold sweat, and the dryness of my mouth.

I had a similar panicky reaction near Ryan Chase. Before sitting next to him, I believed that my social skills were about average for an introvert. Nope. Fear of embarrassing myself rendered me totally mute. My language neurons detached from my brain, leaving me only symbols: ! or ?! or :). My entire presence could have been replaced with a mannequin, and he probably wouldn't have noticed.

In the week that followed the assigned seating, I said four words to Ryan Chase. Total. And that was if you counted "hmm" as a word. They happened on Wednesday.

Ryan: Do you think we'll have a quiz on that play from our summer reading?

Me: Hmm, I don't know.

Ryan: I kind of skimmed it. I mean, the title spoiled the whole thing, right? *Rosencrantz and Guildenstern Are Dead*? Okay, well, now I know. Why would I read it?"

Me: (*Flirtatious laughter, flipping of hair, blanking of mind.*)

I turned back around. *I can't produce dialogue in simple, everyday conversations, but please, screenwriting school: pick me!* At least this way, he had a close-up of my perky ponytail. Paige Hancock: sad sack, social mute, and the uncontested winner of Oakhurst's Most Brushed Hair award. How could he resist?

By Friday, I resigned myself to spending the weekend learning about sports. Preseason football seemed to be Ryan and Tyler's topic of choice, so maybe I would start there. He would be so impressed when I chimed in with my predictions for this year's football Golden Globes, or whatever awards they give out. I'd have to look it up. When Ms. Pepper began class, I scribbled down the terms I heard—zone blitz, 4-3 defense, safety—in the back of my planner, as Ryan and Tyler kept whispering to each other in football language. Ms. Pepper's voice, escalating in volume and pitch, broke into my thoughts.

"Ryan. Tyler. I'm going to be honest with you. This is not working for me, you two having your little guy time back there," she said, turning on her heels to face them.

"Ryan, if you could please switch seats with . . . ," she trailed off, glancing around the room, ". . . Max."

My heart sank.

"Is this permanent?" Tyler asked.

"Like a tattoo," Ms. Pepper said.

Max obediently picked up his books and slid out of his chair in the front.

"Ms. Pepper," Ryan groaned, packing up his things. "I thought we could be friends."

"Okay. Let's be friends." She smiled. "And friends don't let friends fail English."

"My therapist says it's important for me to be social," Ryan joked, clapping Max on the back affectionately as they crossed paths mid-switch. The class laughed.

"That's why I'm putting you in the front, my little problem child," she said, tapping the desk where Ryan was now seated. "So we can have super-fun chats!"

"They're going to be about literature, aren't they?" asked Ryan.

"Yes, yes they are." Ms. Pepper surveyed the new seating arrangement. "I like it. It stays. Now, back to *Rosencrantz and Guildenstern*."

~

Forty-five minutes of Shakespeare-inspired existentialism later, Ms. Pepper faced the class. "One last thing. I'm advising the Oakhurst QuizBowl team this year, and we're looking for at least one more member."

I didn't know much about QuizBowl except that it was a game-show-style student activity, with two teams from different schools answering academic questions. I also knew that it was possibly the least cool activity at Oakhurst High. Even the chess team had more participants.

Despite all that, something inside of me whispered: *do it.*

"We could particularly use strength in the language arts arena, so my Honors students would be well suited," she continued. "Hint, hint."

No hands went up. The bell went off overhead, and as everyone collected their things, Ms. Pepper added, "At least think about it, okay? Come talk to me if you're interested."

When I'd promised myself I'd participate in a school activity this year, I figured I'd rejoin Key Club or French Club or maybe even chorus—something low commitment in a big group, where I could easily be anonymous. There would be no hiding in QuizBowl, which seemed much scarier.

But maybe that—the fear I felt in challenging myself— was exactly why I should do it.

I packed my things up slowly, stalling so that no one would realize I was staying after to talk to Ms. Pepper.

As everyone bustled out of the classroom, Maggie Brennan pointed at me. "You coming to my party tomorrow?"

I almost said maybe, but I caught myself. "Maybe" had carried me as far as it was ever going to. "Yes. For sure."

"Good." She nodded decisively—my RSVP finalized.

Morgan lingered, waiting for me, but I told her I'd meet her in the cafeteria.

Once everyone was gone, I approached Ms. Pepper's desk. She opened her mouth to say something, but I cut her off before I could chicken out. "I, um, had a few questions about QuizBowl. If that's okay."

Ms. Pepper pressed her hands together, almost a clap. "Oh, great! Of course!"

"Is it totally academic?" I asked. "Or more pop culture?"

"Both," she said. "We could really use more support on the pop culture side, though."

That I could do, with the years of novels and TV trivia stored up in my mind. "Do I need to, like, try out or something?"

Her mouth quirked into an amused smile. "What's the last thing you read for pleasure?"

"*Looking for Alaska*," I said. "Well, I *re*read it for pleasure."

"Ha," she said. "You'll be fine."

I squirmed a little, wringing my hands together. "So, are there team practices?"

"Not really. There'll be one sort of organizational meeting, but other than that, QuizBowl is very low commitment. Matches are only once a month, and they last for about an hour. So you can put it on a college application without having to put much time in. Plus, it's fun."

"Okay." I wondered if I'd need a car to get to different meets, but maybe I could work that out. "I have to ask my parents, but I . . . think I'll do it, if that's okay."

"Of course it's okay! It's great!" She pressed her hands together again. "I think you'll be just the right fit for the team, Paige. And if you come up with any other questions, let me or Max know."

"Max?"

"Max Watson. Who sits behind you? He's the team captain."

Oh, of course *he is*, I thought. "Right. Thanks. I'll see you Monday."

"See you Monday," she said.

By the time I got to the cafeteria, I had the feeling of highway hypnosis. I'm sure I passed people in the hallway, but they blurred over. Had I really just volunteered for *QuizBowl*?

When I plopped into my usual seat in the cafeteria next to Kayleigh, Morgan glanced up from unpacking her lunch bag. "Everything okay?"

"Yeah," I said, nestling my books in the middle of the table. "I just had a quick question."

I stood up to go to the lunch line, but not before Tessa sank into an open seat at the table. Our original schedules had the four of us sharing a lunch period, but Tessa had blown through the first few days of precalculus, receiving perfect scores on a homework assignment and the first quiz. The teacher insisted on moving Tessa to senior-level calculus despite her protestations. The advanced class probably wouldn't be that much harder for her, but it meant that her lunch and math periods were now switched.

"Aren't you supposed to be in calc in, like, two minutes?" asked Morgan.

"Yes," Tessa said in a whiny voice. "I'm pretending for a second."

She looked around at each of us.

"Ugh! This sucks," she cried, slapping her palms against the table. "You're all here together, and I'm learning definite integrals."

"We definitely don't know what that means," Kayleigh said, and Morgan laughed.

Tessa gave Morgan a dark look. "Go ahead—laugh it up. I eat lunch alone."

"Not *alone*." Morgan patted her arm. "You'll find people to sit with! It'll be good for you. You'll make more friends!"

Tessa made a face. "I don't need more friends."

I do, I thought, almost laughing bitterly. I wasn't unfriendly with anyone, but I'd dropped off the social sphere. Kayleigh knew girls from volleyball and chorus, while Morgan had friends from church, Empower, and student council. Tessa talked to a strange array of people in the halls: a guy she met in woodworking class who looked like a tree himself—huge and lumbering—some girl with a septum piercing, and the kid who worked as the school mascot.

"All right," Tessa said, glancing up at the clock. "Don't talk about anything good."

Before she could leave, I plunked my news down. "I think I'm joining QuizBowl."

Morgan retracted her head a little, surprised, but a grin spread across Tessa's face.

"I mean, I'm at least going to try it," I said. "Maybe it won't be fun or maybe I'll suck at it, but . . . yeah."

"Look at you, with your beginner's mind," Tessa said, holding her hand up as she stood to go. "Do it. C'mon."

I gave her a high five, feeling a little sheepish.

"Our little nerd," Kayleigh said, pretending to dab at her eye. "All grown up and competing against other nerds."

"Shut up," I said, but I couldn't help but laugh. Sure, QuizBowl wasn't a *cool* activity to join and, yeah, the idea of answering difficult questions in front of an audience terrified me. But it wasn't anything like the fear that accompanied my drowning nightmare—harrowing and visceral. No, this fear made me feel fizzy. Hopeful.

In fact, this fear felt like waking up to discover I am still here.

~

It was just my dad and me for dinner that night, since Cameron had dance class. We talked about my first week of school, and I almost told him about QuizBowl. But I wanted to be sure it would happen before I shared the good news. Instead, when he asked if I had any fun weekend plans, I said, "Yeah, actually. I'm going to a big back-to-school party tomorrow."

"Look at you," he said, putting his fork down. "Out in the world, amongst the people. Proud of you, kid."

"Ha," I said. "Thanks. When I told mom, she said: 'I'm not so sure about that.' She's trying to make me check in with her when I get to the party *and* when I leave. And I have to be home by ten thirty."

"Oh, Paiger." He smiled as he shook his head. "Give your mom a break. It shook her . . . it shook *us* to—"

"I know," I said. And I did know. It shook them that Aaron—a kid my age—could be gone, like that. "But she's driving me insane."

The good-natured smile didn't budge. "Eh, so your mom's a little tightly wound, big deal. It's what keeps her curls in place."

I cracked a smile in spite of myself. That same humor kept him employed as the Life & Arts columnist for our city paper. He cracked jokes about political predicaments, pop culture, and everyday life. Somehow, though, he always managed to throw in a poignant thought.

As I polished off my last bites of coconut curry chili, my dad stayed seated across from me. He was a fast eater, given to cleaning dishes before I even put my fork down.

But he remained, as if waiting for a signal I had yet to give him.

"Listen, kid," he said finally, lacing his fingers in front of him. His voice was uncharacteristically serious, a tone I hadn't heard since he and my mom announced the divorce.

"What?" I blurted out, succumbing to a fear that refused to fade—that terrible news might be just moments away. "What is it?"

"Everything's fine. Totally fine. I was just wondering, if . . ." He trailed off, stricken. "I was wondering if it would bother you if I started dating again."

"Oh." *That* I wasn't expecting. "No. Of course it wouldn't."

His shoulders dropped in relief. "Okay. Great. Good."

"I kind of figured you had been before now," I said. My dad lived alone except for every once in a while when Cameron and I stayed over. He was still good-looking for his age and had a successful career. It would have made sense if he dated without me knowing.

"Well, I have," he admitted. "Very casually. Sporadically. You know."

I didn't know, and I didn't want to know. Gross. No. I nearly shuddered.

"Was that all?" I asked.

"Uh, yeah. I guess that's all."

"Okay."

"Okay," he said, but his eyes were elsewhere, hovering on a thought unspoken.

But I couldn't shake the feeling that something was not okay. When my dad dropped me off after dinner, I turned back. I tried to make out his face in the glare of the headlights, and I waved in a way that I hoped would look cheerful.

For the first time in years, it felt strange to be going home to a place where we all used to belong.

Chapter Four

On Saturday night, I smoothed my hair one last time and glanced at my phone. An hour until Tessa would pick me up. An hour and a half until we'd be at Maggie Brennan's party—my first party in over a year.

My room was already tidy, but I reshelved a few DVDs I had sitting on my nightstand. I put them back into their alphabetical places on my bookcase, where a stuffed animal that Aaron won for me sat on the middle shelf, watching me. The cat, with its beady, plastic gaze and stitched-on smile, lived next to a framed photo of me and Aaron.

Behind both, there was a collage I'd made from magazine clippings in eighth grade. In the center, I'd glued a photo from Morgan's thirteenth birthday celebration:

Kayleigh making a kissy face, Morgan pink-cheeked and wearing a plastic tiara, Tessa with a closed-lip but real smile, and me—squinty-eyed and mid-laugh. It was only three years ago, but I looked so *young*, with that carefree smile. Like I had no idea how vicious the world could be.

I'd surrounded us with glossy magazine clippings—a purple minidress, a bouquet of peonies, the ocean's shoreline, a line of bright-red and pink nail polishes, a three-tiered cake, a pair of ornate earrings, and towering satin heels. I'd also added cutout words—*fun in the sun!*, *GIRLS*, *Love ya!*

Why had I picked these things? I'd never wear a dress that tight, and I'd always been a pastel nail polish kind of girl. I owned a closet full of ballet flats and only three pairs of heels. The cake was beautiful but in an aesthetic way—not in an appetizing way. And the ocean? No longer something I wanted near me. This wasn't what I loved, who I was.

So I pulled the collage from the shelf and gently pried the center photo off. At my desk, I glued it onto the center of a new piece of paper: my friends, still the center of my world. The rest? White space. I thumbed through a stack of old magazines, pausing to snip a picture of a TV and another of a stack of books. I wasn't sure why I hadn't included those things in the first place. Had I been embarrassed of them?

"Paige!" my mom called, piercing the quiet. I glanced at my phone: still twenty minutes until Tessa would be here. "Can you come down here, please?"

I frowned, figuring this would be a lecture about my immovable curfew and the importance of making safe choices when out with friends. Downstairs, I found my mom sitting at the kitchen table with nothing in front of her but a glass of red wine. As the features editor of *Mommyhood* magazine, my mother was rarely without some sort of text—a marked-up draft of an article or a parenting book to review. It jarred me to see her sitting there, just waiting for me.

I mentally reviewed any possible reason that she could be mad at me. But she looked more concerned than mad as I sat down across from her.

"What's up?" I asked, my voice pitchy.

"There's something I'd like to discuss with you." She paused, lifting her wineglass to her lips. The time limit for a "sip" passed and transitioned into a gulp. I stared at her as she swallowed it down, cheeks puffed out. She gave a deep-breathing-exercise exhale. "I'm dating someone."

I felt my eyebrows shoot up. "You are?"

In that first moment, I didn't feel anything but surprise—at the coincidence that my dad had just mentioned the same topic. I wasn't surprised that she would be dating, but that it had slipped past me. I hadn't seen her coming and going at strange hours or spending a lot of time on the phone. Maybe she met him through online dating.

I shook my head to clear my thoughts. "That's great, Mom."

Her expression relaxed. "Really?"

"Yeah! I mean, you and Dad have been divorced for a long time. Cameron and I are old enough to understand that—"

She held up her hand, cutting me off. "There's something else."

Silence settled between us, enough time for my heart to palpitate.

"The person that I'm dating," she said, "is your dad."

At first I thought she meant I had a secret biological dad—like, some guy I'd never met who secretly fathered me sixteen years ago, and she recently reconnected with him. That seemed more likely. But no—no, she meant my actual dad. The guy she divorced over five years ago and, in my estimation, possibly never loved in the first place. My face morphed in total horror as I realized the veracity of her words. "What?"

"Your dad and I," she said, "have been seeing each other. For the past four months."

Four *months*? My mouth lagged open as the whole scene became a freeze-frame. I blinked, speechless, as my mind flipped through the most basic questions: Is this a joke? How had I not known? Why in the world would they think this is okay? Oh my God, this is what my dad had tried to bring up with me! He was talking about my *mom*.

"I know it comes as a surprise. But we didn't want to tell you until we were sure it was worth telling."

"I . . . I . . ."

"And we want you to know that we're happy." That word—"we"—flabbergasted me. They had never been a parenting team, even when they were together. "This is a good thing."

"But . . . I remember back then . . . ," I began, pausing to collect myself. My shoulders felt moments away from collapsing—into sobs or maniacal laughter, I wasn't sure. "You were *miserable*. Neither of you were happy until after the divorce."

"I know it seemed that way." She sighed, relaxing her posture. "And maybe it was that way. We needed some space and time to figure things out for ourselves."

"But . . . when? H-how?" I stuttered. "Why?"

"We started speaking again regularly after . . . Aaron."

I winced, even though I was grateful that my parents dropped their hostility last year. Helping me cope became their mutual priority, and it didn't go unnoticed—by me or my sister.

My mom continued. "Then everything with your grandma's health started to decline, and your dad just . . . understood."

My grandmother's slow-but-steady memory loss had taken a toll on all of us, and I was glad my mom had someone to talk to. But it didn't have to be my dad, of all people.

I sat back, defeated. For years I was forced to sit front row while two people I loved started to hate each other. It felt like the discontent in our house could be absorbed, like cigarette smoke permeating the walls' insulation.

"I can't . . . ," I said, my voice breaking. "I cannot watch it happen again."

"Oh, honey," she said, placing her hand over mine. I retracted it. "It won't. It won't happen again. Not like that."

She couldn't possibly know such a thing. I blinked over and over, but the tears pushed back at my eyelids. Perfect—my face would be puffy in front of the entire junior class.

With watery vision, I stared at my mother, reliving it all: the tense silences that dropped between them like walls, the marked lack of eye contact during family dinners.

"I'm not—it's not . . . ," My mother tripped over her words before giving up with a sigh. "I'm sorry, sweetheart. I thought you'd be happy."

Happy? My disbelief shifted into glowing anger that she'd sprung this on me now, after hiding it all this time. I could already hear the gossip, ricocheting against the lockers and tarnishing what should have been my year, my fresh start. I would be demoted to an even weirder reputation: the Girl Whose Divorced Parents Date Each Other.

"I'm going to go to Tessa's," I said the moment it popped into my head.

"I thought she was picking you up at seven."

"Well, I'm going over there now."

She looked startled, clearly caught between exercising parental authority and allowing me some space to process her news.

"Okay," she said quietly.

But I was already out the door. I wondered how long it would take her to call my dad and report my reaction. The very thought of that conversation made our familiar house feel foreign and off-kilter.

I shut the door behind me and made my way across the street, down the slope, and across the tiny stream to the neighborhood that backed up to mine. It was this same in-between space where I met Tessa when I was seven, a few weeks after each of our families had moved to Oakhurst. I was reading *Anne of Green Gables* at the base of the hill when I saw a tiny blond figure splashing in the stream farther down. The path, like our friendship, had become worn in over time. Now, nine years later, I could have walked the path to Tessa's with my eyes closed, and it hadn't failed me yet.

"Hey," Tessa said, glancing up for a moment as I walked in the side door. She looked back down, digging through her purse. "I was just leaving to get you."

She stood next to the kitchen table, wearing a summer

dress and tall wedge heels that closed the five-inch height difference between us. Her blond hair fell forward, half-way to her waist. Tessa McMahon didn't even own a blow-dryer, and her apathy was rewarded with teenage-years Taylor Swift hair. Because life is not fair.

"Can I borrow something to wear?" If I was going to face all of my classmates after what had just happened, I needed to at least *look* confident.

"Of course. Aha!" She produced a container of lip balm from the depths of her purse and looked up at me.

"Whoa," she breathed. She stepped toward me, squinting to get a better look at my undoubtedly blotchy face. "Hey. What's going on?"

"Let's find me something to wear and then I'll tell you. Okay?"

I riffled through Tessa's walk-in closet until I found a dress that I'd almost borrowed once before. Shopping in Tessa's closet was difficult for two reasons. Her miniature clothes rarely fit totally-average-down-to-my-size-eight-shoes me. And, secondly, Tessa's sense of style only really worked on her. There was a sort of bohemian feel to her wardrobe, effortless and comfortable. Even though most of her clothes and accessories were expensive, she thought exposed labels were tacky. This was part of the reason why she'd never quite fit in with the popular crowd, no matter how many times they'd tried to recruit her.

The dress still fit snugly, a bit too tight in the chest, which was why my mother hadn't let me wear it out earlier in the summer.

"That looks good," Tessa told me when I emerged from the closet. She leaned back on a pile of pillows on her bed, crossing her arms. "I thought you didn't like that dress."

"I like it. My mom just wouldn't let me wear it that one time."

"*That* is cute," Tessa cried, gesturing at the dress. "Why didn't your mom like it?"

"Too skimpy," I said, making air quotes.

"*Ew!* It is not! That is rude of your mom to say!"

I snorted. Only Tessa could turn parental restriction into a personal offense.

"Whatever," she said, shaking her head. "Tell me what's going on."

I took a deep breath. "My parents are dating."

She pursed her lips. "That's okay, right? I mean, they've been divorced for a long time now. You had to figure that they would eventually start—"

I held up my hand to stop her, as my mother had done to me just minutes before. Stringing together the next sentence was like jamming mismatched puzzle pieces together— forced and awkward and wrong. "My parents are dating *each other.*"

"Wait, *what*?" Tessa gawked, sitting up.

"Dating each other," I repeated. "Day-ting."

I held up both my index fingers and touched them together, as if this somehow symbolized "when one's divorced parents date each other." The American Sign Language linguists would have to make up a whole new vernacular for my screwed-up family life. Tessa's eyes boggled in confusion. She was there when my parents separated and divorced. She'd heard me complain about the arguments and even heard a few in person, from the confines of my bedroom during sleepovers.

"Well," she said after a few moments. "That's . . . pretty weird."

I threw my hands up in the air. "I know! God! Everything is going to happen all over again. They'll both wind up unhappy, *again*, and Cameron and I will have to live through it *again*."

Tessa twisted the ends of her hair, apparently not ready to offer advice. And suddenly, it all struck me as so *absurd* that I started laughing—but not the laugh of a person who was cracking up. The laugh of a person who was just plain cracking.

"Are you . . . ," Tessa trailed off. "Is this a weird joke?"

"Nope!" I said, gasping for air as I wiped under my eyes. My nitrous-oxide giggling continued. "This is so real. It's totally fine. My parents are dating each other. Whatever! It's okay!"

"It *will* be okay." She looked me right in eyes. "It will."
My laughter dropped off.

This was not the first time Tessa had sworn to me that everything would work out. After Aaron's funeral, I went to change into my pajamas when it hit me that the funeral wasn't happening. It *had* happened. There was nothing left to do. There was only his unending absence. I fell to my knees on the carpet in my half-unzipped black dress, hysterical, and Tessa pulled me into her arms. As I sobbed, she repeated, over and over, the same words in a rhythmic way that somehow calmed me: *It will not always feel like this. I promise. It will get easier. You will not always feel this way, Paige. I promise.* She never tried to rationalize my pain or fix it. But she planted this idea, that someday it might ease.

"Okay. Okay." I pinched the bridge of my nose. My skin felt ruddy, and I turned to examine the toll that crying had taken on my complexion. I stared at my face in the mirror, thinking of that picture of the four of us from the collage. Same green eyes, same light-brown hair at my shoulders, same everything. Other than a few inches of height and the hint of curves, I looked exactly the same as I did in eighth grade. The sameness suffocated me, like the walls were closing in around me. Inside, I'd changed so much—even in the past year. Yet here I stood, same old Paige. I needed to break free of her.

"Will you cut my hair?"

I glanced back at Tessa in the mirror as her mouth formed the word: "No."

"Just bangs." Turning around, I gave her my best pleading look.

"You want me to cut bangs into your hair?"

"Yes."

"You realize that I have never cut anyone's hair in my life?"

"Yes."

"No."

I groaned. "You're supposed to be my best friend."

"I *am* your best friend," she told me, avoiding my gaze. She was still on her bed, picking at her nails. "Which is why I won't let you make hair-related decisions when you're this upset."

"I'm not upset."

"Okay," she said sarcastically.

"I need a change, Tess." I whined.

"Then change mascaras or something," she said. "Your hair is fine."

"If you don't do it, I'll do it myself." I reached over to her desk, plucking a pair of all-purpose scissors from the drawer.

When she only stared at me, I took the front panel of my hair between my two fingers, sectioning it off.

"God," she muttered after a moment, climbing off the bed. "Fine. Give them here."

I stayed still, unwavering. But this one gesture—this simple, snipping motion—moved me forward all on its own. I stood, breath bated, ready to be changed in even the smallest way.

Chapter Five

On our way to Morgan's house, Tessa and I didn't talk. The bangs tickled my forehead, and I couldn't stop staring at myself in the car's side mirror. This girl, with her new hair and the "skimpy" dress, could handle the next few hours. The radio played over us, and I sang along to myself.

My friends' music preferences diverged and overlapped like a four-part Venn diagram. Kayleigh liked pop and hip-hop, with some classic rock. Tessa also dabbled with classic rock but generally preferred low-key indie music. She enforced a zero-tolerance policy for schmaltz, which always made for bickering if Morgan was in charge of song selection. Morgan favored the kind of lite rock my mother listened to and, also like my mother, disapproved of Kayleigh's hip-hop. We had a house rule that stated you got to pick the music when everyone was at your house or in your car. There were two exceptions: on birthdays or during a life crisis, the other girls abdicated their DJ rights.

House rule was easiest on me. I liked most of the songs my friends did. My only quirk was a shamefully enthusiastic love of pop ballads, which I tried to reign in.

But that's what Tessa played now, a girl-pop anthem that I had always liked. I knew she was quietly enforcing the Crisis Amendment, allowing me this one song as my family life shifted under my feet.

"Hey," I said to Tessa, after she pulled into Morgan's driveway and honked. "I'm not going to tell them yet. About my parents."

Tessa nodded as the front door opened and Kayleigh emerged. Kayleigh is only three inches taller than I am, but with much better curves and a confident sway to her walk, even in heels.

"Morgan!" Kayleigh yelled from the top of the drive-way. "Come *on*."

Morgan ducked out the door, calling good-bye to her parents before it shut. She walked to the driveway in her typical perfect-posture way—shoulders back, chin slightly raised.

"Geez, Kayleigh." I could hear them through the open windows. "I was coming."

Morgan and Kayleigh acted more like sisters than any two people I knew, including me and my actual sister. When Kayleigh's mom died, her dad and three older brothers started attending Morgan's church. Morgan was only five at the time, but she took Kayleigh by the hand and guided her to their Sunday school classroom. They've been best friends ever since.

Kayleigh and I clicked in fifth grade, each intuiting that our lives were harder than other kids'. We didn't talk about my parents' chilly silences or her mom's death, but we sensed that hurt the way that only broken-home kids can. She introduced me to Morgan, whose parents were utterly normal, and somehow, with Tessa, our individually weird lives gelled together and stuck.

"I thought your mom wouldn't let you wear that dress," Morgan said to me, shutting the car door behind them. Her memory contained the entire school's gossip and all four of our wardrobes.

"Well, I'm wearing it anyway." I glanced at Tessa for affirmation, and she gave me a decisive nod as we pulled out of the driveway.

"Wait," Morgan said. "Turn around. Do you have bangs?"

"Yeah, she does!" Tessa said this like a cheer, rallying me as she turned the radio up.

"Okay, seriously—why is the world so weird in here?" Morgan raised her voice over the song. "Paige changed her hair for the first time in human history, and this is *not* Tessa music."

"I like this song," Kayleigh said, drumming on the back of my seat.

"Is there a crisis?" Morgan demanded. "Why are we listening to this in your car?"

"Because we can!" Tessa yelled, giving the volume dial another turn. I glanced over at her, hair wild against the open windows, and smiled, despite the chaos filling my life.

I needed all three girls that night, steeling me. They'd always been my closest friends, but after Aaron died, I folded myself into them completely. We camped out at Tessa's for weekends at a time, with rented movies and Morgan-made snacks. They were normal when I wanted to be normal, and they held me when I wanted to cry. When it all closes in, there are only two kinds of people: best friends and everyone else.

∼

Two hours into the party, Tessa had reminded me at least four times that we could leave whenever I wanted. We'd been working our way through the house, pausing to mingle, and I thought I was doing well. No sign of Leanne Woods and her new college boyfriend. Ryan Chase was around, and, having observed him for an embarrassingly long chunk of my life, I could tell something was different.

His body language sang with even more confidence, like he'd finally discovered his good looks. Maybe it was an attempt to shrug off rumors of Leanne-linked depression, but Ryan Chase seemed fine. Just fine.

After a while, I separated from my friends to socialize on my own and prove I was also fine. Besides, I had a personal score to settle: me versus me. I was going outside to the deck, which overlooked Maggie's pool, and I was going to watch my classmates swim. If I was going to swim myself again someday, I might as well get used to it.

I ran into Maggie herself on my way outside. She was wearing a white cotton dress and cradling a two-liter soda bottle in the crook of her arm.

"Hey, Paige," she said. "I'm so glad you came! Great dress."

"Thanks. It's a great party."

From somewhere inside, a glass shattered.

"Shit," she said, rolling her eyes. "Better get in there. Hey—I hope you have a good time. Really."

She gave me one last meaningful look—that "really" proving that she knew, as much as anyone could, what the past year had been like for me. Maggie, whose grace and directness had gotten her elected class president every year since seventh grade, would never give me That Look.

Without any of my friends beside me, I wove through crowds of people. I situated myself at the edge of the tall deck and took a deep breath. Below, kids in my grade splashed each other, bare skin against blue pool water. The water rippled as it moved, and I imagined the little waves as tiny hands, waiting to grab on and pull them down. My throat thickened, but I forced a slow inhale. No one was going to drown. They were all safe.

The warm breeze lifted my bangs off my forehead, and I didn't bother to fix them.

Someone leaned on the railing next to me, arms crossed the same way as mine. I glanced over to see Ryan Chase, inches away and likewise surveying the swimmers.

"Hey," he said, smiling over at me. His eyes looked as wildly blue as the pool.

"Hey."

"Is your hair different?"

Words, Paige. Say them. "Bangs."

"Nice." When he smiled, crinkles formed at the sides of his eyes. I'd never noticed before. Maybe they made him look a little older, but I was charmed—here was a boy whose happiness had already left its mark on his face.

Through fluttering eyelashes and a shy smile, I managed, "Thanks."

Step back, ladies: eyelash batting and monosyllabic responses. Obviously, I had this completely under control.

Before I could recover from this verbal blundering, Ryan Chase's face morphed. His mouth creased in concern and worst of all, he touched my elbow. It was, undeniably, That Look. Voice drenched in pity, he said, "I think it's great that you came tonight."

My head sagged, shoulders slumping. But then I remembered: the gossip and watchful eyes found Ryan Chase here, too—everyone, even me, silently evaluating how he was doing post-Leanne. So I took a chance. "Thanks. You, too."

This caught him off guard, his eyebrows flinching. Oh, God—I'd overstepped. And the award for World's Clunkiest Flirtation goes to . . . Paige "the Social Boundary Violator" Hancock! But then Ryan flashed me a sad, knowing smile. "I'm trying."

I nodded, trying not to show my relief. "Yeah. I am, too."

We stood there together, kindred for a moment—here but separate from our classmates, each dealing with something private in a public setting. I understood, and he knew I did.

"There you are." Tessa leaned in beside me, and Ryan's eyes shifted to her. Morgan and Kayleigh weren't far behind.

"Here I am," I said weakly.

"Hey, Tessa." Ryan stood up straighter.

"Hey," she said, not bothering to make eye contact. She spun around, back against the railing.

"Tessa and I are new lunch table buddies," Ryan told me.

My whole body seared with jealousy, and I wondered

why she hadn't told me about sitting with Ryan at lunch. Probably because it wasn't a big deal to her.

"You just missed Tessa schooling every guy here in darts," Kayleigh said.

Tessa smiled to herself.

"Dart aficionado, eh?" Ryan Chase asked.

"There's a dartboard at the Carmichael," she said, as if he knew how much time she spent there.

He grinned, zeroing in on her completely. "So what's your secret?"

Only then did she cast him a look. She mimed throwing a dart and then smiled smugly. "I've got the touch."

"Oh, hey," Kayleigh said to her. "Are you seeing Ursa Major at the Carmichael next month? My brother's going to that."

Tessa exhaled sharply, almost a snort. "Of course I'm going."

She blocked Ryan Chase out as if he'd never been there and continued to chat with Kayleigh. Morgan glanced around the deck, combing the crowd for prospects. This seemed as good a time as any to duck out to the bathroom. Ryan Chase and I had shared a moment. Yes, Tessa's tiny, blasé presence trumped me in an instant. But, eventually, he'd realize she wasn't interested. Or so I told myself, as I made my way upstairs, where I was pleased to find no line at the bathroom door.

The door was already open a crack, so I didn't even knock. But this wasn't a bathroom at all. I took in a spacious office with a wide desk and a bookcase lining the entire back wall. And, in the back corner, a tall figure with dark hair, sitting perfectly still in a wingback chair.

"Oh my God." I gasped, my hand flying to my chest in surprise. But I recognized him: Max Watson, Ryan Chase's cousin.

"Uh . . . hey," he said, looking up.

I exhaled. "You scared me."

"I got bored," he said, holding up the book in his hand so I could infer the rest.

"So you came in here to read?"

"Well, not exactly. I was looking for the bathroom, but it turns out that someone who lives here is really into John Irving. And so am I."

I leaned closer to get a view of the book's cover. "Is that *Owen Meany*?"

"It is," he said, his eyebrows rising. "You're on a first-name basis with this book?"

"I guess so. I love the closing lines."

"Yeah," Max said. "All the longing in the book is right there in the last two sentences."

Barely repressing an amused smile, I crossed my arms. "You've read it before?"

"I have." He pushed his glasses farther up on his nose.

"So you're sitting in this office, alone, reading a book you've already read . . . ?"

He thought for a moment. "Seems that way."

There was a pause, and I realized I was out of things to say. So I stumbled into an introduction. "I'm Paige, by the way."

"I know," he said. "I'm Max."

"Right. English class."

"Ms. Pepper told me you were considering QuizBowl."

"Oh, right." In all the drama with my parents, I'd totally forgotten. "Yeah, I am. You're the captain, right?"

He saluted. "Aye-aye. I'm really only captain by default, though. The other two team members are super busy. I just have robotics team and Latin Club, so they said I should do it."

"Robotics?" I asked. "Is that, like, building robots?"

"Pretty much," he said, shrugging, and I decided I'd hit my awkwardness capacity.

"Well, have fun with John and Owen," I said, backing out of the room. I knew Max was smart, but this was a committed and impressive display of nerdiness.

"Oh, I will," he called as I shut the door.

I shook my head, brushing off our weird encounter. Even though Ryan had always been popular in school, it was common knowledge that Max was his closest friend. I'd even heard rumors that Max transferred back to Oakhurst because Ryan was having a rough time. During the first week of school, I'd certainly noticed that Ryan wasn't running with his usual crowd. Leanne still walked down the hallways flanked by the same group Ryan had always belonged to. Ryan seemed separate now, chatting with random track buddies or student council people in the hallway instead of his big clique of so-called friends.

By the time I found the real restroom and made my way back to my friends, Tessa had texted me: *This party is dead. Meet you at the car.*

I found Maggie to say good-bye and then made my way through the crowd. But, once outside, I was distracted by the black Jeep parked immediately in front of the house—Ryan Chase's Jeep.

And leaning against Ryan Chase's Jeep was Max Watson, arms crossed.

"You again," I said, slowing my pace. I'd never seen Max Watson at a party before, and now he seemed to be everywhere.

"Me again," he agreed. "Slightly less creepy this time."

I smiled. "How was the book?"

"Excellent, as you know."

"Well," I said. "You missed an excellent party." It wasn't true, really, and my time probably would have been better spent reading or watching TV.

He shrugged. "I only came because my mom is on my

case about being 'actively social' now that I'm back at Oakhurst. Compared to Ryan, I think I seem like a recluse to her."

"Ha," I said, almost fully laughing at how close my own thoughts had been to his mother's thoughts.

"Why is that funny?" He frowned. I stood close enough to see my reflection in his glasses. The bangs surprised me; an already forgotten addition.

"Only because . . ." My mind stumbled, searching. "My mom wishes I was more social, too."

That wasn't exactly true. After what happened with Aaron, my mom wanted me to have "healthy relationships," but she preferred that I have friends over to our house, where she'd know I was safe. She almost forbade me from riding in Tessa's car entirely. "Teen drivers have such a high rate of accidents," she'd said.

"Ah," Max said. "I thought you were making fun of me."

"Never," I lied, as a pang of guilt hit me. This was not good. I really needed Ryan Chase's cousin to like me. Plus, if I stayed here talking to him long enough, Ryan Chase was bound to come to his car eventually. My friends could wait.

"Actually," I said, buying some time, "when I was younger, I would sneak off at slumber parties to read whatever book I'd brought. My friends still make fun of me for it."

He smiled genuinely now, but his eyes traveled above my head.

"You ready?" he asked someone behind me. I turned my head to find Ryan Chase, striding toward us.

"Yep," Ryan said, jingling his car keys as evidence.

"See you Monday," Max said to me as Morgan appeared on the sidewalk near the car, flagging me down.

"You coming?" she called to me.

"Yeah." To the guys, I said, "See you later."

"Bye, Paige," Ryan said, like we were friends. I half expected his grin to have an actual glint to it, with a *Ding*! like a toothpaste commercial.

I hurried to a coy-looking Morgan. She crossed her arms. "They sent me on a search-and-rescue mission but, clearly, you needed no rescue. What did Ryan Chase say to you?"

"Um, he said, 'Bye Paige.' "

"Oh. Well, he totally gave you the eyes."

"I think that's just . . . how his eyes are."

"Dreamy? True." She laughed as she pulled me toward Tessa's car.

"Coffee?" Tessa asked, once we'd climbed in. It wasn't really a question. She took the back roads with the windows down, and I closed my eyes, feeling my hair dance all around me.

~

I spilled my family drama to my friends after all, in two numb sentences. "My mom and dad have been dating each other for four months. My mom told me tonight."

"Oh my *God*," Kayleigh whispered, and Morgan elbowed her.

"Are you okay?" I knew Morgan well enough to expect this question first, along with her hand on my arm. Kayleigh slurped at her drink, and Tessa leaned a bit closer, our shoulders touching.

I shrugged. "I don't think it matters. They're dating, and that's it."

We were in the corner booth at Alcott's, our usual spot on the nights when Tessa's parents were actually at home. Sometimes we got drinks and talked the whole time. Other nights, we gathered our books or magazines of choice, alternately reading and laughing—at Kayleigh's dramatic readings from *Cosmo* or Tessa's scandalous facts from a rock star's autobiography. This could go on for hours, tucked away from the rest of the world.

"Why didn't you tell us earlier tonight?" Kayleigh frowned. "We could have skipped the party."

I shrugged again. "I didn't really want to talk about it."

"That's okay," Morgan said. She twisted one pearl earring. "We don't have to talk about it. We just want to make sure you're okay."

"It's okay if you're not okay," Kayleigh added. There were too many okays flying around, and it was becoming glaringly obvious that I was not, in fact, okay.

I glanced around at each of them, their eyes on mine,

and sighed. "It's just that everything I thought I knew seems different. It's like, when my parents divorced, it was a period. Not an ellipsis."

Morgan shook her head after a moment. "I don't follow."

"It wasn't 'Divorced, dot-dot-dot,'" I said. "It was 'Divorced, period.' That's what divorce *is*. The ending punctuation."

"Maybe it's a new sentence," Tessa suggested. "A new story."

"Or maybe it was a semicolon before," Morgan said.

I had to smile at this, their additions to my loose metaphor. "Please don't take this the wrong way, but do any of you guys have problems that we can talk about instead?"

Morgan heaved a dramatic sigh. "I have *many* problems. For example, I was talking to Brandon Trevino—total potential, right?—while Tessa was throwing darts, and it was going so well until he made this comment about girls and competitive sports that had, frankly, misogynistic undertones. So *that* was a waste of time."

"Brandon Trevino is a ratbag," I said, recalling things I'd overheard him saying in the hallway once. Misogynistic was an understatement.

"It's true," Kayleigh said. "He once asked me, 'So, what are you, anyway?' He doesn't even know me!"

We all made grossed-out noises. People had always been

blunt in asking Kayleigh's ethnicity. If someone was polite enough about it, Kayleigh told them the truth: that her dad's side was French and Polish, and her mom was African American. If people asked rudely—like, "So, what are you, anyway?"—Kayleigh would say, "I'm fabulous; what are you?"

"I'm telling you," Tessa said, "high school guys are a waste of time. Go college or go home."

"Hey," Kayleigh said. "Eric's still in high school!"

"Then maybe the guys at Carmel are salvageable," Tessa said.

"Salvageable?" Kayleigh laughed. "Thanks a lot."

"I haven't met him yet!" Tessa said, grinning. "I don't know if he's acceptable."

"Geez, Tessa," Morgan said. "They're guys, not troll people."

"That," Tessa said, pointing at her, "shows exactly how much you know about high school guys. Let me take you on a little trip down memory lane. To Shawn Puker."

Shawn's last name was not Puker. But, the year before, he took Tessa to a party and got so drunk that he puked. Tessa recounted the total horror—*My shoes, Morgan! It got on my shoes!*—and I propped my chin against my hand, sinking into their easy laughter. Whatever happened next with my parents, my friends and I would still be here trading stories and sips of our lattes. Together, we made four walls, holding each other up even as the world around us shifted.

~

When I got home, I found my sister brushing her teeth in our adjoining bathroom. I hadn't talked to her about our parents yet, but if I had been upset, I expected catatonic from Cameron. At thirteen, my sister was primarily into glittery nail polish and phone conversations where she essentially contributed: "Oh my God. Nuh-uh."

She was bent over the bathroom sink, wrapped in a towel. Beyond her, the bathtub gurgled with nearly drained water, a sickening *glug-glug* that made me shudder. I hadn't used our tub in a year. My sister's girly bath products were lined up in a neat row by the edge of the tub, each chosen for its cute bottle and fruity smell.

"Hey," I said, leaning against the door frame. She looked up, wiping some sort of green gel off her face. Her hair, the same soft brown as mine, was pulled back with a headband.

"I heard you flipped out at Mom." She blotted her face with a towel. "What's your problem?"

My jaw dropped, as if to speak, but no words came out. Cameron stared at me, waiting.

"What is *my* problem?" I asked. "My problem is that they're going to wind up hurting each other all over again."

She rolled her eyes at me. "You don't know that."

"Yeah, Cameron. I do."

"Oh, c'mon," she scoffed. "They've had some time apart, and they're good now. You should be happy for them."

I rubbed at my temples. "You don't remember what it was like."

"I remember," she said, frowning. "I'm only three years younger than you."

"Then you'd remember they were *so* unhappy together. When we were little, they hardly talked. They only fought."

Her expression became a full-on scowl. "No, they didn't."

"Cameron, they did. They got divorced because they bring out the worst in each other."

She glared, refusing to break eye contact for a few beats. "Well, I think you're being super negative. It'll be better this time."

I glanced between our faces, reflected back at me in the bathroom mirror. We looked so alike, the same green eyes and pale skin dotted with freckles, only she was shorter and bonier like I had been at that age.

"Maybe," I conceded, finally, but only because she looked like a little kid to me in that moment. A little kid whose security blanket I had tried to yank away. "Good night."

Once inside my room, I opened my planner to my How to Begin Again list. I'd done it—gone to a party, despite a massive curveball from my mom. I slashed a line through

~~1. Parties/social events.~~

I smiled down at the list, pride spreading through me like warmth. I'd already done one of the five things. It wasn't even that hard. Enamored by my success, I made a quick edit to number three. Because it couldn't be just any random guy. I needed to go out with someone who *got* me, someone I connected with. Someone who made my insides fluttery.

3. Date (RC)

Chapter Six

Three months after Aaron died, my grandmother moved into an assisted-living community—*not* a nursing home, as the brochure was careful to state. I could hardly bear to say good-bye to her house, on top of everything else I was trying to let go of. But after her Alzheimer's diagnosis was official, she wanted an apartment here.

I found that her new place comforted me the way her old house did. The decor was mostly the same—vines of linen roses crawling up the drapes, herbs blooming in their windowsill pots, china figurines curtsying to each other inside a glass hutch. She still stocked ginger ale and my favorite snacks, and she still kept the TV on mute while we talked, always Nick at Nite.

It was my grandmother who taught me that TV shows start with writing. We were watching *I Love Lucy* when I was eleven, and I said, "Lucy is the funniest lady ever."

"Lucille Ball was a magnificent talent," she told me. "But, you know, she was said to be very serious in real life."

"And she could just turn on the funny for TV?"

"Well," my grandmother had said, "almost every episode was cowritten by the same person, who was very funny herself."

"By Lucy, you mean?" I asked.

"No, by a woman named Madelyn Pugh. It was very unusual in the 1950s, to have a woman as a main writer for a show. I think she really understood Lucy."

When I expressed how confused I was, she explained how TV shows are written in advance, by a room full of writers. At first, that new information took away some of the magic for me. But then we watched *30 Rock*, a show about writing for TV, and my grandmother gave me Madelyn Pugh's memoir for Christmas the next year. She made me want to be a part of it all.

Now I roamed around the living room, waiting for my grandmother to "put on her face." She did her full hair and makeup before entertaining company, even if it was only me. And it was often me, carrying plenty of emotional baggage to unpack on her floor.

The mantel showcased my school pictures, framed next

to Cameron's. Nestled between them was the picture of my grandma twirling in front of the Eiffel Tower—her arms slightly out, skirt in a bell shape around her legs, face blurred from the spinning motion. I know now that she was fifty in the photo, but she looked so young and free.

I sat down at the kitchen table, picking through the ever-present dish of trail mix. I liked sweet and Cameron liked salty. Our grandmother mediated between us even with snacks.

"Hi, sweet girl," she said, emerging from her bedroom. She bent to kiss my cheek, and the smell of powdery lavender enveloped me.

"Hi, Grammy," I said.

"New haircut?" She squinted at me as she lowered herself into a chair.

I nodded. "Bangs."

She gave a sagely nod. "I've always said bangs would look good on you, Katie."

"Paige." This only happened once in a while, my grandmother calling me by my mother's name.

My grandma blinked a few times and then laughed, a bit embarrassed. "Silly me. Did I call you Katie? You just look so much like your mother did when she was a girl. Only now you have bangs."

"Bangs that my mother *hates*," I said. "Of course."

"She said that?" Her frown deepened the delicate wrinkles by her mouth.

I sighed, remembering my mother's terse tone in the car on the way here. "Well, she hates that I cut them without asking her."

"Oh, she'll get over it."

Sometimes I couldn't believe that it was my grandmother who raised my mom. I didn't remember my grandfather, but I knew he was a marine. Maybe that's where my mom got her strict rules and military-grade enforcement of a curfew. We were quiet for a few moments while I lost myself in thinking about my mom. And my dad. And my mom and dad.

"My goodness, dear." My grandmother peered at me from across the kitchen table. "You look like you have something heavy on your mind. Is it the dream again?"

She meant the drowning nightmare, which only she and the therapist knew about. As far as I could tell, it was one of the last things my grandmother retained before her memory loss worsened.

"No. It's not that. Did you know," I began, trying to sound calm, "that my mom and dad. Are dating. Each other?"

She sucked in her breath. "I think I may have heard something about that. Are you sure?"

This was the Alzheimer's at work. My mom had surely told her already, but that conversation would seem dreamlike, confusing for my grandmother to recollect.

"I'm positive."

"Goodness me."

"I . . . feel . . ." The words scattered in my mind, and I

held my hands up in bewildered surrender. My mouth was still halfway open, thoughts stillborn. But no matter how I searched, there was no candy coating on the truth of my feelings. "I feel like a horrible daughter."

With my free hand, I began plucking more M&M'S out of the trail mix in front of me and lining them up beside the bowl. "I know I'm supposed to be happy. *All* divorce-casualty kids want their parents to get back together."

Her lips curved into a sad smile. "You're afraid to get your hopes up."

"Yes." I exhaled all the air from my lungs, forming a more dramatic sigh than I intended. "I am. Because I already know how this ends."

She tightened her hand over mine. Her nonchalance alarmed me, given that this should feel like new information to her.

"Don't you think it's a mistake?" I asked. I needed to know what she remembered, now that her long-term memory was stronger than the final years of my parents' marriage. "Like . . . they're not compatible, no matter how much they want to be?"

"Oh, honey," my grandmother said. "It's more complicated than that. Your parents, they were so happy together those first few years."

"They were?" I started arranging the blue M&M'S into a line.

My grandmother nodded.

I'd once found a photo of my parents on their wedding day, in the bottom of my mother's jewelry drawer. I sneaked back in dozens of times over the years to study it. In the soft light of the photograph, they were exiting the church, beaming sideways at the camera. They looked at ease beside each other, young and golden. They weren't the parents that I knew.

"Then what *happened*?" It's a morbid curiosity, the search for relationship fissures—like searching for a cause of death. I knew it wouldn't change anything, but I still had to know.

"Things change. There are so many outside forces coming at marriage; finances and jobs and houses and children. You can lose each other if you're not careful. It doesn't mean it was all a wash."

I shook my head slowly, disbelieving. I scooped up the blue M&M'S and popped them into my mouth.

"Oh, my little girl," she said, patting my hand. "Not everything ends so badly."

I wanted to live in Lucy and Ricky's world, where the blunders of life were righted in one neat half hour. They made it look easy.

"Come on now." My grandmother's eyes had the glimmer of intrigue. "There must be some nice boy who makes you want to change your tune."

This got a smile out of me. "I guess, maybe."

My grandmother smiled back, settling back into her chair. "Tell me everything."

"Well, you know how you told me that dating kind of helped you, after Gramps?" Her eyebrows dropped, and I scolded myself for phrasing it as a question. She didn't remember. "It was a while ago. Anyway, that's my plan now. And there's this guy, Ryan Chase, whom I've liked since forever, and he's the perfect person to go out with."

"Why him?" she asked, still smiling. "What makes this boy good enough for my girl?"

I'd told her before, of course, but I started at the beginning all over again—with the cereal aisle.

"It was such a hard time for his sister and their family," I said. "But there he was, dancing anyway."

"Ah," she said. "Joy in the face of destruction. A very admirable quality."

"I think so, too. He had a bad breakup this summer, but he's still so confident and positive. I know that if we went out, everyone would see that we're both doing really well."

"So he's the plan," said my grandmother.

"He's the plan," I agreed. "Or at least part of it."

I told her my other goals, inspired so much by her. "I don't think I can actually swim—not any time soon. But I put it on the list for someday. And travel might be harder to plan, too, but I'll figure it out. I'm not sure where yet. Why did you pick Paris?"

She smiled. "Why not Paris? My world had crumbled around me. Like your friend Mr. Chase, I found a place to dance."

~

"So," my dad said, pulling the passenger's side seat belt over his chest. "Are we on speaking terms?"

"Nope." I could barely look at him because my mind refused to compute: he's dating *Mom*. Did they go on actual dates? Hold hands? I recoiled.

My mom had dropped me off at my grandma's, but it was my dad's turn to pick me up for dinner at his place, making it impossible to avoid him. I'd already dodged a phone call from him because talking about their relationship made it real. And I *liked* my denial. It was cozy here, in the land where divorced parents just didn't touch each other.

I drove with rigid posture, square shoulders and chin held high. My dad stayed quiet for a few minutes, honoring my request for silence.

"The dating thing is bad enough," I said, finally. "But it really, really sucks that you kept it from me."

I could see him nodding in my peripheral vision.

"You're right," he said. "I'm sorry about that."

I blinked. My father, famously verbose, was leaving it at that. If he was aiming for reverse psychology, it worked. I felt like a pessimistic brat.

"I know you don't mean for it to affect me." My shoulders drooped. "But it does."

"I know that, Paiger," he said, a sigh escaping. "I do. But your mom and I are going to do everything in our power to keep this as normal as possible."

I wrinkled my nose. "What does that even mean?"

"Whatever you want it to mean. You and Cameron will still come over for dinner twice a week and stay with me when your mom's out of town. We don't have to talk about it. I won't come over to the house at first if that will make the transition easier."

My mom gave me a similar speech earlier that day, only hers had more parenting magazine phraseology: "defined boundaries" and "respecting everyone's comfort levels." In reality, I was the only one with any level of discomfort, but I had earned it—all those nights, squinting my eyes in fake sleep while their bickering voices carried into my bedroom.

"You know," my dad said, "when you fall for someone, it's involuntary, kiddo. Even when it's for the second time with the same person. You'll see someday."

Also involuntary: my scowl. I was the one in high school. *I* was supposed to be giddily going on dates and looking hazed over with happiness—not my middle-aged parents. All I had were a few hopeful conversations with Ryan Chase and a list of things that might make me feel happy again. It usually took being with my friends or my grandma to make me feel happy. But last night, when I took my list down to only four? It was the happiest I'd felt, being alone, in a long time. I needed the satisfaction of crossing off another item—it had felt so charged, so definite.

I glanced over at my dad, desperate for a subject change. "So . . . I'm thinking about doing QuizBowl at school. It's like a game-show-type trivia thing."

He sat up straighter. QuizBowl was squarely inside my dad's wheelhouse. I'd heard stories of his victories at bar Trivia Nights in college, and he tried to get Cameron and me to play Trivial Pursuit Junior for years when we were little. "Really, kiddo? That's *great*!"

Once I saw the excited look on his face, I knew I really had to do it. My parents watched me suffer so much sadness that they couldn't take away. I think I wanted them to see that I was doing better these days. And maybe I wanted to make myself see it, too.

Chapter Seven

"All right," Ms. Pepper called, after the bell rang. "This isn't the first week of school anymore. Time to get down to business."

The chattering died down, and she picked up papers from off her desk.

"On the first day of class I told you that I had two goals for this year," she said as she passed a handful of papers down the first row. "For you to learn about one another and literature. This in-class assignment will serve as a refresher on Shakespearean themes you've previously studied in *Romeo and Juliet* and *Julius Caesar*. It will also help you get to know a fellow classmate, as you'll be working in twos. You're not in kindergarten, so pair yourselves off. I'll trust you to pick someone you don't already know well."

Max poked me in the back before Ms. Pepper even finished talking. "Wanna work together?"

Morgan was already chatting with Maggie Brennan. Ryan Chase was too far away to ask, and I didn't want to get stuck without a partner.

"Sure." I spun in my seat to face Max, noticing the faint imprint across his cheeks and forehead—the remnant of chemistry lab goggles.

"What?" he asked.

"Nothing," I said, not wanting to embarrass him.

The first section read: WHAT'S IN A NAME?

"Full Name," I read aloud. "Is it Max*well*? Or Maxi-*millian*?"

"Neither. Just Max." His mouth pulled into a half smile. "Max Oliver Watson."

"Paige Elizabeth Hancock," I said, watching him write it down. "Okay, next question. Are you named after anyone?"

"My grandfather and my godfather." He pushed up the cuffs of his shirt. "Although, when I was little, I thought I was named after Max from *Where the Wild Things Are*."

I smirked at the idea of Max being anything like Max from the children's book. Highly unlikely. Max Watson was more "volunteer tutor" than "king of all wild things."

"What about you? Are you named after anyone?"

"My parents just liked the name Paige, I think, but Elizabeth is because my mom is a huge *Pride and Prejudice* fan." I thought for a second. "I don't think I've ever told anyone that, actually."

His head jerked toward me. "Really?"

"Yeah. Guess it never came up. Elizabeth is a pretty standard middle name."

"No," he said. "I mean really 'Elizabeth'? You seem much more like a Jane Bennet."

My jaw dropped in offense. "That's kind of mean!"

"No, it's not! Jane is deeply underappreciated."

"Because she's *boring*," I said, surprised at how much this bothered me.

"As opposed to Elizabeth, who judges everyone?"

"Elizabeth is smart! She's . . . a critical thinker!"

"Jane is also smart. She's just not critical of other people. And she has much better taste in men."

"Now you're insulting Mr. Darcy?" I sat back in my chair, arms crossed. "Well, *this* should be interesting."

"He's mean and moody."

"He's misunderstood," I said. "He has a good heart."

"*Bingley* has a good heart." He laughed, apparently not realizing that his volume was now significantly above the general buzz of our classmates.

I opened my mouth for a counterargument, but people were starting to look at us—because we were heatedly and publicly disagreeing about Jane Austen. *Not* winning any cool points here. So I mumbled, "I *guess*."

"I'm sorry," he conceded. "I meant it as a compliment. Jane's quiet and kind, you know."

My cheeks flushed, and I looked down at my paper, wondering if they taught awkward, literature-based flattery at the Coventry School.

"Childhood nicknames, whether endearing or mean," I recited from the page.

Max stayed silent. He cleared his throat and averted my glance.

"None," he said, but his voice was too high.

I narrowed my eyes at him. "I don't believe you."

"You first."

"Okay . . ." I would definitely be omitting Grammar Girl. "I don't really have any. Oh, except my dad calls me Paiger. I kind of hate it, but he calls everyone by nicknames. Also, my last name's Hancock, so . . . there were never *nicknames* with that. But plenty of jokes involving the second syllable."

Max laughed a little. "You can probably guess mine. It may or may not be related to a feminine hygiene product."

I wrinkled my nose. "Maxi-pad?"

"Oh yeah." He grinned ruefully. "Thanks, older kids on the bus. But that nickname faded off before junior high, at which point it was replaced with 'nerd.' "

I stifled the smile that wanted to creep onto my face. It was sort of endearing how comfortable Max seemed with the nerd label. He glanced back down at the page and read, "Are there any names that have negative connotations for you and why?"

"Ugh." I made a face. "Yes. Chrissie."

He wrote it down. "Why?"

"Chrissie Cohen was my next-door neighbor, and she antagonized me every day until she moved away."

"Antagonized you how?"

"She mocked me for reading on the bus, mostly."

"Well," he said. "If we're talking about bullies' names, I have at least a dozen you can write in. Mike, Brandon, Clark—"

My head snapped up. "Clark Driscoll?"

"Yeah," Max said. "Biggest jerk to me. Made gym class total hell."

I'd never understood Aaron's friendship with Clark, which Aaron summarized as "I don't know. We've been best friends since we were in diapers." Where Aaron's sense of humor was goofy, Clark's had a meanness that over-stepped teasing. He didn't talk to me a lot when I was going out with Aaron, and even less after he died. I noticed him in the hallway, though—the way he stared down at the floor these days. When he did make eye contact, he'd say, "Hey, Paige" in this defeated voice. He'd lost weight in the past year, the round curve of his face diminishing to a defined jawline. But he didn't look healthier for it. He looked withered, like a plant away from sunlight. I worried about him at a distance, afraid that I had no right to talk to him about our shared loss. His loss was so much greater.

"Paige?" Max's voice cut into my thoughts.

"Yeah? Sorry. What did you say?"

"Do you want to move on to the next section?"

"Sure," I said, affecting a false smile that drooped right back down. Part of me wanted to know if Aaron had ever been there when Clark bullied Max. I knew he'd never contribute, but I hoped that, even in middle school, he wouldn't have stood by and watched. "Yes."

We went through the section on surname origins and their implications, then a section on pet names, where I learned that Max once had a guinea pig named Milo, after the main character in *The Phantom Tollbooth*.

"So," Max said, after we'd finished the last item on the worksheet. "Have you decided about QuizBowl?"

"Well, I had a few questions. I, um . . . actually don't even know who the other people on the team are."

"Oh. Malcolm Park, who's in our grade. He's awesome—you'll like him. We've been friends since before I left for Coventry. The other is Lauren Mathers. She's a senior."

I knew who Malcolm was, but not Lauren. And that wasn't my only concern. "So, is there . . . a bus?"

"A bus?"

"Well, we stay after school for matches, right? And travel to away meets?"

"Oh," he said. "It's only the four of us, so we just drive."

My cheeks flashed with heat. "Well, I don't have a car, so that might be a problem."

"I can drive you. No problem."

With Ryan Chase sitting a few seats away, I still felt torn. Maybe QuizBowl would help me get to know Max, and therefore Ryan. But maybe it would be social suicide. *Beginner's mind*, I repeated to myself. No more maybes. "Then okay."

"Wait, seriously?" Max's eyebrows shot up above the dark frame of his glasses. "You'll do it?"

"I'll do it."

"Wrap it up!" Ms. Pepper called. "We need to talk about starting *Hamlet* tomorrow."

"Awesome!" Max continued. "We're having one practice next Sunday, just to get team strategy clear before matches start. So, do you want to come over a little early? We can go over game structure and that kind of thing?"

"I guess. Sure."

"Quiet, people!" Ms. Pepper said. "It's Bard time. Your favorite time."

I turned back around, settling in for the remainder of class. A few minutes later, I stifled a gasp as something brushed the back of my arm. It was Max's hand, tossing a note onto my desk. The note was folded into a tiny paper airplane, impossibly small and precise. Inside, he'd written his address and the time 6:00 p.m. I folded the airplane back up and flicked it gently, watching it spin like a compass needle gone awry. It only took three tries until the plane pointed toward Ryan Chase.

~

At the end of the week, I found myself walking in the same direction as Max after class.

"What happened to your fingers?" he asked.

I glanced down at the two burn marks. "Hot-glue gun. I was making something for my best friend's birthday. It's kind of hard to explain."

"I'm smart," he said.

I rolled my eyes. "When we were little, my dad took us to the Renaissance Fair, and we got these flower crowns. We wore them for *months*, I swear. I don't know what happened to mine, but I made us new ones for her birthday."

"Tessa, right?" Max asked. "She's your best friend? We sit together at lunch."

"Yeah." That made sense, since I knew she'd been sitting with Ryan Chase.

"She was talking nonstop yesterday about eating at whatever restaurant tomorrow."

"Barrett House?" I asked, laughing. "Yeah. Her parents

are taking us. She's been dying to eat there since it opened and already has every course picked out. She, uh . . . likes food."

"I've noticed," he said. "She ate, like, half my fries yesterday after eating all of her own. So, flower crowns and a huge dinner sound pretty perfect."

"That's the plan," I said as we parted ways.

~

It was a disaster.

The text came Saturday morning, around the time I woke up. *Dinner's off tonight. Can you tell the girls?*

I called Tessa, not even bothering to text back.

"Hey." Her voice fell completely flat.

"What happened?"

"Oh, you know. The same thing that always does. My parents left me a message some time overnight, saying they can't leave China because their meeting with investors got pushed back. Or something. I don't know." She sighed. "They said we could still go downtown with Gram, but . . . I don't feel like it anymore."

"I'm sorry," I said. The phrase felt weak and watery, just two words trying to fill such a deep void.

"Yeah," she said. "Me, too."

"I'll tell Morgan and Kayleigh."

"Thanks. You wanna come over later? Just watch TV or something?"

"Of course. Five o'clock?"

"Okay. See you then."

I struggled to visualize a plan B, something perfect and Tessa-ish. She deserved those five courses—especially after everything she'd been through with me in the past year.

A month after Aaron died, I had a breakdown at Alcott's. I felt the panic attack coming on, invisible walls closing in around me, and I excused myself to the bathroom. Instead, I hid in the tree house in the children's-book section, crying into my bent-up knees. It took only a few minutes before Tessa crawled in beside me, her inner compass mapping in five directions: north, south, east, west, Paige. She didn't say a word or even try to comfort me. Of all Tessa's qualities, that was maybe the one I admired the most: she knew how to sit inside my sadness with me. I wouldn't have survived without her.

So yes, she deserved those five courses, plus every dessert on the menu.

And that's when it snapped to my mind: a dessert buffet. We could set it up on Tessa's back patio. Morgan made killer cupcakes, and Kayleigh could at least cover ice cream and brownies from a box. I'd go to the grocery store and buy all Tessa's other favorites. It still didn't feel like enough, but it was better than nothing. I texted the girls frantically as I raced downstairs, filling them in.

On it, Morgan sent back. *I'll make a cake.*

Kayleigh chimed in, too. *Brownies: check. Will stop at Kemper's for ice-cream pints.*

Perfect, I replied. *And we're totally still dressing up.*

Duh, Morgan said.

I'm always dressed up, Kayleigh added.

I found my mom editing an article at the kitchen table. "Can I borrow your car?"

"To go where?"

"The grocery store. Tessa's parents are stuck in China, so dinner's off. We're trying to make her a dessert buffet."

"Oh no. You're kidding." My mom liked Norah and Roger, but she could barely resist her own urge to mother Tessa. "Of course, take the car. And here."

She pulled her wallet from her purse and handed me two twenties. "Drive safe. I mean it."

Forty bucks bought me a bunch of Tessa's favorites: a blackberry pie, four little crème brûlées from the bakery, two bottles of sparkling grape juice, and two bouquets of sunflowers—plus, sparklers from the clearance bin, which she'd prefer to candles. At home, my mom helped me rummage through the Christmas supplies in the basement until we found the strings of white lights.

Kayleigh, Morgan, and I sneaked around the back of Tessa's house to the patio overlooking the pool. On the outdoor table, Morgan set up the cake—two-tier funfetti—on one of her mom's cake plates. She unloaded other fancy dishes she'd brought "for presentation" while I arranged the sunflowers in two vases my mom let me borrow. Kayleigh maneuvered the strings of lights around the patio railings.

When we were ready, I knocked on the back door until Gram McMahon let me in. I'd called her cell earlier to fill her in.

"You girls are gems," her gram said. "She's in quite a mood."

I found Tessa in her room. She lay in a fetal position on the bed, blankly staring at the TV.

"Hey." I lay down on the other side of the bed, facing her. "Happy birthday."

"Yeah," she said drily. "Super happy."

"Your parents suck at being parents sometimes," I said. "But don't let them ruin your day."

"Sometimes I think they didn't even mean to have me," she said, with a little snort of derision. "I know, I know. I'm being melodramatic. What seventeen-year-old pouts over their mommy and daddy? Maybe I'll throw a huge party tonight, kegs and all. That's what I'm supposed to do, right? Act out for attention?"

"Sure," I said. "But first, I need you to put on your party dress."

"Why?" She sounded exhausted and utterly unamused.

"We have plans. Good ones."

My best friend narrowed her eyes at me. "You don't have to do this."

"I know. It's not even really for you. It's for me."

This made her smile a little. "Oh yeah?"

"Yeah. Planning makes me feel happy. Look at how happy I am." I gave her a creepy-big smile, eyes unblinking like a clown serial killer.

"God," she said, laughing. "Fine. Anything to get you to stop making that face."

She put on her pale-pink maxidress, and, in the kitchen downstairs, I presented her with a flower crown.

"Oh my God," she said, placing it on her head. Her expression went thoughtful, reaching up to touch the synthetic petals. "Do you know why I loved these so much when we were little? They made me feel invincible. Like, what terrible thing could happen to you when you're wearing a crown of flowers?"

We were not invincible. But I wanted to pretend—to remember that innocent freedom—if only for the night.

I led Tessa out the back door, where Morgan and Kayleigh stood by our dessert table, amid twinkle lights and speckled frosting and sparklers that crackled in the setting sun. "Happy birthday!" we yelled, and I swear I saw wetness in Tessa's eyes as she leaned forward to blow out her Roman candles. We sat there in our flower crowns until the world went dark, until we were half-sick from sugar but still laughing, laughing, laughing like the almost-invincible girls we were.

Happy 17th! I'd written in Tessa's card. *Thank goodness you were born. I don't think I would have lasted without you.*

Chapter Eight

"You're sure Max's mother is home?" my mom asked on Sunday, as I slid my bag onto my shoulder. I'd slept till noon at Tessa's house, in a sugar coma, and I still felt too groggy to tolerate my mom's inquisition.

"It's Sunday," I said. "Why wouldn't she be?"

"Well, I don't know." She frowned. "A doctor . . . could work strange hours."

"I mean, do you remember Max Watson from before he transferred schools? Gangly, dark hair, glasses . . . ?"

"Oh, right," she said. Even if his mom wasn't home, Max Watson took the prize for World's Least Likely to Corrupt Your Daughter. "Okay. Find out how late this will go and text me so I know when to pick you up."

She idled in the driveway as I made my way to the front door, waiting until I got in okay. I glared back at her, visually begging her to drive away.

Before I could knock, Max opened the door, his tall frame propping the screen open for me.

"Hey," he said, as if he didn't notice I was just awkwardly standing there, glowering at my mom. "I thought I heard a car. Come on in."

"Thanks." I stepped past him and into the house. I turned to see him waving at my mom, who waved back as she reversed down the driveway. Just when you think you can't embarrass yourself in front of a guy who used to build model airplanes during inside recess.

Inside, light streamed into the foyer from tall windows, reflecting against a dozen silver frames on a wall by the stairs. I couldn't make out the faces in the photos, but they were all of people holding one another close. The dining room, to the left, had a beautiful painting and a long table with upholstered chairs. I'm not sure what I expected, but it wasn't this comfortable sophistication. All I knew about Max's family was that his mother was a pediatrician and his cousin was the love of my life.

"Ready?"

"Sure," I said, snapping out of my tactless staring, and we stood there in the foyer for a moment as I glanced at his shirt—a black tee with some sort of spacecraft and the word "FIREFLY" across the top. I followed him into the kitchen, where the smell of something warm and savory lingered. There were two pots on the stove with steam still rising from them.

He gestured toward the kitchen table, where a half-eaten plate of spaghetti sat. His laptop sat closed, next to a small orange box. "You can have a seat. Sorry to eat in front of you. I got home later than I thought I would."

I glanced around as I sat down. "Where's your mom?"

"Working." Max took his place and picked up the waiting fork.

"You can cook?"

"It's just spaghetti. Do you want some?"

"No thanks." I gave a puzzled smile, more to myself than to him—dorky Max Watson, fixing Italian for one. The most I could do was heat up leftovers in the microwave, and even then I usually under- or overheated it on my first try.

"Oh my God," I said, staring at the orange box on the table. I hadn't noticed at first, but there they were. Do-Si-Dos, the most underappreciated and delicious Girl Scout cookie of them all. "How do you *have* these? It's fall!"

Max eyed me suspiciously. "I stockpile them in the spring and freeze them."

"No *way*," I said. "These are my favorite cookies in the world."

"Not possible," he said bluntly. "I am the only person on planet Earth who likes these more than the mint ones."

"No, I do, too," I said. "You can verify that with Tessa."

He eyed me, smiling a little. "I guess that means you'd like one?"

"Yes, please," I managed to say—when really I was thinking about grabbing the whole box and making a run for it.

"Go ahead," he said. "Raid my rations. I guess I owe you for jumping into QuizBowl."

I grabbed the box. "I've tried so many other peanut-butter cookies. Why are these so much better than all the others?"

"Sorcery," Max answered through a bite of spaghetti. "It's a Girl Scout badge."

The peanut-buttery goodness released as I bit down, and I sighed happily. *Savor it*, I reminded myself.

I chewed for a moment, and, high on cookie, blurted out, "Cool shirt, by the way."

It hit me after the words left my mouth: I'd mocked a virtual stranger to his face. After he shared his precious cookies.

But he just looked up at me from his plate, smiling as he shook his head. "Shut up."

I smiled, too, though half in relief. "What's *Firefly* anyway?"

"Only the best sci-fi show of all time. It was canceled after one glorious season. A travesty. It's my favorite show—and shirt—of all time."

"Then why don't you wear it to school?" I'd only noticed Max wearing collared shirts at school: pale-blue oxford or green with tiny gingham checks, rolled at the sleeves and untucked.

He didn't meet my eyes. "I'm, uh . . . I guess I'm still used to the Coventry school uniform. I can't quite bring myself to wear an old T-shirt to school. It's nice that I can wear my Converse, though. I hated wearing dress shoes."

We ate in silence for a minute before I asked, "So, how late do you think we'll go? I need to let my mom know."

"Malcolm and Lauren will be here at seven, so probably around eight. But I can take you home."

"Oh no, you don't have to." That was the worst part of not having a car—being a burden to everyone.

"It's really no problem. I said I'd drive you to QuizBowl stuff."

True enough. "Okay. Thanks."

I texted my mom, hoping she wouldn't forbid me from driving in a car with a boy she didn't know.

The garage door shuddered open, startling me. As I looked toward the sound, Max's mom walked in, holding a briefcase. She almost looked more like Ryan—shorter, with dark-honey hair. But when she turned to face me, her green eyes and wide smile reminded me of Max.

"Oh, hi there!" she said. "I'm Julie."

Up close, she looked too young to be a doctor. I'd imagined Max's mom would be professorial and kind of solemn, like a foreign news correspondent—not the Disney Channel mom standing before me. "I'm Paige."

"Also known as Janie." This was from Max, who was smirking over his pasta. I almost kicked him under the table.

"It's nice to meet you," she said, ignoring Max. "I remember your parents from before Max transferred to Coventry. I was so excited to hear you'd joined QuizBowl!"

"Nice to meet you, too," I said. She didn't give me That Look—not even a hint of it. I wondered if she knew about Aaron. She stood behind Max, wrapping one arm around his neck and kissing the top of his head.

"Hey, baby," she said to him. "Smells good in here."

Max's expression didn't change, but I saw the hint of a blush on his cheeks. "There's plenty left. Still warm."

"Great. Did you just get started?" she asked.

Max spun some spaghetti around his fork. "We had barely started, really. Paige was just telling me how much she likes my shirt."

I almost choked on my bite of cookie.

"Well, that's nice." His mom smiled over at me so earnestly that I felt guilty right away. I tried to give Max a *What is wrong with you?* look, but he was looking down at his plate. And grinning.

"Well, I'm going to eat this in the office." She balanced

the plate on one hand, still holding her briefcase in the other. "The paperwork is never done. Have fun!"

When she was out of earshot, I leaned my hand against my cheek and stared at Max. He chewed purposefully, avoiding my gaze.

"Um," I began, my voice incredulous. "Did you just *tattle* on me?"

"No!" he said, laughing. "I really wanted my mom to know that someone other than me likes this T-shirt."

"God," I grumbled. "Now I feel guilty for teasing you."

"That was the idea." He set his plate aside. "Okay. So. QuizBowl format. You ready?"

My mental image of a QuizBowl tournament flashed in my mind—me, seated at a table on a stage, trying to buzz in answers as hot auditorium lights beat down. But I squared my shoulders, nodding. "I'm ready."

Max explained the four rounds, toss-up questions and point values. We could jump in and answer questions if the other team got them wrong—except in the third round, when each team would pick from a few categories and answer ten related questions.

"Okay." I knew all this already from my Internet searches. Max kept going: when to answer questions the other team missed, when it's allowable to answer without being acknowledged by the moderator, and other various rules.

"Consultation between players is only allowed during

the third round, so it's best to know your fellow players' strengths as well as you can," he continued. "I buzz in and guess sometimes because there's no penalty for a wrong answer. But I only guess in my 'home' categories. That's why Malcolm and Lauren are coming over, to discuss how we'll split up our expertise areas. Any questions so far?"

I shook my head. "I think I understand the format. I'm more curious about the kinds of questions to expect."

"Gotcha." He set his plate aside and opened his laptop. "Just give me one second to find the website."

As he typed, I let my eyes stray around the kitchen. There were three pictures on the nearest patch of wall: one of Max's mom and another woman who looked like her, one of what seemed to be grandparents, and one of Max and Ryan at the beach. They were six or so, facing the camera head-on with their arms slung around each other's shoulders and each missing a few teeth. Ryan's hair was blonder then, and Max was wearing a swim shirt and snorkel goggles.

"I like all the pictures around," I said, gesturing at the one of him and Ryan. "That one's cute."

I hoped the word choice came off as the "Aw, little kids are cute" way instead of the "Your cousin is still cute and I want him to love me" way.

"Thanks. It's one of my mom's favorites."

"You and Ryan seem so different." I eyed him closely to

make sure that my comment registered as normal. I didn't want to pry or bring up Ryan where he had no place. The last thing I needed was Max suspecting my crush.

"Yeah, I get that a lot. I think that's why we get along so well."

"That's nice," I said decidedly. "Being friends with someone since you were little, I mean."

"Like you and Tessa," he said. Tessa must have said something at the lunch table. I wondered what else they talked about during that hour.

"Yeah," I said. "Like me and Tessa."

"I like her a lot," he said, glancing over at me. "She's so laid-back and cool—plus she has the best taste in music. I would never have guessed that her parents own a hotel chain."

I bit down a frown, thinking of the night before. "Yeah, well. It's hard sometimes. Her parents aren't around very much. She spent a lot of time at my house when we were kids."

"Yeah, she mentioned that." His eyes returned to the screen. "Same for me. Single mom in medical school and all. I half lived at my aunt and uncle's house."

"Oh." I felt awkward, unsure of what to say about that. "I'm sorry."

He looked up. "About what?"

"Um. About your dad?" I nearly cringed, regretting my words.

"Oh." He snorted. "Don't be. I'm not."

I nodded, feeling stupid and intrusive.

"He's still alive or whatever," Max said. "But I never see him. He and my mom were together in college. When she got pregnant, he bailed."

I felt my eyes widen. I assumed that Max's dad lived here, some tall guy with dark hair and a crisp suit. I was also surprised that Max would divulge all this to someone he barely knew. Maybe he could sense that my family situation was weird, too.

"So your mom graduated from college and raised you by herself while going to medical school?" I hadn't exactly meant to say this. And now it seemed like I was prying. Again. With Ryan Chase around, sentences crumbled into disjointed words before they could leave my mouth. If only that was happening now.

"She did indeed."

I shook my head in disbelief. "Wow."

"Yep. She's pretty cool."

"Wait," I said. "So she's . . . Dr. Watson?"

He laughed. "Yep. Just hasn't found her Sherlock yet. And look at you, with the literature references! QuizBowl suits you already."

I tilted my head to one side, giving him a disbelieving look. "Everyone knows Holmes and Watson."

"Maybe," he said. "But I assure you, we need the pop culture expertise."

"So, when you say 'pop culture,' are we talking current pop culture?"

"I'd say last fifty years or so with TV shows and movies. But sometimes they ask about current-day celebrities and stuff. Some leagues do all pop-culture questions. Those are called trash tournaments."

"So, let me get this straight," I said, lacing my fingers together. "So, what I'm bringing to the team is *trash*?"

"No!" Max held his hands up in a halt motion. "Well, okay, kind of. But 'trash' isn't meant to be derogatory. That's just QuizBowl jargon."

"Great," I muttered. The Trash Collector could be a new nickname. Get in line, boys. My dance card is filling up fast.

An hour passed quickly once the others arrived. I'd had a couple of classes with Malcolm Park in the past. He was the kind of friendly that you noticed—a student-council extrovert, involved in everything. He always had a travel mug of coffee with him, like an adult going to his office instead of a kid going to school. I'd always assumed that the caffeine was the source of his power. He and Maggie Brennan would have made a winning ticket in any election.

Malcolm greeted me so enthusiastically that I felt like I'd been his dream choice for a fourth player. Lauren Mathers leveled that feeling out. She shook my hand firmly and said, "I'm glad to have a fourth seat filler. I want Quiz-Bowl on my résumé for every year of high school."

Lauren was petite, with sandy-blond hair that fell to her shoulders. Based on a picture of her, she could have been typecast as a cheerleader in a TV show. Except that she moved in purposeful jerks of motion, as if she were an alien learning to navigate with a human body. It didn't help that she spoke in flat tones and, as far as I could tell, did not smile.

"Coventry must be so mad that we stole you," Malcolm said, settling in.

"They're fine without me," Max replied. "More than fine. They'll be tough to beat."

They divvied up subjects: physics, chemistry, and history to Max, biology and math to Lauren, political science and economics to Malcolm, literature and pop culture to me. Then the categories got way more nuanced. Max: computers/technology, Latin. Malcolm: military stratagem, plant life, business practices. Lauren: medical terms and pharmaceuticals, instrumentation.

"Not all music," Lauren said, eyes flashing at me. "I know key signatures, famous classical musicians, and some Broadway musicals. Popular music will be on you."

She pronounced it pop-u-lar, as if she herself were enunciating from a Broadway stage.

"Paige," Malcolm said. "What subtopics do you feel comfortable with?"

Um, none? God. I wasn't an expert in *anything*. But I

did have topics I'd been obsessed with as a kid. And I did read a lot about embarrassingly uncool things. Here those things might be, if not cool, then at least helpful. I took a deep breath. "Astronomy—constellations, number of moons and their names, that kind of thing. Um, state trivia. Like, mottoes and birds. Flags. Horses. Astrology. Greek gods. I know a bit of French and French culture. Some basic theology and philosophy."

The last two became subjects of my expertise as I desperately grappled for some kind of comfort in Aaron's death. Not that I'd tell them that.

We divided up the world piece by piece, splitting by continents to study locations, populations, and basic facts. I got North America, which proved they were going easy on me. Max led us through a mock match, reading questions from the website, and I sat stunned by the specificity of the questions. Why the hell would I know the Malaysian port city of Malacca? Or that there was a pope named Formosus? I didn't even know those were *words*.

Suddenly, this all felt like a massive mistake—the excruciating uptick of a roller-coaster hill as you start to doubt your safety and sanity. I wanted to bail out.

I excused myself to the bathroom, where I stared at my own face and tried to calm down. Anxiety wasn't a new part of my life—it had come and gone in crippling bursts for some time. But I couldn't weigh which would make me more panicky: going through with QuizBowl or quitting. *Focus on the plan*, I told myself. *And how good it will feel to cross something off.*

As I exited the bathroom, I couldn't help but glance in the nearest room. There was a bed with a blue comforter tangled on top of striped sheets. Above it, a large "M" hung on the wall. So this was Max's room. I peered in without stepping any closer. I didn't mean to be nosy, but I had never really seen the inside of a boy's room before.

There were at least fifty paper airplanes that I could see, made from all different patterns of paper. They were attached to a string, suspended around the room, as if flying in neat lines. I thought of the note Max had passed me earlier in the week, folded into a tiny plane.

A built-in bookshelf covered the whole left wall, with textbooks stacked at every level. There was a poster from a sci-fi-looking movie I'd never seen and a tabletop globe and a record player with vinyl stacked beside it. Yep. This was Max's room all right. For some reason, it made me smile. The space was so lived in, so clearly someone's happy place.

When I returned downstairs, my new teammates were packing up.

"I look forward to working with you." Lauren shook my hand again. "I hope you'll be able to contribute meaningfully."

She nodded at Max and Malcolm, the brisk acknowledgment of a drill sergeant, and walked out the door. My mouth hung open a bit.

"Don't mind her. You'll get used to it," Malcolm whispered before ducking out behind her. "Glad to have you, Paige."

"Sorry about Lauren," Max said. "She doesn't really have a filter."

"No big deal," I lied. In one sentence, Lauren had homed in on my exact fear: that I wouldn't be able to contribute meaningfully.

"Mom!" Max yelled into the hallway. "I'm taking Paige home."

"Oh!" I heard from the other room. By the time I pulled my bag onto my shoulder, Julie—Ms. Watson? Dr. Watson?—had appeared from the hallway, smiling.

"How did it go?" The eye contact suggested that the question was directed at me, but I had no idea how it'd gone. Or if the rest of the team was regretting their decision like I was.

"Good," I said, glancing at Max for confirmation. "I think."

"Great! You'll have so much fun. Max *loves* QuizBowl."

"We should go," he said.

She stepped closer to me. "It was so nice to meet you, Paige. You're welcome over any time."

And then, she was hugging me. It didn't last long enough

for me to react, but the perma-smile remained when she stepped back. Maybe hugs and excessive smiling were her version of That Look. I smiled back anyway, and glanced at Max, whose face was tinged with pink again.

"Okay," he said, tugging at my arm. "Seriously. Leaving now."

"Sorry about my mom," Max said once we were in his SUV. "She's been worried about me readjusting to public school. She probably thinks you're a harbinger of social normalcy for me."

I gave a bitter laugh, because social normalcy eluded me at every turn. "And, hey, I socialized with you despite your *Firefly* shirt."

This made him smile. "Yeah, that couldn't have hurt."

We were quiet for a few moments. It didn't feel awkward, exactly, but I wasn't sure what to say. We pulled onto the main drag, beneath the shade of the wide oak trees. The very tips of the leaves were the color of a just-lit match. Soon, the whole line of trees would explode in fiery yellows and reds, engulfing the town in autumn.

"I know she doesn't mean to compare us," Max said, pausing to bite at the thumbnail on his left hand. "But Ryan and I are the same age. It's hard not to compare or, I guess, contrast."

I nodded, my ears perking up at the possibility of talking about Ryan Chase.

Max sighed. "Ryan always had this big group of friends

all around him, and a serious girlfriend. Not that it worked out or whatever."

I looked over at him. He was still steering with one hand. "Yeah, that must have been hard on him."

"Yeah. Leanne isn't my favorite person, but he really cares about her."

Present tense. My whole body prickled with jealousy, but I felt validated in Max's dislike of her. This proved that being friendly with Max would give me the upper hand.

"Anyway." Max shook his head, glancing over at me. "Do you have your driver's license?"

"Of course I do." I felt myself blush, even though I was speaking to a guy in a sci-fi fandom shirt. "I just don't have a car."

"Oh," he said. "Sorry; that was rude of me."

I blew my bangs out of my face. "It's not so bad, really. I mean, Tessa's almost a year older than I am anyway, so she's been driving me around for a while."

"Yeah, Ryan and I drive together a lot even though we both have our own cars. It's just more fun. Even though he has the *worst* taste in music."

We turned down my street, and I pointed toward my house.

"I'm the third house on the right," I said. Before I could stop myself, I let out a groan. My dad's car was parked in the driveway.

"What's wrong?" Max asked, frowning as he pulled into the driveway.

"Nothing. My dad's just . . . here."

"And that's bad?"

"It's a long story."

He shrugged, sliding the gear shift into park. "I've got time."

I considered telling him, for reasons I didn't understand. Maybe it was because he'd told me personal stuff about his own family. Maybe it was that, as far as I could tell, he didn't know about Aaron—so he didn't see me through a lens of pity.

"You won't tell anyone?" I sounded like a little kid, bartering in secrecy.

"Of course not. I'm really good with secrets."

"Me, too," I said. I settled back in my seat, propping up my knees on the dashboard. "My parents divorced when I was ten."

"I'm sorry," Max said automatically, the way I'd said it when he mentioned that his dad wasn't around.

"Don't be," I said, quoting him. "I'm not."

He cocked his head, waiting for me to explain.

"I know. It's weird that their divorce never upset me . . . ," I trailed off, realizing my attitude must have sounded heartless to Max, who had only ever known one parent. So I rephrased.

"My parents, as a couple, were miserable. They were only happy apart. They were better—"

"Parents?" Max finished for me.

"Exactly. Anyway, a little over a week ago my mom told me that she was seeing someone," I said. "And that someone is my dad."

". . . You're kidding."

"I wish. They've been dating for four months."

"Wow." Max shook his head, mouthing "wow" again.

"At first, I thought I could commiserate with my younger sister, but she doesn't even think it's weird. I feel like I'm the only person in the history of time who has experienced the awful phenomenon of watching your divorced parents date."

He glanced over at me.

"Sorry," I said, giving a little laugh. "I didn't mean for that to sound so solipsistic."

I paused, now embarrassed. It was an old tendency, a habit I thought I had broken, to use bigger words when I got worked up. "I meant that—"

"I know what 'solipsistic' means."

I sighed, regaining my fervor. "It's like I've floated out of my body and I'm watching my parents flirt with each other. My original plan was to ignore it and pretend they were both dating someone I didn't know."

"Until . . . ," Max guessed.

"Until yesterday, when my mom announced that she wants the four of us to go to dinner next weekend, and attendance is not optional."

"Yikes!" he said. "What are you going to do?"

Max and I sat there together for the next half hour, as the sun dropped in the sky—tangerine smearing into fading blue. I should have been embarrassed about unloading on a stranger, but that was just it: he hardly knew me, let alone my family, so his opinion was unbiased. He listened as I detailed all of the ways my parents' relationship would go wrong and hurt everyone involved.

"But," Max said, after I had wound down from the last part of my rant. "What if it doesn't go wrong?"

"This isn't *The Parent Trap*. Stuff like that doesn't happen in real life."

A small smile spread across Max's face. "It does, though. Not very often, but it does."

I gave him the same disbelieving look I gave Morgan when she said that this season of *The Bachelor* was going to end in true love. "Believe me, my parents are not going to wind up as a 'happily ever after.'"

"Maybe not. But even if they don't, that doesn't mean it wasn't worth it for them."

"How do you figure?"

He twisted in his seat, turning toward me. "Do you ever go back and reread books that you really love?"

"Yes." This was probably so much of an understatement that it was actually a lie.

"And you know what happens, right? Even in the tragedies."

I narrowed my eyes instead of responding.

"Look," he said, gesturing with his hands now. "Romeo and Juliet manage a double suicide, Beth dies and Laurie marries Amy, Rhett leaves Scarlett . . ."

"You read really girly books."

He paused to roll his eyes at me. "I was trying to use examples you would know."

"Sure."

"The point is that we already know it doesn't work out, but we reread them anyway, because the good stuff that comes before the ending is worth it."

This took me aback. It was a compelling argument—one I'd never considered.

"Also!" Max shook his finger as if giving a lecture. "In books, sometimes the foreshadowing is so obvious that you know what's going to happen. But knowing *what* happens isn't the same as knowing *how* it happens. Getting there is the best part."

It made sense, I had to admit. Max stayed silent, waiting for me to respond. I stared down at my lap. He'd handed me a new mind-set, wrapped in literary references.

Maybe it was the near darkness, protecting this conversation in a way that daylight never could. I felt cocooned, separate from home and school and everywhere else.

"Thank you." The words were hushed in the dark space between us, and I looked his way.

His eyes found mine. "You're welcome."

Chapter Nine

The night before my first QuizBowl match, I dreamed of drowning. As usual, I plummeted under the water—clear pool water this time instead of a murky river—until my whole head was submerged. My gasps for air became gulps of liquid, my lungs nearly burst, and my open eyes stung and blurred.

After what felt like an hour, I startled awake in the darkness, heart slamming against my rib cage. I wiped my palms against my duvet cover and tried to slow my breathing. Tears rolled, as they always did—the ending credits to this nightmare. I cried out of relief that it wasn't real. I cried because Aaron was still gone, and it would always be so achingly unfair.

I got my laptop from my desk and reread script dialogue. In the glow of the screen's light, I mouthed the words
I'd written, trying to imagine them acted out. And, for
the thousandth time, I pulled up NYU's web page and found
the screen-writing program. The deadline was approaching, and I already had my *Mission District* script polished.
I'd need a school transcript, a teacher recommendation, and
the hundred-dollar application fee, which would take a
serious chunk out of my birthday-and-Christmas-money
bank account. But I wanted to do it for myself. And I wanted
to do it for my grandma, to show her I could be as brave as
she was.

When I finally fell back asleep, I dreamed of Ryan
Chase. *That's more like it*, I told my brain after the alarm
woke me up. I spent extra time getting ready, hoping that
looking good would give me more confidence going into
QuizBowl. But I couldn't find the shirt I'd decided on. I
tugged a sweater on and opened my door. "Mom! Have you
seen my plaid button-down shirt? The blue-and-white
checked one?"

"No, sorry, honey," my mom called. I had only a minute
or two before Tessa picked me up, and I searched frantically through my hamper. Finally, it dawned on me.

"Cameron!" I yelled.

I heard her footsteps padding down the hall, but she
didn't answer.

128

"What?" she said, crossing her arms from the doorway of my room.

"Did you borrow a plaid shirt without asking?"

She avoided my gaze. "Well, you weren't home for me to ask."

"God, Cameron. You *know* I plan my outfits out." I picked out my outfits the Sunday before each school week, to make sure everything was clean and ironed. "You're not even allowed in my room!"

"So wear something else—what's the big deal?"

"Where did you put the shirt?"

"It's in my hamper."

"Cameron!" I shrilled.

"God, chill out," she said, rolling her eyes. "Drama queen."

"Girls," my mom said, ducking in to referee. "Enough. Cameron, apologize to your sister and go finish getting ready."

"Sorry," Cameron said over her shoulder.

"I bet," I grumbled, pulling my bag onto my shoulder. I'd have to wear this stupid sweater.

My mom sighed. "I'll have a talk with her about staying out of your room. No exceptions. But you could cut her some slack, you know. I don't know why you girls can't get along."

I looked at her as if this were one of the dumbest

comments ever made. "Maybe because Cameron only thinks about Cameron. And we have nothing in common."

"What about the fact that you're sisters?"

I thought about this for a moment. I didn't really see how this bonded us, other than genetically. Sure, we had inherited a few of the same physical qualities, but in terms of interests and even personality, Cameron and I had no common ground whatsoever. My mom sighed again, seeing that she was getting nowhere with me.

"She looks up to you, you know."

"No, she doesn't."

"Yes, Paige. She does. You should try to remember what it's like to be in junior high."

"Pass," I said. "High school sucks enough, thanks."

And with that, Tessa's car horn beckoned me to school.

~

"You know where my locker is, right?" Max asked as we left English class. I nodded. "Meet me there after school, and I'll walk with you to the QuizBowl match room."

"Okay," I said. "Thanks."

"Are you nervous?"

"A little," I admitted. "I—"

"Hey," a guy said from near us. He was leaning against a locker, wearing an oversize sweatshirt and looking right at me. I recognized him—Josh something, a stoner kid who used to live in my neighborhood. Nice enough, but a total burnout. His eyes were always bloodshot, and as far as I could remember, he'd never spoken to me directly. He sat in the back of my math class and always had his head down, hoodie up. "Hey . . . Grammar Girl."

I closed my eyes, trying to convince myself that this had not just happened. Josh rode the same bus as I did during the Chrissie Cohen years. I opened my eyes to find Max staring at me, wide-eyed with delight.

Grammar Girl? he mouthed at me.

"Did you take notes in math yesterday?" Stoner Josh asked. "My dad's gonna kill me if I don't pull a C."

"Yeah," I said, even though a part of me wanted to punish him for calling me Grammar Girl. "You can look at them before class if you want."

"Cool. Thanks."

I turned away, not caring whether Max caught up. I felt the heat of humiliation creeping up my neck.

"Um," Max began, easily lengthening his strides to keep up with me. I could see him in my peripheral vision, suppressing a grin again. "When do I get to meet Grammar Girl?"

"Never."

"Are you sure?" he asked, eyes following me as I stared ahead. "Because she sounds awesome."

I glanced over at him as he dodged the crowd, struggling to keep pace with me.

"Ow!" he cried as his elbow connected with an open locker door. "Look, I am in physical pain because I am so dedicated to the genesis of Grammar Girl!"

"Fine." I sighed as we made the turn toward the cafeteria. He was still walking with me, even though this wasn't his lunch period. I stopped, crossing my arms. "Do you remember me telling you how much I hated Chrissie Cohen? Because she used to make fun of me on the bus?"

Max nodded.

"Morgan rode the bus home with me one day in sixth grade. My usual seat was taken, so we sat in the last open seats near Chrissie and her sidekick. She turned to us and said, 'Hell no. Sixth graders do not sit next to Amber and I.'"

His grin widened. "And you corrected her?"

The memory still made me shudder. I'd thought it was my moment—I was smart, and I could stand up to her. "I said, 'It's Amber and *me*. Don't they teach you that by eighth grade?' But it backfired. By the end of the week, she had everyone on Bus 84 calling me Grammar Girl. She moved away later that year, but it sort of stuck. Apparently, it's *still* stuck . . ."

I glanced up at Max, who was beaming as if he'd discovered a pile of gold.

"Grammar Girl," he repeated, entranced. "I love it."

"That's enough out of you."

"Not quite. I can't believe you lied to me!"

"What?" My eyebrows scrunched together. "When?"

"You," he said, pointing at me, "were supposed to tell me any and all nicknames."

I opened my mouth to protest, but I had no defense. "Grammar Girl" had entered my mind that day we did the name work sheet in class, but I hadn't mentioned it. I never, ever thought it would come up again.

Max looked incredulous. "I gave you "Maxi-Pad," and you held out on me!"

"I . . . I . . . ," I stuttered while I tried to think of an excuse. But Max was already stepping away from me, walking backward as he shook his head.

"I'm disappointed, Janie," he said. Raising his voice so it would carry amid the bustle of the hallway, he repeated, "Disappointed!"

People turned to look at me, but I laughed, despite myself.

"Hey," Morgan said, now standing by my side. "What was that about?"

I rolled my eyes. "Nothing."

She peered down the hallway at Max. "Why did he call you Janie?"

"Long story. Not important." We turned toward the lunchroom, where our table was empty. Normally Kayleigh got there first, claiming it for us.

I sat down next to Morgan, who busied herself with unpacking her homemade, healthy lunch. She was concentrating a little too hard on unwrapping her turkey and hummus pita. "Morgan? Everything okay?"

She sighed. "We got into a fight this morning. Kayleigh and me."

I resisted saying "Kayleigh and I." Now was not the time. I'd sensed some underlying friction between Morgan and Kayleigh for a few days now. "About what?"

"On the way to school, I was telling her about some feminist advocacy projects I'm spearheading for Empower this year, and when I looked over, she was texting Eric! While I was talking to her about stuff that is *really* important to me." Morgan's face flushed with the remembrance of it. "And it's like—you know me—I've wanted to fall in love since the first time I saw *Mulan*. But not at the expense of being emotionally unavailable to my friends! Then Kayleigh accused me of being oversensitive, which made it worse, of course."

I twisted the ends of my hair. They fought occasionally— we all did—but where Morgan wanted to talk it through, Kayleigh shut down.

"I'm sure she was just embarrassed that you called her out, and she bit back."

"Maybe." She took a big bite of her pita and chewed with particular determination. "But it's like . . . ever since she got back from camp, she hasn't been fully *here* with us. And I'm happy for her—I really am. But we've been her primary people for most of her *life* . . . and when this random guy shows up, we're secondary? That *sucks*."

I chewed on my lower lip. It was always a treacherous middle ground, making one friend feel heard and understood without piling on against another friend. "You know what? I think this is still really new for her. And, since Eric goes to a different school, I bet Kayleigh just wants to make sure they're still connecting. But that'll wear off, you know? With time."

"I guess I didn't think about it like that." Morgan sighed. "I know you're right. It's just hard."

When Kayleigh showed up a few minutes late, Morgan's head jerked up.

"Look, about this morning . . . ," Morgan started.

"Let's not," Kayleigh said, cutting her off. "We were both cranky. No big deal."

I spent the rest of the period being overly chatty to compensate for the tension.

~

The first QuizBowl match was a "home game." I don't know why I imagined us sitting on the stage in the auditorium. We were just in a senior-hallway classroom, with long tables facing each other. Max chatted to me after we sat down, but I could barely hear him. My palms were sweaty, even though there was no audience except the other team and their faculty adviser. Lauren strode in and took her place, nodding to Max and me.

The informality surprised me. Malcolm stood over with the other team, meeting a new member and laughing with the other team's captain until the match started. The moderator was the other team's coach, as decided by a coin toss, and I wished Ms. Pepper would have won. The room was strangely quiet. When I had imagined the match, I'd heard game show music. Max showed me how to use the buzzer, and I wiped my hands on my jeans under the table.

We began with no ceremony but the other team's coach saying, "Okay, let's begin."

Max crushed a few toss-ups right off the bat—Copernicus, ergs, Kalinin, and Bardo Thodol, and a few other words that had absolutely no meaning to me. Malcolm chimed in with the president of the Sudan and a medal winner from the—I kid you not—1896 Olympic Games. Lauren named Hopper as the painter of *Summer Interior*, which I'd never heard of. When we got a computational math question about slopes, she barely scratched the equation onto her notepad before answering, correctly: negative three.

St. John's went on a streak toward the end of the second round. They beat us to the punch a number of times, and Malcolm and Max each got one question wrong. Lauren only buzzed in when she was sure. St. John's flubbed their last bonus question, which was literature related. Max glanced at me and, seeing my wide-eyed ignorance, quickly answered, "the O. Henry Awards." Twenty points to Gryffindor.

The longer I went without answering, the more claustrophobic I felt. I wanted to slink from my seat to the floor, and then slither out the door. I doubted anyone would notice my absence. A few times an answer popped into my mind right away, but I never felt sure enough to buzz in. My guesses were only right about half the time.

I contributed nothing to the lightning round. We got to pick from four possible categories, including one about the periodic table. The moderator could have asked my teammates those questions in their sleep, and they would have answered them between snores.

Before the last round, Max leaned over to me. "Answer the next one, no matter what it is. You've gotta get your first buzz over with."

I looked at him with what I'm sure was total horror. "I *can't.*"

Malcolm leaned in on my other side. "He's right, Paige. Next time St. John's answers one wrong, push it. We have nothing to lose."

My opportunity came soon after.

The moderator began, "This female frontiersman, born Martha Canary—"

Buzz from St. John's. "Annie Oakley!"

"Incorrect. Oakhurst?"

Max leaned back in his chair, and Lauren folded her hands together. Malcolm nudged me. I hadn't even heard the whole question! I only knew one other woman from the Wild West, but they were giving me no choice.

My heart tried to escape through my rib cage. My mouth went so dry that I could barely speak the words. "Calamity Jane?"

"That is correct." The moderator said this in his same monotone, but my mind heard: THAT IS CORRECT! Malcolm nudged me again, twice this time—excited. Max didn't look at me but smiled knowingly.

We won, with no pomp but a weak round of applause from the other team and Ms. Pepper. I sat back in my chair, taking an exhale that felt like my first since before the match began.

"I wouldn't have remembered Calamity Jane," Lauren said. I didn't know how to respond, but she didn't wait for me. "Good work. You were more useful than I thought you'd be."

"Thank . . . you?" I said, and she gave a nod.

"Max, Malcolm, pleasure as always," Lauren said, and she saw herself out.

Malcolm got up to chat with the other team, and Max stayed next to me as I came down from the adrenaline rush. I glanced at my phone. "That was only forty-five minutes? It felt like two hours."

"It gets less stressful," Max said. "You were great."

"Oh, be serious. I got *one*."

Ms. Pepper broke away from the other team's adviser and came to our table. "Paige, excellent first showing! Most first-timers don't even buzz in."

I threw a sidelong glance at Max. "I was peer pressured."

He shrugged, unrepentant. "My grandpa always said you learn to swim when someone pushes you in the deep end."

A shiver went through me, cold and bracing, but I tried to maintain an impassive facial expression. Max went on chatting with Ms. Pepper while last night's nightmare replayed on loop.

"You okay?" I heard Max ask.

"Me?" I said, looking up. "Yeah! Fine. Just thinking."

I had the nightmare again that night. When I awoke, I wiped my tears on my pajama sleeve and went to my desk. I put a line on my plan, through item number 2: ~~New group~~. And, as I tried to fall back asleep, I told myself this: I may still be stumbling through these steps, but at least I'm stumbling forward.

Chapter Ten

"Remind me what we're doing here again," Tessa said, taking in the wide scope of the stadium before us.

I had suggested that we attend the homecoming football game. In truth, my motive was mostly Chase-based, but I'd convinced Tessa to come on the grounds of it being a quintessential high school experience. Besides, the October homecoming game was always the most attended game of the year, so it was sort of like a party. Or so I told them.

"I'm participating in a school event," I said.

Tessa jerked her head toward me, her expression softening as she realized I was referencing my plan. "You're right. Maybe it'll be fun."

"It *will* be fun!" Morgan said, linking arms with Tessa.

Morgan loved school spirit so much that she broke her cardinal redhead rule: no red clothes. Her red polo shirt was the one exception, and it came complete with a warrior insignia on the lapel. Tessa didn't own a single item of Oakhurst Warriors apparel but still wore a simple red V-neck with jeans.

Kayleigh was coming separately, but at least she was coming to the game and sleeping over at Tessa's afterward. It seemed like every other weekend she was busy with Eric, whom we still hadn't met. At least tonight, it wasn't Eric who was keeping her from us. Her brother was home from his first semester of college and had offered to drop her off after they had family dinner. We beat her there and immediately agreed that we should have showed up sooner. The stands were packed, lined edge to edge with fans in red and gold.

"There," Morgan said, pointing to the right side of the stands, where the bleacher space left was barely enough to fit four people, and we hurried toward it.

"Paige!" a voice from somewhere in the stands called as we neared our seats. My eyes searched in between the rows, wondering who I knew at a sporting event. But then I saw Max, tall above the people in front of him, waving at me to come over. And standing right next to him: Ryan Chase. I headed over to them as the girls set up camp in the bleachers.

"Hey!" Max said. He was wearing an Oakhurst Warriors T-shirt that looked certifiably vintage, its press-on letters curling up at the edges.

Ryan Chase grinned over at me. "Hey, Paige."

"Hey, Ryan." I attempted to flash him a flirty, yet unassuming smile. I had no way of telling, of course, but I probably looked deranged. And then, the inevitable question.

"Is Tessa here?" Ryan asked.

"Yeah," I said, gesturing toward my friends. Ryan and Max waved up at them, and they waved back.

"I didn't have you pegged as the sports type," Max told me.

"Right back at you."

"That's true," Ryan said. "Hates sports, likes school."

I looked Max up and down. "And yet it doesn't seem that you've brought a book."

"My mom wants me to be 'actively social,' remember?" he said, using air quotes.

"Hates sports but likes hanging out with me." Ryan reached up to ruffle Max's hair, as though Max were his younger brother. I continued grinning like an idiot, thrilled to be on the inside of Ryan's conversational trivialities.

"You should have worn the *Firefly* T-shirt, too." I gave Max a sly smile.

Ryan laughed. "Oh man, she's seen that?"

Max scoffed at me. "Low blow, Janie."

"That," I said, "was for tattling to your mom."

The clock was down to less than five minutes until the start of the game. People were still cramming into the stands, and I should have played it cool and gone back to my friends. But I felt like I'd been given a real opportunity.

"I'm going to get a hot dog," Max announced. "Anyone else want one?"

"Definitely." Ryan pulled a few bills from his wallet. "Paige?"

I *was* hungry, and it would mean that I could stay here for a few more minutes without it being weird. "Sure, why not?"

I reached into my pocket to find a five-dollar bill that I knew was there somewhere.

"Let me get it," Ryan said, handing cash to Max. I opened my mouth to protest, but he cut me off. "Seriously, hot dogs are a buck or something. I would like to pay, as a thank you for razzing Max about his spaceship apparel."

"Thank you, Ryan," Max said sarcastically.

"Okay." I beamed at Ryan. "Well, thank you."

"Condiments?" Max yelled back the question as he made his way down the metal steps.

"Just mustard!" I called to him.

"Hey, that's how I eat mine, too!" Ryan said, as if there was a one-in-a-million chance of this. Given the football snack-stand offerings, there were exactly four ways to eat hot dogs: ketchup, mustard, both or neither. But hey, common ground was common ground, so I matched his enthusiasm anyway.

"Cool!" I said.

There was silence between us for a moment, and my mind went totally blank. I couldn't think of anything except for the phrase: *Think of something to say. Think of something to say.*

"Hot dogs are so good," I said, after what felt like minutes. *What. Did. I. Just. Say?* I could almost hear a studio audience laughing uncomfortably.

"Oh, totally." Ryan nodded, as if what I said was a legitimate contribution to the conversation. "Perfect game-day food."

I was talking to Ryan Chase about hot dogs. Hot dogs. I assured myself it was better than nothing, but I had to think of something better. *Okay*, I told myself. *I don't have to craft deeply meaningful banter here. I just have to string together words. Any words.*

"Did you ever think about playing football?" I asked. "Since track's in the spring?"

"Nah," he said. "Not really."

Cue crickets. If I couldn't think of anything, what did Leanne Woods talk to him about for two years? Maybe they just looked into each other's eyes for hours, occasionally remarking at their own attractiveness.

"What about running cross-country in the fall?" I asked.

Apparently, my idea of chatting with Ryan Chase meant conducting an impromptu interview about his interest in sports. But maybe this would turn into a British sitcom—painful awkwardness somehow becomes humor. And then those two awkward people fall adorably in love.

"Eh. I like the speed of track and field, the different events and all that."

I already knew this of course, from obsessively eavesdropping in English class for the first week. "Cool."

A loud whistle blew overhead, and a roar erupted from the crowd as the team took to the field. Ryan cheered, with one hand on either side of his mouth, and I clapped, trying to fit in. Max pushed his way back toward us with a stack of hot dogs wrapped in foil.

"Thanks, man," Ryan said, his eyes glued to the field. He had rotated his body away from me, already engrossed in the game.

I took my hot dog and mustard from Max. "I should probably get back to my friends. Thanks for the hot dog."

"No problem," Ryan said.

"Thanks, Max."

"Yep. See ya, Janie."

"There you are!" Morgan called as I apologized to the at least twenty people I had to climb over.

"Did you go down to concessions without us?" Tessa pointed to the foil-clad hot dog in my hand.

"No." I paused for a minute, deliberating. I couldn't keep it to myself, so I blurted out, "Ryan Chase bought it for me."

Morgan gasped. "Jealous!"

"Ryan Chase bought you a hot dog," Tessa repeated, her voice flat.

I bobbed my head happily as I sat between them. "Yeah."

"Are you going to eat it?" Morgan glanced at the hot dog.

Tessa's face crumpled in disgust. "As opposed to *what*?"

"I don't know! Saving it, as a memento or something."

We both stared at her. Tessa found words first. "That is sick, Morgan."

I made a show of unwrapping the foil and distributing the mustard. I chewed exaggeratedly. *"Mmmm."*

"Kayleigh!" Morgan yelled near my ear. She waved her arms wildly until Kayleigh spotted us and jogged up the bleachers. They'd bounced back from their tiff, like they always did. The people in our row parted to let her through, and Kayleigh shimmied over them. Her tote bag was bloated with, I assumed, pajamas and sleepover supplies for the night we had planned at Tessa's house.

"God, finally," Tessa commented as Kayleigh sat down.

"I know," she said. "It's my brother's fault. What did I miss?"

"Ryan Chase gave Paige a hot dog," Morgan said.

Kayleigh looked confused. "Is that some sort of metaphor?"

"Kayleigh!" I shrieked, reaching over to smack her leg. "No! Perv!"

I shrank into myself with embarrassment as they burst into giggles. They could laugh all they wanted. Ryan Chase had purchased a gift for me. And now the foil was wadded up in my pocket, proof that it had happened.

I hardly paid attention to the game, sneaking glances down at him. My friends chattered through most of the game, pausing to clap along with the school cheers, and it felt wonderfully normal. I, Paige Hancock, was hanging out at a football game with my friends.

"So," Morgan said as we filed down the bleachers. "Has the hot dog charmed you into a crush on Ryan Chase?"

"No," I lied. "It was nice, but it was just a hot dog."

"Ryan Chase's hot dog isn't enough for Paige." Kayleigh snorted with laughter, and so did Tessa. "Oh, Morgan, don't look at me like that. You make it too easy."

"Whatever," Morgan said. "Besides, Ryan Chase is busy going after the one girl who couldn't care less."

"Me?" Kayleigh fluffed her hair. "I don't blame him."

"No," Morgan said. "Tessa."

Tessa rolled her eyes. "Oh, please. I'm just an ego bruise to him. The less I care, the more he tries to win me over. And I know this because yesterday, he said, 'Tessa, the less you care, the harder I'm gonna try to win you over.'"

My skin burned with envy. I couldn't master this kind of apathy, no matter how hard I tried. I was built to care—to notice, to overanalyze, to try—in a way that felt inalterable.

When we finally hit the track at the bottom of the bleachers, Kayleigh announced that she needed a bathroom stop.

"Me, too," Morgan said. "Meet you guys by the concession stand?"

Tessa and I made our way into a more open area where we could walk side by side. I parted my lips to say something, but the words dissipated in my mouth.

Across the walkway, I saw . . . Aaron. Standing with some friends. The people between us went blurry, moving past. *Not possible. Am I hallucinating—did I hit my head?* My hand flew to my chest, as if I could hold my racing heart inside of me. I almost cried out and ran to him.

But no. Of course not. It was Jacob. His younger brother. My thoughts became disjointed. The dark hair, the same chin and nose. But he was a little shorter, a little skinnier. Longer hair. Of course it was his brother. But the Rosenthals moved. Homecoming. He must be here visiting friends. A freshman now.

I wanted him to disappear. I'd only ever met him a few times, so I had nothing to say. I didn't even want him to see me. But I stood, paralyzed.

Without warning, Tessa linked our hands and said, "Hey, I'm kind of chilly. Let's go back to the car."

She pulled me forward before I could respond.

"Do you know what I was just thinking about? The Fourth of July carnival when we were twelve—do you remember?" she asked, chattering in this weird, nervous way.

I blinked, confused by the tangent, but she kept going, tugging me. "Remember how I wanted to go on the Ferris wheel because I'd never tried it?"

We were already at the edge of the parking lot, hurrying past the crowds. I wanted to ask why the hell she was being so frenzied, but she didn't stop talking long enough for me to try. "We got all latched in and, even though I didn't think I was afraid of heights because I'm in airplanes all the time, I got woozy before the ride even started. Do you remember?"

"Yeah. We couldn't get off because people were still getting loaded on the ride. But, Tess, I—"

"By the time we're stopped at the top, I was almost hyperventilating, so dizzy and sick . . . and you leaned over the edge of our cart and yelled to the guy running it, asking if we could come down."

"And he ignored me." I was breathing hard from our pace.

"He ignored you," Tessa agreed. "I begged you to distract me from how panicked I felt, and so you recounted the entire—"

"Ferris wheel scene from *The Notebook*," I said. "I remember."

"And it helped for a while. Then you tried to yell down to the guy again, and when he ignored you again, do you remember what you yelled?"

My mouth formed a shaky smile. I did remember.

We had reached her car, now standing right behind it. Tessa said, " 'Excuse me, sir . . . WE HAVE A BARFER UP HERE.' And he let us right out. I ran off the ride, so overwhelmed with adrenaline and relief that I started sobbing. You walked me over to the area behind the snow-cone stand, so no one would see me cry. You stood with me and hugged me until I was done."

"I remember," I said, shivering against the chill in the air. "What does this have to do with anything, Tess? I just . . . I just . . . saw . . ."

My voice broke, imagining his face again, and tears filled my eyes.

"Jacob Rosenthal," she said. "I know. And I was getting you to the snow-cone stand, where no one would see you."

I was crying into my hands before she'd even finished talking.

"I thought he was a ghost," I whispered, between breaths like hiccups. "He looks . . . so much . . . like Aaron."

"I know." She hugged me, letting me lean against her shoulder. "It startled me, too."

I couldn't believe how easily my brain believed it was him. That single second felt like how the world should be, and I wanted that feeling back—wanted *him* back. We stood there until I felt cried out, and I straightened, wiping my eyes. We both leaned back on the bumper of her SUV. Tessa slung her arm around me.

"Can you talk to me about something again?" I asked. "Literally anything. Just to keep my mind off it."

"Sure," she said. "Question: do you have a real crush on Ryan Chase or just an oh-he's-so-cute crush, the way Morgan does?"

Well, *that* took my mind off it. There didn't seem to be a point in totally denying it, so I just sighed and settled on a fib. "The latter. He's just nice and fun to talk to. Nothing else."

Tessa opened her mouth to ask more, but I was saved by a familiar voice, angrily calling out.

"What the heck, you guys?" Morgan demanded. Kayleigh was right beside her. "You just took off!"

We stood up, and I looked at Morgan. Her voice went quiet. "Oh no. What's wrong?"

"Jacob Rosenthal was at the game," Tessa said.

Neither girl said a word, but they both winced, shoulders drooping.

Before I could tell them I was fine, Morgan's arms engulfed me and Kayleigh was right beside us, pulling Tessa in, too. I could pick out their scents—the soft vanilla of Morgan's perfume and the floral of Kayleigh's hair and the spearmint gum that Tess chewed any time we were outside of school. With our arms around each other, I almost believed that strength could travel between us like the heat of our bodies. Nothing, not even sadness, could be greater than the sum of us.

Chapter Eleven

"'Don't let schooling get in the way of your education.' Who said it?" Ms. Pepper asked, looking at us expectantly.

Her in-class questions were like daily QuizBowl practice. We'd lost one match and won another since the first, but I hadn't lost my apprehension. The answer was Mark Twain; I was 99.9 percent sure. Of course, I'd never risk the .1 percent chance of being wrong in front of Ryan Chase. Even after three months of sharing a class with him, I still feared embarrassment at every turn.

Seeing that no one else was going for it, Max—Mr. QuizBowl himself—answered from behind me. "It was Mark Twain."

"Very nice, Max," she said. "For a bonus point . . . know any of his other quotes?"

I turned to look at Max, glad it wasn't me on the spot. He gave me a quick, private smile before reciting, "A person who *won't* read has no advantage over one who *can't* read."

Ms. Pepper raised her eyebrows. "Impressive! Anyone else?"

To my surprise, Morgan's hand shot up. Ms. Pepper nodded at her.

"Something like . . . 'When red-haired people are above a certain social class, they call it auburn,'" Morgan said, self-consciously touching the tips of her own red hair.

"Excellent. And for the last point, does anyone know Mark Twain's real name?"

"Mark Twain!" yelled Tyler, which elicited a few giggles.

"Thank you for that, Mr. Roberts," Ms. Pepper said. "But no."

I raised my hand before I could change my mind. "Samuel Clemens."

"Samuel Clemens, indeed!" she said, marking the bonus point down.

Max pushed my elbow with his index finger from behind me. "Nice one, nerd."

I felt myself smile, even though it was a dorky thing to know, let alone share.

"I'm talking about Mark Twain," Ms. Pepper said, "because we finished *Grendel* a day early. Since this is an honors class, we will be cramming in another piece of literature today. And there'll be another assigned over the weekend."

Everyone groaned. It was Friday, so this was especially cruel.

"I like your enthusiasm!" Ms. Pepper said. "So here's the plan. Today, we'll read one of Mark Twain's short stories in class and talk about it. Your assignment for the weekend is to read another one of Mark Twain's short stories, whichever one you want. On Monday, we'll have a short in-class writing assignment in which you'll draw from both texts. It might benefit you to read more than one short story, but only one is required."

More groaning.

Ms. Pepper deflated. "Oh, c'mon, guys. Give Mark Twain a chance. He's actually really funny."

By the time the bell rang, I had to agree with her. I was sort of excited to read another short story over the weekend. I had read *Huckleberry Finn* and *Tom Sawyer*, of course, but nothing else of his.

"Surprise assignments are the worst," Morgan said once we were in the hallway. She turned to Max. "Paige has to plan ahead or she goes crazy."

Max smiled. "She's already a little crazy."

"I know." Morgan smiled back, as if I wasn't there.

"Hey!" I said.

"Love ya!" Morgan said, turning toward the hall. "See you in a few."

Max and I had gotten into the habit of walking together toward lunch and math class, respectively. Morgan always stopped at her locker on the other side of the building, so I was glad to have the company. Walking alone to class often made me think of Aaron. Would we still be together, holding hands in the hall? Sometimes, standing alone at my locker, I half expected to feel a little jab at my waist. Aaron used to come up behind me and poke my side, just to watch me jump. We'd both laugh, and I'd push his shoulder as if I was mad.

"I like your friends," Max announced. He'd gotten to know them a little better the weekend before. He invited us over to his house, along with a few other people, to watch scary movies and hand out Halloween candy. I was surprised at how well everyone got along and thrilled that I had spent my Friday night with Ryan Chase, sneaking candy and bonding over a mutual hatred of Skittles.

I eyed Max. "Um. I like my friends, too."

He rolled his eyes at me. "No, I mean . . . I guess I'm surprised by how much I like being around a group of girls."

"Yes. That is shocking, teenage boy," I said, and Max laughed.

I got this little buzz every time I made Max laugh. His eyebrows shot up in tandem with every grin, like he was perpetually surprised that I could amuse him. "They were the girls I went to elementary school with, but I never thought I'd be able to talk to them like friends. They're really easy to talk to."

"Yeah, they're good like that."

"I already knew I liked Tessa. But Kayleigh is just cool," he said. "And Morgan . . . I mean, she *looks* like . . ."

". . . a ginger 1950s housewife?" I guessed.

He laughed again, eyebrows lifting. "Yeah. But then she rattles off feminist ideology in her prim voice. It's awesome."

I nodded. "She's wanted to major in women's studies since we were, like, ten."

"How does that work, exactly? Isn't she . . . I mean, she's religious, right?"

"Yeah. She believes in personal freedom, God, and true love. In that order," I said, quoting Morgan's oft-repeated explanation.

"That sounds about right," Max said. "Considering that, in history class yesterday, she raised her hand to politely suggest that the teacher was slut-shaming Anne Boleyn."

"Ha!" Only Morgan would defend a known mistress.

"Anyway," Max said as we reached the point where our paths diverged. "Ryan and I were talking about catching a movie tonight. If you want to come, you—"

"Yes. I mean. Sure." I didn't even bother to ask which movie.

"Cool," he said. "I'll tell Tessa in math. You should invite Kayleigh and Morgan if they're around. I'll text you later."

I was jittery for the rest of the day, running my

wardrobe through my mind. All that stood in my way was a cute outfit. And my mother. After school, I mentioned it to her casually.

"This is a bit last minute," she said, sighing. I regretted telling her that it was a group of people. If I had said I was going with Tessa, she wouldn't have blinked. Now she wanted to know the names of everyone going. What are parents looking for when they ask for that information? Is there a secret list of Bad Kids passed out like a phone tree? I rattled off a few names in one breath, hoping none of them would stick in her memory.

"Are you dating one of these people?" she asked, arching an eyebrow.

"No," I said hotly. "Ugh, Mom, seriously."

"Well, how would I know? You never talk about boys to me anymore." It was an offhand comment, but she paused when she realized its implication. I hadn't talked to her about boys since Aaron. She cleared her throat. "You can go. Just be home by ten."

"Mom, the movie starts at eight. With previews, I don't even know when it'll be over." I was about three seconds from throwing my trump card: if you're allowed to date Dad, I'm allowed to stay out until eleven.

"Fine," she said, looking back down at her magazine. "Then ten thirty. The later you're out, the more people are leaving bars and driving drunk."

I gave her an eye roll so extended that Cameron would have been proud. "At least give me eleven."

"You have to be at your grandmother's early tomorrow. Ten thirty is my final offer."

"Fine," I said, turning my back so she couldn't see my follow-up eye roll. I considered fighting her on this, telling her that Dad would totally let me stay out. Unfortunately, pitting them against each other—the one perk of being a divorce kid—was useless these days.

At seven thirty, I heard a honk in my driveway, but I was surprised to find Max's SUV instead of Tessa's. I glanced back at the house, hoping my mom wouldn't look out the window. She would probably come out and grill Max about his driving record and intentions.

I climbed in the backseat and shut the door behind me. "Hey. What's going on?"

Tess glanced back at me. "We decided to carpool. Max was over at my house anyway. We had a math project."

"That we were using as an excuse to watch Mystery Science Theater," Max said.

Their connection made sense to me. Tessa couldn't stand to be around anyone who was trying too hard, and Max was never trying to be anyone he wasn't. And I could see how he'd gravitate toward Tessa, who loved music and yoga as passionately as he loved trivia and cult-favorite sci-fi and who knows what else.

I hoped we were picking Ryan up too, but Max drove us straight to the theater. I could barely hear him and Tessa talking over the radio as they discussed the many merits of Ryan Adams's music.

"I mean," Max said as he parked the car. "I'm usually not much for cover songs, but his cover—"

"Of 'Wonderwall'?" Tessa finished. "I know. I *know*. Almost as good as the original."

"I actually think it's better," Max said, unbuckling his seat belt. "Janie, what do you think?"

"The cover's better," I said. And it was—sadder than the original, full of longing.

"Don't listen to her," Tessa said. When I made a face, she added, "I'm sorry, Paige, but you listen to girl-pop anthems, not ironically."

"Hey!" I said. "You have *every* Lilah Montgomery song on your iPod."

"That's different. She writes her own music, and it's folk inspired."

"Some pop anthems are well written," Max offered, and I looked at Tessa like: *Ha!*

When we walked into the theater, Ryan was already waiting with Morgan, who looked starstruck by his presence. I had to remind myself that Morgan didn't like Ryan—at least, not any more than she liked every other cute guy in school. Kayleigh was out with Eric, of course, though none of us was sure why they couldn't come to the movie with us.

"Hey!" Ryan said, spreading his arms open. "My other two dates. Thanks for dropping them off, Max—see ya later."

Tessa stepped past him.

His eyes followed her, and he called out, "I know you love me, Tessa."

I hoped his affection toward her was only joking between friends. She certainly wasn't interested in him, and he probably wasn't used to that. I made a mental note that I should try to play hard to get, if I ever had the opportunity. While everyone stood in line for snacks, I leaned against the nearest railing, my appetite suddenly absent.

Other than Alcott's, a decrepit bowling alley, and the frozen-yogurt shop, Cinema 12 was all Oakhurst had in the way of hangouts. It opened when we were in junior high, with high-tech screens, a deluxe snack counter, and even a small arcade area. I'd spent countless nights there, giggling with my friends in the dark theater.

My eyes wandered to the arcade area, which was usually filled with unruly little kids. I blinked, a memory fluttering into my mind before I could push it out. When I opened my eyes, I could almost see Aaron there, relentlessly maneuvering the claw machine, just a week before he was gone for good.

The air was that sticky, July hot, and I was sunburned from a long day at the pool. The icy air-conditioning of the theater felt like a salve against my skin. Aaron's dad had dropped us off, and, for some reason, Aaron set his sights on a stuffed cat in the claw machine. He must have spent five dollars in quarters, determined to win it for me, and we missed the beginning of the movie. But when that claw finally grasped the cat's plush head, he grinned in triumph.

I got it on my first try! he announced to everyone in earshot, even though it was an obvious lie to anyone who'd seen him there for half an hour straight. He presented the stuffed cat to me with bravado. I didn't even really like cats, but I liked Aaron. I liked the mischievous glint in his brown eyes, his throaty laugh, and the easy way he could turn anything ordinary into an event—so that somehow a wait in the movie theater lobby became a battle with a claw machine.

"Hey," Tessa whispered, standing close so that her shoulder touched mine. Her arms were stuffed full with a jumbo popcorn, Sno-Caps, and a soft drink as big as her head.

"Hey," I said, snapping back into the present.

Her eyes traveled the length of my face. "You good?"

"Yeah."

There were weeks—months, even—when these memories would have dissolved me. When I would have curled up in bed, my mind battling this impossible question: How could someone be here one day and be *gone*, forever, the next? The question held me to the ground, demanding answers, and I still had none. But I did have a group of friends, laughing together and waiting by the theater door. Waiting for me.

"You comin' or what, Hancock?" Ryan Chase hollered at me. Around us, grown-ups turned to frown at his unnecessary volume.

His grin broke through the cloud of sad memories, and I stepped forward.

I tried to hang back as we entered the dark theater, so that I was strategically sitting between Ryan and Tessa. This was fine anyway, since Max and Tessa were still talking music. Morgan sat on Max's other side, settling in with her Junior Mints.

"Hey, man!" Ryan called toward the entrance. Tyler Roberts was walking in our direction, decked out in his letter jacket. "Over here."

"What's up, everyone?" Tyler said, taking a seat on the end of the row, next to Morgan. "Sorry I'm late."

Tessa and I waved to him as the theater went dark. The first preview began, the surround sound crackling to life with the jaunty melody of an animated film.

"Is it cool if I sit here?" Tyler was asking Morgan. "Not waiting for another guy or something?"

"Nope," Morgan said, giggling at nothing.

"Cool," he told her. "I'd sit on the other side next to Chase, but people might think we're on a date."

Morgan's laughter stopped. "And what's wrong with that?"

"Nothing," Tyler said. "Except that I'm way out of his league. I mean, he's a good-lookin' guy, but . . . c'mon."

"*Shhh!*" someone hissed from a row behind us.

"Yeah, Paige," Max said, his voice too loud. He looked over at me, bringing a finger to his lips. "*Shhhh!*"

I could feel every head turning to look at me. Between us, Tessa muffled a laugh. My face burned as I whispered back, "I'm not even talking."

Max grinned, leaning back in his seat. The next preview began, touting a new rom-com out at Christmas.

"Oh my God!" Morgan said, her eyes transfixed on the screen. She spoke loudly enough that we could all hear her. "This looks so good. I'm totally going to see this."

Max gave Morgan a thumbs-down and Ryan feigned loud snoring noises, which prompted another outburst from behind us.

"Quiet down there!" a voice bellowed from the back.

"For the last time, Paige Hancock," Max said loudly, turning to me again. He was doing this on purpose. "Pipe down!"

Ryan and Morgan snickered over their popcorn as I sank down in my seat, face aflame. Max's face, however, was downright gleeful. Tessa patted my knee, but I could tell she was holding her breath to keep from laughing.

As the movie began, another feeling replaced my mortification: surprise. Someone other than my best friends had given me a hard time—embarrassed me, even. And other people laughed. It had been so long since anyone had done that. Everyone had been treating me like a porcelain doll, with sad eyes painted on her unmoving face. They were so careful not to break me, tiptoeing around the fault lines caused by Aaron's death.

Not Max. He got close enough to poke at me, to nudge me out of my comfort zone. I wondered—of course I wondered—if he knew about Aaron. I still couldn't tell, but I desperately hoped that he didn't. Maybe he'd never heard because he was still at Coventry, and maybe Ryan never mentioned it.

Eventually, I forced my attention toward the movie in front of me. In the past year, I had streamed nearly every movie and TV series available online. Sometimes, when the credits rolled, I felt almost sick with dread that I had to return to real life.

But, that night, when the lights went up, I didn't feel the overpowering urge to stay planted in the seat. I wasn't desperate to keep living in a character's contained, well-lit world. I stretched my arms as we filed out of our row.

"Very funny, jerk," I said to Max when we were in the lobby of the theater, batting his arm.

Max shook his head but couldn't keep the grin off his face. "You should really learn to use your inside voice."

Tessa had peeled off to use the bathroom, and she returned in a flurry.

"You guys," she said. This was the most excited I'd seen

her since Thelonious and Sons announced their US tour. "There's a *Rocky Horror Picture Show* happening here tonight."

Tessa had a bizarre and long-standing love for *Rocky*. I found it creepily sexual, and the audience participation factor made me squirm.

"Uh," Ryan said. "What is that?"

Tessa's jaw dropped. "Only, like, the most amazing, interactive experience you could ever possibly have."

"It's creepy," I told Ryan.

"Can we stay for it?" Tessa was all-out pleading to everyone. Since Max drove us, she had no way of getting home. But there's no way my mom would let me. Tessa *knew* that. "Please? It starts in half an hour."

"I'll stay." Ryan shrugged, and Tyler nodded, saying, "I'll see what it's all about."

Crap, I thought. I'd rather sacrifice my DVD collection to the volcano gods than let Ryan Chase know that my mother treats me like a child.

"I should get home. I've got stuff going on early tomorrow," I lied. "So I'll just ride home with you, Morgan."

"Oh, I . . . ," She trailed off, glancing over at Tyler. "I was going to stay, but I could run you home real quick."

I hated my mother. For the first time in my life, I considered not going home, just texting her that I was staying out late, too bad.

"I'll take you," Max said from behind us.

"No, I'll just call my mom. Really, I . . ."

He held up his hand, twirling his keys around one finger. "Janie. It's no big deal."

I pushed my bangs off my face. "I mean, if you're *sure* you don't mind . . ."

"I don't," he said, and then added in a lower voice, "Please get me out of here. *Rocky Horror* scares the hell out of me."

I smiled genuinely, and he called out, "Hey, Ry!"

Ryan glanced up at us from his conversation with Tyler. Max pointed at him. "Can you take Tessa home?"

"Sure," Ryan said. Tessa nodded at us, waving. I called my good-byes to everyone and followed Max toward the exit. As we walked to the car, I looked over my shoulder back into the theater lobby. They were already talking again, Morgan's head thrown back in laughter at something Tyler said. Now it was a double date, and I was *so* not on it.

Inside the car, I pulled my phone out of my purse and pushed the Power button.

"What's with the mood, dude?" Max asked as he turned on the engine.

I sighed again as we pulled out of the parking lot. "It's just that my mom is so lame about my curfew. When I get home, my dad's going to be there anyway. And they'll stay up late, and yet I have to be home now? It's so unfair."

I glanced down at my phone. Nine missed calls—Mom.

Mom. Dad. Cam. Dad. I stopped scrolling as my heart throbbed in panic. Max had only picked me up three hours ago. My phone had been off in the theater. The only text said, "Call when you get this," from my dad. I couldn't bear to listen to the three messages, so I dialed, hands shaking.

"Is everything okay?" Max asked, glancing over at me.

"I . . . I don't know." My dad's phone was ringing—once, twice, three times.

"Paige?"

"Dad? Wh-what's going on?"

"Paige, honey," he said. "Your grandmother had a stroke."

The word reverberated against my brain—*stroke, stroke, stroke*, colliding with any neurons that would have otherwise helped me process the word. My lower lip trembled, and my vision tunneled around me, all sense of time and space lost.

"What?" I could hear my own voice in my ears, choked and childlike.

"She's doing all right," he continued, "but it's too soon to tell what damage has been done."

My throat restricted, and I gasped for air to compensate.

"It's okay, kiddo. We're all here at the hospital with her, and I'm going to come get you now."

"Okay," I breathed. My whole world went blurry, like I wasn't fully inhabiting my body.

"Paiger, listen to me," my dad said. "It'll be all right. I'll be there as soon as I can."

The line went dead. This situation didn't necessitate a good-bye. In fact, "good-bye" was the absolute last word I wanted to hear.

"Paige?" Max asked quietly. I could feel him looking between me and the road ahead of us.

I moved my lips, forcing them to form the words. I held up my phone as if it were some sort of explanation. "My grandma had a stroke. She's alive, but . . . I don't . . . know. My family's at the hospital."

My voice cracked twice as I said it. Speaking the words out loud, having to tell someone else, made it real. My eyes filled with tears, even as I begged them to remain dry. I covered my face even though I still held my phone in one hand, embarrassed and exposed.

"Listen, Paige," Max said. "I'm sure it's going to be okay. She's already at the hospital, and medical technology is so advanced when it comes to strokes. Call your dad back. Find out which hospital and tell him I'm driving you now."

Before I could even attempt to protest, he made a U-turn, back toward the highway. I wiped at my wet face, nodding. That's what I needed, to be with my family immediately. To see my grandma, to know that she was okay.

I quickly dialed my dad's cell phone number.

"Dad," I croaked. "My friend Max is bringing me now, okay?"

We were mostly quiet during the drive to the hospital. I wasn't even really thinking, just staring out the window at nothing as tears kept slipping out. It was late November, and the trees were finally bare. I hadn't noticed until now, how sullen they looked.

At one point, Max said, "It might help if you take deep breaths and let them out slowly. The oxygen expands your bronchioles, which will activate your parasympathetic nervous system and slow your heart rate."

Using science to comfort me. I wanted to tease him for it, but I was too busy holding my breath and letting it out slowly.

As soon as the tires hit the parking lot, I called my dad, and he described how to get to the waiting room. I unhooked my seat belt, nearly bailing out of the car before it had come to a full stop. I could see my quick breaths in the air, but I couldn't feel the cold. I was already numb.

Max leaned across the seat. "Do you want me to stay?"

"No, I'm okay." I glanced back at him across the car. "Could you not tell anyone about this?"

Even though my paramount concern was, of course, my grandma, I still couldn't shake the thought of Max relaying my embarrassing meltdown to Ryan Chase.

"Of course, I won't. Promise," he said. I nodded and shut the door behind me, bolting toward the hospital. It felt, however foolishly, like everything would be okay, if I could just get to her.

~

She looked so small in the hospital bed. I wished she could hear my thoughts through her drugged slumber: *I'm going to apply for screen-writing school, Grammy. Get better so I can tell you all about it.*

The little room closed in around us, too many machines looming against the walls. I wasn't used to my grandmother being silent or still. An oxygen tube curled across her cheeks, under her nose. After almost two hours of sitting in the room, I was beginning to feel like I needed some extra air myself.

My mom was in a chair next to the bed, her hand clasping my grandmother's. Her head rested on the bed, and I couldn't tell if she was even awake. Cameron was curled up in a seat, texting or playing a game on her phone. My dad was pacing around the room, unable to stop moving. Since I'd arrived, he'd left at least six times, going for more coffee or to the bathroom or to find the doctor for another question he'd come up with. The doctor had no answers. We just had to wait for her to wake up. It was too much for me, the pacing and the machines and the beeping.

I pointed out into the hallway, gesturing to my dad that I would be outside. I teetered out of the room, running my hand along the wall to steady myself. The hallway felt just as stifling as the little room where my grandmother lay sleeping. I glanced around at the hospital, struck by its drab walls and antiseptic smell. Only a shock of blond hair stood out in the colorless hallway. It belonged to a tiny, familiar form, seated on a bench with her elbows propped on her knees.

"Tess?"

She looked up and, seeing me, leaped off the bench toward me. She grasped both my arms.

"Is she okay?" she asked.

"W-wait," I sputtered. "How did you know I was here?"

"Max came and got me."

"You left *Rocky Horror*?"

"Yeah," she said. "Are you okay? Is your grandma okay?"

"But you didn't . . . have your car?"

"Max took me to get it," she said impatiently. *"Is she okay?"*

"She's stable. Okay for now," I told her, so relieved to have her in front of me. Her presence made the hospital less foreign. "And I'm . . . I don't know. Fine."

"Good." Tessa nodded. She eased her grip on my arms. "Good."

"You left *Rocky* for me."

She lagged her head to the side. "Of course, I did."

My lower lip wavered, fresh tears forming. Tessa lived through losing Aaron right beside me. It seemed unfair that she was always the one supporting me. Her life would have been so much lighter if it weren't entwined with mine.

"So," Tessa said. "Is there a plan?"

"My mom's going to stay." I gestured back at the room. "And I think my dad wants to stay with her."

"Do you want to go home? I can take you."

"I want to stay, but my dad said earlier that he was going to take Cam and me back. I don't think he wants us to be here if they get bad news."

Tessa winced. "Do you want to stay longer, or do you want me to take you back now? I can do whatever."

"Let me check with my dad."

Tessa walked back with me and stood outside the room. Cameron was curled up with a pillow on the ledge by the window, nodding off. She looked so harmless this way, like when she was a baby. When I nudged her arm, she startled awake with the same childlike expression of sleepiness. My dad stood up, gesturing for me to move toward the hallway. He hugged Cameron and me at the same time, his arms stretching wide to fit both of us into one embrace.

"It'll be okay," he said for the hundredth time that night. "Go home and get some sleep."

Cameron opened her mouth to say something, but my dad cut her off.

"I'll call you if anything changes," he said.

"But what if Mom . . . ," I began. He clasped my shoulders firmly, quieting my question.

"I'll be with her the whole time," he said.

I nodded. It was strange, letting go of my worries about my mother to my father, of all people.

"Thanks, Tessie," my dad said over our heads. "Call my cell if you girls need anything."

I watched as my dad walked back into the room, settling in for a long night of watching my mother sleep. He sat in the chair, no longer pacing—staying steady for her now. Maybe this was how it was supposed to be. Tessa grasped my hand as we turned to exit. She put her other arm over Cameron's shoulder, guiding us both toward home.

Chapter Twelve

When Tess and I arrived at school on Monday, I hesitated before getting out of the car. My grandmother had woken up over the weekend, but the doctors were still running tests and monitoring her. My dad stayed with my mom at all times, and it was strange to be home without them. I'd always envied Tessa's parentless lifestyle, but not like this. This felt lonely and hollow.

Tessa stayed over all weekend, leaving only to shower and grab more clothes. I wasn't sure how it had turned out this way, that Tessa, who was less than a year older than me, became my guardian in times of emergency. She was quiet now, waiting for a cue from me. As I pushed the car door open, biting wind hit my face.

"If you change your mind, I can take you home at lunch," she said. "Or before. I'll just cut class."

"I know," I said. My dad had already called the office to excuse me, if I felt I needed to leave. But school provided a welcome distraction, with my familiar routine of classes. I couldn't bear to be alone, at home, in the silence.

People bustled into the doors beside us, but it all looked different to me now, like the world shouldn't be moving on while my grandmother lay in that hospital bed. As I made my way down the hall, my eyes found Max. He stood in front of my locker, searching the approaching crowd. I saw him before he saw me. I felt myself smile at the familiarity of him—dark mop of hair and the shirt cuffs jammed up his forearms like an exasperated young professor.

"Paige," he said, straightening up. This unsettled me, hearing him use my actual first name. "Is your grandma okay?"

"She's fine for now. And I—"

"Good. Because I was going to text you, but I didn't want to interrupt whatever was going on with your family, and . . . I just wanted to apologize because I know I said I wouldn't tell anyone, but I thought—"

My hand almost moved to his chest as an effort to calm him, but I hesitated. "Max."

"Yeah?" He blinked, green eyes like mine, behind the rectangular frames of his glasses.

"Thank you. For driving me and for knowing to go back and get Tessa."

"Oh." He stared at his omnipresent Converse. "No big deal."

"It was to me."

When he glanced back at me, his expression had relaxed. "So . . . how're you doing?"

"I . . . ," I considered my usual refrain, the almost-convincing chorus of "I'm fine!" But my mind flashed backward to our driveway conversations. It was a little late for pretense. "I don't know."

He looked so genuinely sad for me, but it wasn't pity or That Look. He chewed on his thumbnail, as if racking his brain for a solution to this equation. But life is not evens and odds and solving for x. And sadness? Sadness is an equation made of all variables.

I realized then that Max Watson and I were staring at each other, not speaking, amid one of the busiest hallways in the school. And almost everyone was looking at us as they walked by, gawking at the intensity of our conversation.

"Hey," a deep voice said, and I felt a hand on my arm. "How's she doin'?"

I turned to Ryan, nodding. "Better. The doctors are . . . hopeful."

"Oh, that's great." The creases formed at the sides of

his eyes, but the blue of them still sparkled through. "I'm so glad."

I tried on a smile, glancing from Ryan to Max. "Well, I guess I'll see you in English."

As I walked away, a lump rose in my throat. Max and Ryan didn't look related, but they must have shared a gene that made them unabashedly kind. I felt so lucky to be on the receiving end of it. I'd never really been friends with guys before—especially not with two guys who would seek me out to check on me.

I ducked into the bathroom on my way to my first class to double-check my makeup. My eyes were still a little bloodshot from crying so much the night before, but at least I was smudge-free. On the way out, my upper body collided with someone coming out of the boy's bathroom.

"*Oof,*" I muttered, stepping back. When I opened my eyes, Clark Driscoll's eyes were on mine.

"Hey, Paige," he said. "Sorry about that."

"No, it was my fault. I wasn't looking." I remembered the puffed-up jerk he used to be—the guy who picked on kids like Max. But I couldn't see even a glimmer of that guy in the Clark Driscoll that stood in front of me. The purplish shadows under his eyes made his skin look sallow.

"Rough morning?" he asked. His voice was quiet, carried across the desert landscape of sadness that we both knew too well. I'd been fighting my way out of this waste-land, but Clark, it seemed, had made a home there.

"Yeah," I said. "You could say that."

"I have bad days with it, too." He said this with such softness that I realized he thought I was upset about Aaron. He delivered his brief eulogy for Aaron the same way, resigned and with a crack in his voice. It was, then and now, like watching a wild beast too grief-stricken to protect himself—rolling over to expose a soft underbelly.

"And feel guilty when you have good days?" This popped out of my mouth, unscripted. I would have been horrified if he hadn't given me a wistful smile.

"Every time," he said. Then he looked away, like he'd said too much. "See ya."

The day dragged as my thoughts lingered on my grand-mother and my mother, but I stayed at school. Months before, my encounter with Clark would have deepened my sadness. Instead, that day, it reminded me that I'd survived worse. I could be strong for my grandmother because I knew what it meant to be strong now. That's something I couldn't have said last year.

~

"The left side of Grammy's face does droop a little, and she'll need to rest more," my mother explained later in the week. My dad sat beside her, their hands linked. "But, other than that, things won't be that different. Just physical therapy, some medical equipment in her apartment, and the nurses will be there more often, monitoring everything."

"But," I said, swallowing hard. I'd been worrying about what I was going to ask for the past week, but I needed to know. Of course I shouldn't have Googled "stroke complications," but I was nothing if not a worst-case-scenario kind of girl. "Now that she's had one stroke, isn't it likely that she'll have another one?"

"Maybe," my mother said, her expression falling.

My dad jumped in. "Maybe not."

Cameron was sitting next to me at the kitchen table, her hands fidgeting in her lap.

"So that's all that will change? She's mostly okay?" Cameron asked.

My mother nodded. "She'll probably be a lot more tired between new medicines and trying to recover, but yes, everything should be fine."

"When can we go see her?"

"As soon as she's settled again," my mother told me. "But she knows that you are thinking about her."

∼

With all the worry surrounding my grandma, I almost forgot about our QuizBowl match against Coventry. I'd made myself flash cards for all kinds of subjects, but I still felt unprepared. Max drove me to the away match, and I read our practice questions the whole way.

The Coventry School was beautiful inside—small but stately. We were in a classroom that smelled like polished wood and chalk, without Oakhurst's gross undertones of industrial cleaner and mold spores. I watched Max greet the Coventry team, who all wore the standard school uniform and seemed thrilled to see him.

No one was more thrilled than a girl with a platinum-blond pixie cut. She launched herself into Max's arms, hugging him tightly. She grinned as they talked, adjusting her glasses, and I smiled at the idea of Max having a nerd-girl counterpart. When she took her place at Coventry's table, her nameplate read, "Nicolette." Different, but beautiful. Fitting.

Coventry took us to task in the first round. Nicolette answered three questions, two of which I didn't know the answer to. But, in the second round, Max came alive. Even though he answered each question almost apologetically, he racked up dozens of points against his former team. The energy caught on, and soon Lauren and Malcolm lobbed a few correct answers of their own.

The third round meant choosing one of four topics. We'd be asked ten questions based around that topic, and we got to pick before Coventry.

"Okay," Max said, whispering as he leaned in. "I think we could do well with the Bay of Pigs or Voter Rights one, but here's the thing: if we don't take the "Music from the Movies—1980s" category, Coventry will. And believe me, Nic and James won't miss a single one."

The three of them looked at me. The stress of my grandma's stroke wore down on me, but somewhere in between exhaustion and resignation, I felt devil-may-care, like I had nothing to lose. "Pick it."

"Are you sure?" Lauren asked, nearly glaring at me. "You need to be sure because we'd do well with the other two."

"I'm sure." I thought back to all the times I'd raided my mom's DVD collection to watch those movies, snickering at the hairstyles and clothing choices. When we were little, Cameron and I sang along and mimicked trademark dance moves. I'd been unknowingly studying this pop-culture topic for years.

Max articulated our choice, and the questions began. I didn't need to consult my teammates. I rattled off the answers without overthinking, for once. I didn't even realize when I'd answered the tenth question; I sat poised, waiting for the next.

"That's all of them," Ms. Pepper said. She was moderating the match but failing to moderate her grin. "All one hundred points, plus the twenty-point bonus for getting them all correct."

Malcolm slapped my back, and Lauren gave me a prim smile. I leaned back in my chair, proud and relieved. Max knocked his knee into mine under the table, a quiet I-told-you-so.

We won, narrowly, which meant we actually needed my third round cleanup. After the match, our team went right back to mingling with Coventry as if we'd been seeing a movie together instead of competing. Max was catching up with his Coventry adviser, while Malcolm and even Lauren chatted with the other team. I stood back a bit, not sure where I fit in.

"So," Ms. Pepper said from beside me. "Are you liking QuizBowl so far?"

"I am," I said. "It's nerve-racking, but . . . it's also an adrenaline rush."

I recognized my moment. We stood away from the crowd, where no one could overhear.

"Um, I wanted to ask you," I said, already bumbling. "I'm applying for a summer writing program and was hoping maybe you'd write a recommendation letter for me?"

Ms. Pepper all-out beamed. "I'd love to. What program?"

"It's, um, screen writing, actually," I said. "At NYU. I mean, I probably won't get in, but . . . I'm applying."

"That's fantastic," she said. "Just e-mail me the contact info, and I'll send in a recommendation right away. When will you find out?"

"Not until the spring," I said.

She turned to me fully. "You know . . . I've been trying to convince the school to let me teach a creative writing class next year. Do you think you'd be interested in that?"

"Yeah. Definitely."

"Janie," Max called, leaning back from his conversation to make eye contact with me. "You ready to go?"

I nodded, then glanced at Ms. Pepper. "He's my ride."

"Ah." Her eyes were on Max. "If you don't mind me asking, why does he call you Janie?"

"It's stupid," I told her, unsure of how I could possibly explain the nickname's origin. But she still looked at me, waiting. "A stupid *Pride and Prejudice* reference."

She smirked and tilted her head, trying to get a different perspective of me. "He thinks you're a Jane, huh? Interesting."

"I'm not, though," I said. "I'm an Elizabeth."

Her mouth formed a knowing smile. "Well, we're all Elizabeths, I suppose. When we need to be."

I opened my mouth to ask what she meant, but Max came up to us, keys in hand. We grabbed our coats, and I took once last glance at Ms. Pepper, hoping for a hint. She smiled, shaking her head ever so slightly, as I left with Max.

When we were out the classroom door, I asked him, "So, do you miss Coventry?"

"Nah." He shrugged. "I mean, a little, but I'm glad I'm at Oakhurst."

"Well, it seems like they miss you. Especially Nicolette." I raised my eyebrows suggestively, poking his arm. "I think she likes you."

"Yeah. We went out a few times at the end of summer." This shocked me away from my juvenile grin. I'd never pictured Max as someone's boyfriend. He was . . . Max. "I ended things. It wasn't a big deal, and we're still friends, obviously."

I studied him now, imagining him on a date with Nicolette. "Did you end it because you were leaving Coventry?"

"Partially, yeah." He frowned but didn't elaborate.

I had to know more, but a voice called, "Hey! Paige and Max!"

We turned to see Malcolm at the door, waving his arm widely. Lauren was beside him, arms crossed over her pea coat. They met up with us beside Max's car.

"Do you guys want to go get ice cream? We were gonna stop on the way home." Malcolm smiled brightly, balancing—as always—Lauren's stoicism.

"Ice cream?" I asked, with a little laugh. "That's an intuitive choice, on this frigid night."

The look on Lauren's face wasn't exactly annoyed. Formal as she was, Lauren could only look cross. Or vexed. "I like peppermint ice cream. It's a seasonal flavor at Kemper's, owing to peppermint's association with Christmas. It only became available this week."

My comment seemed like pretty basic sarcasm, so I wasn't sure if I should apologize or explain myself. Instead, I stood there with my mouth opening and closing like a guppy.

Max looked down at me. "Sounds good, yeah?"

I nodded, then spent the car ride trying to guess Max's favorite ice-cream flavor. Coffee, as it turned out. With hot fudge. Malcolm got dark-chocolate ice cream with marshmallow topping.

The sight of the butter-pecan ice cream made me think of my grandmother. I was out with friends, indulging, and she was in physical therapy every day. So I got one scoop of butter pecan, an act of sugary solidarity, and one of black-raspberry chip, which I'd always wondered about.

When Lauren ate the first spoonful of her peppermint ice cream, she sighed contentedly. We sat at a little parlor table and, at one point, Malcolm made me laugh so hard that I almost dribbled ice cream out of my mouth.

"So black-raspberry chip," Max said on our way out. "That's your favorite?"

"Well, it was really good," I said. "I only got it because I'd never tried it before. But I don't know if it's my favorite. I think I'd have to taste them all to be sure."

"Look at you," he said. "Beginner's mind–ing your ice-cream selections."

A few weeks before, I'd mentioned beginner's mind to him accidentally, and I'd fumbled through an explanation. It was hard to explain without mentioning Aaron, but I still didn't want to bring him up with Max. We'd become friends on the other side of tragedy, and he only knew the girl I was now.

"We should all come here again after the next match," Max said. "You can sample everything you've never tried before."

Malcolm honked on his way out of the parking lot, and Lauren raised her hand in a slight wave from the passenger's seat. We waved back, and I smiled a little to myself. The four of us didn't necessarily have a lot in common, but they made me feel like one of them, and they made me laugh—even Lauren. When I joined QuizBowl, I hadn't expected to like it so much.

But then, that's the sweetness of trying something new.

Chapter Thirteen

I stared out the front window, breathing against the cold glass as a black Jeep appeared on my street. In the past few months, we had all hung out together a number of times, but it was always Max who picked me up if Tessa couldn't. Not that I minded; Max was punctual and never complained about having to cart me around.

But tonight I was climbing into the passenger's seat of Ryan Chase's Jeep. Tessa was coming to Alcott's straight from yoga class, and Max would be late, too.

"Hey," I said, clicking my seat belt into place.

"Hey," Ryan Chase said, and smiled at me as he backed out of the driveway.

"Thanks for picking me up." I figured I would get the

precursory gratitude out of the way so we could talk about more important things. Like the two of us dating, for example.

"No problem."

There were a few beats of silence as we pulled out onto the main road. Now that we knew each other a little and had some mutual friends, our conversation would probably come much more easily. My mind flashed back to the Talking about Hot Dogs Incident, and I shuddered.

"So," I said, resting my hands in my lap, "where is Max, anyway?"

"Babysitting."

"Babysitting?" Max had only told me that he was meeting up with everyone later and that Ryan said he would pick me up.

"Yeah." Ryan chuckled. "He didn't tell you?"

I shook my head.

"He babysits for a family in his neighborhood. He has since we were thirteen."

"Huh," I said. "I didn't even know he had a job."

"Well, it's barely a job. I swear—he'd probably do it for free. They're good kids, and he just goes over and goofs around with them for a few hours."

"You go over with him sometimes?"

"Once in a while."

I smiled back at him, knowing my next comment would

teeter between complimentary and flirty. "I bet they love getting to hang out with a track star."

"Ha," Ryan said. "They prefer Max. He reads them stories, and he knows a lot about airplanes."

"Yeah, what is the *deal* with the airplanes?" I'd been wondering since his first paper airplane note in class. "Is it just paper airplanes? Or, like, all airplanes?"

"All airplanes. It's always been a thing with him. You should have seen his bedroom when we were kids. Airplane wallpaper, airplane comforter. Craziness."

I kept it to myself that I had seen Max's bedroom once, with the airplanes soaring over his bed.

"He never grew out of that phase. He says that even though airplanes are now a commonplace form of transportation, they're still a baffling feat of science and human will."

I laughed. It sounded like he was quoting Max exactly. "You've heard that speech more than once, I take it?"

"More than twice." Ryan grinned. "One time, when we were little, he ate birdseed because he thought it would make him fly like a plane."

"No way," I said, giggling. "No. Way."

He looked over at me, his expression fading to a small smile. "It's nice to hear you laugh."

I felt hot all over. What did my laugh even sound like? Was it dorky?

"You seem like you're doin' good," Ryan continued. *Doing well*, I corrected in my mind.

"I feel better than I have in a while," I admitted. "Which makes me feel guilty sometimes, but . . . I'm working on it."

We were in Alcott's parking lot by then, and Ryan pulled into a parking spot.

"You know, Aaron and I had Spanish together freshman year." He looked over at me, hesitating. "I didn't know him that well, but I really liked him. And . . . I'm sure he'd want you to be happy again."

This wasn't pity and, furthermore, it was true. Aaron's mom even told me this, before they moved to Georgia. She hugged me good-bye and said, *He'd want you to be happy again, sweetie. I hope you will be.*

"I'm sure, too," I told Ryan. "Aaron could make anything fun, so I try to remind myself that having fun again is—"

"A good way to honor his memory," Ryan finished.

"Exactly. It can be hard, though."

"Yeah." He frowned, looking down at the steering wheel. "I remember, after my grandpa died, one of the hardest parts was all the firsts without him. The first ski trip, trying to remember that he wasn't back at the lodge complaining about the weak coffee. The first family wedding without him. I kept looking around for him, kept forgetting."

I didn't know Aaron well enough to have mile markers like that. We'd never celebrated a holiday together. But I still knew exactly what Ryan meant. The first time I went to Snyder's Diner, where Aaron and I had our first real date, I had to get up and wipe my eyes in the bathroom twice.

"Yeah," I said. "I'm still working on that."

"What firsts do you have left?" he asked. "If you don't mind my asking."

"I—uh . . ." My heart had its very own panic attack. I couldn't think of a single lie. "Well, I haven't gone out with anyone since Aaron. So, that's probably the biggest one."

Yep, my brain said. *You just said that to Ryan Chase. Out loud.*

"You're out with me!" Ryan said.

Mortified, I tried to make my laugh sound natural and relaxed. I probably sounded like a mental patient cackling over a joke that a bird told her. "You know what I mean."

"Yeah, I do," he said, smiling. "And I get it. You have to promise not to tell anyone this, but I still haven't kissed anyone since Leanne."

"Really?"

"Really. I went out with a few girls over the summer— mostly to spite Leanne. Terrible, I know. But, when it came down to it, I couldn't kiss any of them because it just—"

"Wasn't for the right reason." I hoped that God—or Cupid—took notice that Ryan Chase and I were finishing each other's sentences. "I understand. I think I've accidentally built everything up too much after Aaron. I wish I would have gotten it over with—just kissed someone early on and freed myself from the who and when."

"Me, too," Ryan said. "You know what?"

"What?" I asked, looking over at him.

Before I could even register what was happening, he leaned across the car and pressed his lips against my cheek. I almost jerked back in surprise.

"All right," he said, pointing at his cheek. "Lay one on me."

Before I could think twice, I planted a kiss right on his cheek. He smelled like pine trees.

"There." He grinned, sitting back just as fast as he'd leaned over. "That fixes it for both of us. Which seems like exactly the right reason."

And that's when I fainted.

Okay, I didn't really faint. But something inside me snapped like an elevator cable, my heart plummeting to my feet. I felt light-headed and combustible, my neck hot beneath my collar.

"Thanks," I said, laughing a little. *Thanks?! Someone kisses you and you say thanks?! Did you learn nothing from Rory Gilmore?* "That takes the pressure off."

No, it doesn't! Now I have no idea what's going on! Do you like me or are you just being a good friend in the most confusing, lip-touching possible way?!

"Hey," he said. "What are friends for, right?"

Not this! I climbed out of the car onto shaky legs. Ryan Chase kissed me. Ryan. Chase. Kissed. Me.

∿

An hour later, I found myself searching through the fiction aisles in Alcott's while everyone else sat in the coffee shop part of the store. Max had arrived a few minutes before, but he immediately excused himself to pick out a novel before the book counter closed. In my seat at the corner booth, I couldn't hear myself think. Ryan was making Tessa laugh despite herself, Morgan was batting her eyelashes at Tyler, and I was in a confused near panic. Ryan Chase had kissed me. What did that even mean?

I needed what Kayleigh called my "Introvert Time-out"—a few minutes to reenergize and collect my thoughts.

I passed most of the alphabetical-by-author shelves before I found Max sitting on the floor. He was leaning against the shelf, long legs crossed in front of him. There was a small pile of books at his side, presumably those that were under consideration for purchase.

"Hey," I said, turning into the aisle.

He looked up from the book he was holding. "Hey, girl."

The first time he said this to me—in his simple, cheerful way—the phrase struck me. It was something I expected to hear from Morgan or Kayleigh, not from a cerebral teenage guy.

"Can I sit?"

"Of course," he said. He slid the pile of books to his other side, making room for me. "Is Ryan boring you with sports talk?"

My face flushed at the mention of his name. I sat down, wondering if Ryan would tell Max about kissing me. He seemed so casual about it—he probably wouldn't even *think* about it again. "Nope. I just need a little quiet for a minute."

My eyes followed the spines of the books across from us. I had always found comfort between rows and rows of books: some familiar, some foreign, stacks of old friends and piles of new friends to be found. I looked at the book in Max's lap.

"*The Amateur Marriage*," I read out loud. "I didn't know Anne Tyler wrote a book about my parents!"

Max laughed that delighted laugh of his. I felt that rush of pride, like a tiny shock to my system—a flashbulb going off.

"How's that going?" he asked. His voice went quiet, and even though I was still glancing down at the books, I could feel his eyes on me. "Your parents, I mean."

I shrugged, glancing up at him. "Still weird. I can't think about it too hard or the entire universe shifts a degree, like everything's a smidge off."

He nodded. "Makes sense. It's disorienting."

"Yeah. A divorce is supposed to be final. Period."

"No semicolons."

"Precisely," I said, unsurprised that he'd get it. "No ellipses either."

I pulled my knees up against my chest, content to sit still. Max continued flipping through his stack of books, occasionally pausing to put one back.

After a while, Max scooped up *The Accidental Tourist.*

"Ready?" he asked, but I wasn't—not quite.

"In a minute," I said. And so we stayed.

~

Ryan went home early to rest up for a morning workout, and I left with Max, feeling dejected. I was banking on Ryan driving me home, so I could figure out where the hell that kiss had come from. Now Max and I were in my driveway, engine running. We'd spent most of our conversation talking about his airplane obsession—Newton's third law of motion! Bernoulli's equation! The Wright brothers! But we'd moved on to discussing my other Max revelation of the night.

"I can't believe you kept babysitting a secret from me," I told him, leaning back against the headrest.

He made a face at me. "I wasn't keeping a secret. I was just . . . not mentioning."

"Same thing."

"Not the same thing at all."

I rested my legs against the dashboard, relaxing against the seat. "Not telling is a secret, period."

He arched one eyebrow. "Stated like someone who keeps some good secrets."

I smiled and shrugged my shoulders.

"So you admit it?"

I thought about this for a moment. Of course I kept secrets, but I wasn't sure if I was willing to own up to it. There was something about Max's expression that made me talk, though. Like he already knew anyway. "Yes."

"You have secrets you don't even tell Tessa? Like *no one* knows?"

"I tell my grandmother everything," I said, tilting the vent until the heat blasted against my face. "But she has Alzheimer's, so she doesn't remember half the time."

This seemed to catch Max off guard. The look on his face was one I'd seen a hundred times from Tessa—a focused gaze, gauging whether she should change the subject to keep me from getting upset. In an attempt to lighten the mood, I said, "You tell me a secret."

"You already got one. Max Watson, Babysitter."

"Oh yeah." I smiled over at him, still completely tickled by this new information.

He turned his face to me. "You tell *me* a secret."

"Umm . . ." I searched my mind for a good one. "Okay. I did not like *Indiana Jones*."

"*What?* Which one?"

"There's more than one?"

Max pressed his face into his hands and groaned.

"It starts in a temple or something? I don't know. I watched it with my dad when I was little, and I fell asleep."

He swiped his hands through the air, making a pronouncement. "All right, it's settled. I own all of them, and you at least have to give *Raiders of the Lost Ark* a chance."

"No way!" I said, laughing. "This is why it's a secret! So no one tries to make me watch it!"

He gave me a challenging look. "But maybe you'll *love* it. What happened to beginner's mind?"

I wished I hadn't told him about that. "Your turn. Secret: go."

"Hmm," he said. "Okay. I hate all hot tea. I think it tastes like bathwater."

"Interesting." I saw my window of opportunity. "Okay. Take it or leave it: I watch your movie *if* you try at least two teas, of my choosing."

He groaned again, tipping his head back. "Deal. Your turn."

"I . . ." I hesitated, already feeling a burst of embarrassment. "I'm applying to a summer program in New York. To study screen writing for TV. Which I think I might want to study in college, but I don't know."

"Whoa," Max said. "That is . . . awesome."

I smiled a little. "Not that awesome. I haven't even told my mom, and there's no way she'd let me go even if I did get in."

"Why not?"

"It's expensive, for starters. And she's really overprotective."

"Well," he said. "Maybe you should write yourself a script of what you plan to say to her. Work on that rhetoric."

I wasn't sure if he meant it as a joke, but I seriously considered it. "That's actually a really good idea. Okay, your turn."

"I also applied to a summer program. In Italy. To study Latin. And history. And pasta."

I laughed. "So, do you want to study history in college? Or, like, Italian or something?"

He leaned his head against the steering wheel. "God. I don't *know*."

"You don't have to answer! Sorry, I didn't realize it was—"

"An endless source of angst for me?" His laugh sounded self-deprecating and even a little bitter. "Nah, it's okay. I just . . . I have the grades, and I have the test scores. But I have no idea what I want to do, which means I have no idea what schools I'm interested in. I thought if I got some distance, with this study-abroad trip, maybe I'd have a better idea."

"And Italy's a secret? Does your mom know?"

"She's the only one who does. And now you. I'm pretty sure I'll get in, but I'm waiting to hear before I tell Ryan. I sort of feel like I'm bailing on him." He sighed. "Okay, enough cousin guilt. Your turn."

I don't know what compelled me to say what I said next.

Maybe I was thinking of him and Ryan, of me and Tessa. "Sometimes it sucks to be Tessa's best friend."

"Why?" Max asked. I thought he would look surprised at such a radical statement about one of our mutual friends, but he didn't.

I brushed my bangs to the side. "Because that's my identity to people: Tessa's best friend. And, like, every guy is in love with her. She's beautiful and interesting and . . . you know."

"I'm not in love with her," Max volunteered.

"Oh no?" I asked. Max and Tessa seemed to enjoy each other's company so much that I couldn't help but wonder if there was more to it for him.

"I mean, I do think she's beautiful and interesting," he said. My stomach seared with that old, familiar jealousy. "But, that's just, you know . . . pulchritude and conversation."

"Pulchritude," I repeated.

"Yeah. It means—"

"I know what it means." I stared at him for a moment. "And those two things seem like plenty."

"For some people maybe. I don't know. I just don't think of her like that."

"Then you're the only one who doesn't." I shouldn't have expected him to get it anyway. "Never mind. It's not something a guy would understand."

"Really."

"Really."

He turned to me, his eyes steady on my face. "I don't understand what it's like to feel eclipsed by a charismatic best friend even though she—or he—doesn't mean to?"

My mouth fell open a little, and I snapped it shut. I'd never thought of his relationship with Ryan that way. After a moment, I said, "Maybe you do."

He smiled, smoothing his hands against the steering wheel. "Maybe."

As we sat there for a moment, I wondered what had compelled me to tell Max such a private, embarrassing thing. I almost wished I could snatch the words back from the air. Or that I could wiggle my nose like Samantha in *Bewitched* and turn time back a few minutes.

"Have you ever noticed," he asked, "that you sing the backup parts in songs?"

I jerked my head over to him. "I do *not*."

"Yeah. You do. Last week, when we were driving to the away match at Beech Grove, there was an Aretha Franklin song on the radio. You hummed along with the backup singers."

"First of all," I said, "I deny this accusation. Secondly, what does that have to do with anything?"

He shrugged. "You're not Tessa's backup singer. And I'm not Ryan's sidekick, either. So I don't think either of us should act like it."

We'd only really met a few months ago, but Max knew more about my life than almost anyone. It was easy for me to be honest with him because there was nothing to lose. With Ryan, I was always afraid of embarrassing myself, wary to state any opinion or try to be funny. Max was just Max, and he was a solid friend to have in my corner.

"Here's a secret." I turned my head toward him. "You don't completely suck at giving advice."

"That," he said, "is not a secret."

Max Watson had a few secrets of his own. Most of them were silly, admitted through laughter: he cried more than once reading *The Hunger Games*, he dressed up as Harry Potter for every single elementary school Halloween, and even the smallest amount of coconut would make him break out in hives.

I told him about my irrational fear of bees—I'd never been stung, so I had no idea if I was as allergic as Tessa. That I thought the phrase was "a blessing in the skies" until I was thirteen and that I insisted on being called "Jessie" in kindergarten because I was so obsessed with *Toy Story 2*. But I couldn't quite bring myself to tell him about Aaron, and I couldn't tell him about my drowning nightmare either. Maybe those secrets would tumble out eventually, but for now, like any good secret, I was safe with Max.

Chapter Fourteen

By Christmastime, my parents were all but fused at the hip. "Defined boundaries" and my comfort level fell by the wayside in favor of perpetual togetherness. I was forced to spend the holidays doing every clichéd, family-oriented event that the season had to offer. We picked out a tree, decorated it, made cookies, decorated them, and watched what felt like a hundred Christmas movies—all while enduring my parents' shameless flirtation. I visited my grandmother three times in four days just to get a break from them. She was doing well, if a little confused and very tired, and her recovery was better than all of my Christmas presents combined.

By the day after Christmas, I'd already been coerced

into one game night, which was ameliorated only by Tessa's presence. But since Tessa was in Santorini with her parents until the New Year, I was not about to agree to a reprise of game night. I needed an excuse or at least an ally for the evening. Morgan, I knew, was at church choir practice, so I only had one shot left.

"I'm going to a party with Eric," Kayleigh said through the phone line. "Sorry."

My desperation won out, and I was reduced to begging. "Can't you cancel? He'll understand, right?"

"I would, but things have been a little rocky between us. I really need to spend some time with him."

"Fine," I grumbled. It wasn't an exaggeration on her part. Tension between her and Eric seemed to flare up and settle in a less-than-twenty-four-hour cycle. Normal, fun-loving Kayleigh was gone, and she'd been replaced by Girlfriend Kayleigh, whom I didn't like nearly as much. Even when she was with us, she had one eye on her phone and one foot out the door.

When the doorbell rang less than an hour later, I hoped she'd changed her mind. My parents were setting up the Fact-O-Mazing board, prepping for a night of family trivia. I was calculating how many of my possessions I would have to sell in order to buy a ticket to Santorini.

"I'll get it," my mother called. *Please be Kayleigh*, I pleaded with the universe. A few moments passed before

I heard the sound of "Deck the Halls" echoing through the house. It wasn't a choir; it sounded like only a couple of voices, all male. We exchanged confused glances, and my dad stood up to see what was going on. But the singing cut off abruptly to the sound of laughter. Another moment passed, and my mother came back into view, ushering in two guys: Max and Ryan, decked out in holiday sweaters.

"You know these people?" my dad asked.

"Um, yeah," I stammered. "I do."

"My mom channels her holiday stress into cookie baking," Ryan said, holding up the tin in his hands. "She sent us out to spread the Christmas cheer."

"She's like a very bossy Keebler Elf," Max added.

"Well," my dad said, brows furrowed. "That's nice."

"Oh my goodness," Ryan said, surveying the room. *Oh my goodness?* He was clearly putting on a nicey-nice-boy-next-door routine for my parents. "Are we barging in on family time? I do apologize."

"No trouble! You should stay awhile! We're having a game night," my mom said, beaming at them. She was always complaining that I spent all my time at friends' houses, never bringing them over to our house anymore. My philosophy was, if you want your daughter to have guests over, don't divorce her dad and then flirt with him in your home.

"Oh, we wouldn't want to intrude," Max said.

"No!" my mom said. "It would be perfect. We were

about to play a trivia game to prep Paige for QuizBowl matches."

Max cocked an eyebrow at me. My Christmas wish became this: let me disappear from this place. "Oh, really."

I wasn't sure if I wanted them to stay. On the one hand, I was actually friendly enough with Ryan Chase that he would drop cookies off at my house and stay for family game night. But he'd be there for a family game night with my drama queen sister and divorced-but-dating parents. It could turn out to be mortifying, a total step back in seeming datable.

"Well," Ryan said, clasping his hands together. "That would be lovely."

I shook my head, but grinned anyway. My dad stood up taller, a fatherly instinct meant to intimidate. He eyed each of them.

"Ryan Chase," Ryan said, sticking out his hand. My dad shook it.

"Honey," my mom said, addressing my dad. "You probably recognize Ryan from the newspaper. There's always a picture of him in the spring, for track. And this is Max, Julie Watson's son."

"Big fan of your column," Max said, shaking my dad's hand. He turned to my sister, who was looking particularly sulky. "Cameron, right?"

A look of surprise registered on Cameron's face, and

she glanced at me like she couldn't believe I would tell my friends about her.

"Right," she said, narrowing her eyes, probably suspicious that I complained about her to Max. "Hey."

"All right." Ryan stretched his arms as if preparing for a race. "What are we playing?"

It took an hour and four cookies apiece for our game of Fact-O-Mazing to really hit full stride. I took a deep breath in and closed my eyes. It was little better than a guess, and it was very possible that I was about to be dead wrong about who was arrested for voting in the 1872 election.

"Susan B. Anthony," I said in one quick breath, before I could change my mind.

My dad hung his head and muttered, "Crap. Yes."

"Boom!" Ryan said from beside me. He sat up in his chair and pointed at Max. "What now?"

It had been an even game so far, a competition between evenly matched teams. We'd pulled partners from a hat at my mom's suggestion. I wound up with Ryan as my teammate, while Max and Cameron paired up. That left my parents as a duo, solidifying their campaign to become the world's only divorced Siamese twins.

My parents, beyond being generally academic, had the advantage by years. They were old enough to remember events that were taught as history to the rest of us, but young enough to answer many of the pop-culture questions with ease. Many, but not all. They missed a question about a sit-com that I of course stole, bumping them out of the game. My mom patted my dad's leg, smiling. My gag reflex trilled in my throat.

Four questions went back and forth between our remaining two teams, and we answered all of them correctly. It was an impasse, which, by the game's rules, called for a lightning round. My mom fished out a bright yellow card for the sudden-death face-off.

"It's all yours," Cameron told Max.

I glanced at Ryan. He nodded confidently at me. "You can do it."

"You'll go back and forth listing answers," my mom explained. "The first to repeat an answer or not come up with one is the losing team. Roll for who answers first—highest number."

Max and I both nodded solemnly, facing each other across the table. He smiled at me, but I kept my competitive face on, lips pressed into a flat line. I rolled a five. He rolled a two.

"For the win," my dad said, reading over my mom's shoulder. "Name the novels of Charles Dickens."

"Oh, it is on," Ryan said, pumping his arm in a whooping motion like he was in the bleachers of a football game. "Clash of the titans."

"*Great Expectations*," I said.

"*A Tale of Two Cities.*"

"*A Christmas Carol.*"

"*Nicholas Nickleby.*"

No one spoke as I inhaled and exhaled audibly, searching the outer reaches of my brain. I could see the intense look on my face, reflected back at me in Max's glasses. He arched an eyebrow at me, daring me to be wrong.

"*Hard Times!*"

"*Oliver Twist,*" Max replied easily. How had I forgotten that one?

"*Little . . . ,*" I began. Oh, what was it? I closed my eyes, looking for a mental image of "D" section of Alcott's fiction shelves. "*Little . . . Dora?*"

My mom winced. "It's Dorrit, actually. Max?"

"*David Copperfield,*" he said, no trace of gloating in his voice.

"That means Max and Cameron are our champions."

"Boo! Bad call, ref," Ryan joked while Max and Cameron performed the team handshake they had come up with at the beginning of the game.

My dad patted me on the shoulder. "Wow, Paiger. Guess you met your match."

I shook my head, which felt clearer now that I wasn't under pressure.

"*Bleak House,*" I muttered. "I forgot *Bleak House.* That was on my flash cards, too!"

"I know," Max told me. "You had me quiz you with them!"

I stuck out my tongue at him, but I wasn't really mad. In fact, I was grateful that they happened to stop by on the night when I could most use the company. They had turned what could have been an awful game night into a fun Friday. We played another round, and my parents emerged victorious.

"This was so fun!" my mom said. "When are you going to let us come to one of your QuizBowl matches, Paige? Max, she keeps telling us that parents don't go."

"*Mom* . . . ," I said.

"That's true, actually," Max said. "Because it's right after school and just in a random classroom. But parents are allowed to come to regional semifinals, if we make it."

"Well, if you do," my dad said, "we'll definitely be there. Front row!"

Great. I shoved another one of Mrs. Chase's sugar cookies into my mouth.

"I'm really glad you came," I told the guys when I walked them to the door. "I was in need of the company."

"Yeah, Kayleigh told us," Ryan said.

I cocked my head, confused.

Max laughed. "She texted me to say we should crash your family's party."

This situation sort of made me sound like a loser, but it was a good night all the same.

"This was fun," Ryan said as he wrapped one arm around me. "We're leaving for our ski trip tomorrow, so . . . Happy New Year, Paige."

He kissed the top of my head before starting down the driveway.

"Happy New Year," I repeated, almost dumbfounded. Sure, it was a tiny peck—totally platonic—but it felt like a day-after-Christmas miracle.

"Happy New Year, Janie," Max said, smiling.

Soon, I'd put the New Year's refill into my planner—another fresh start. I held out my arms and hugged him through his coat. "Happy New Year. Be safe."

They waved as they backed out of the driveway. Max honked twice before driving off, and, even amid the falling snowflakes, I had never felt less cold.

∿

That night, I startled awake to the sound of my phone vibrating. The screen blared in the darkness, glowing with Kayleigh's name. "Kayleigh?"

"Paige?" She sounded tearful or near to it.

I sat straight up. "What's wrong?"

"I was at a party with Eric in Carmel, and the cops broke it up." There was a pause, and I could hear her muffled crying. "Everyone went running, and I think they must have caught Eric because he isn't answering his phone, and—"

"Tell me where you are." I spoke as loudly as I dared. If my mom heard, she'd call Kayleigh's dad, and Kayleigh would be in so much trouble.

"In a neighborhood in Carmel. Where the party was. I'm like, hiding in some random woods." Her voice broke, giving way to a sob. "My phone battery is low, and I just don't know what to do."

Call Tessa—that's what she would have done, if Tessa wasn't in Greece. Tessa could have handled this.

I considered calling a cab, but I'd never even seen a cab in Oakhurst. Maybe one could drive here from Indianapolis, but that would take too long. And riding with a cabbie at 2:00 a.m. didn't seem safe. I swore in my mind, long strings of the worst words I knew, as I paced the carpet and worked up a sweat.

"Paige?" Kayleigh's voice was small.

"Give me a sec," I said. "I'm thinking."

I knew the McMahons' garage code. And I had Tessa's spare car key. When she gave it to me, she said it was in case I left anything in the car that I needed during the school day. The only time I used it was when she misplaced her own keys in her massive purse.

"If I can get you home, can you sneak back in without waking your dad up?"

"Yeah," Kayleigh said. "For sure."

My feet hit the floor, even though my plan was basic

at best. Sneak out of the house, use Tessa's garage code to get in, and take her car. "Drop a pin and send me the closest address to you. Then stay there, in case your phone dies."

"You can't tell your mom, Paige! She'd call my—"

"I know," I whispered, cutting her off. "I'm not telling my mom. Trust me, okay?"

"Okay. I'm so sorry, Paige. I didn't know what else to do."

"Don't be sorry. I'm on my way."

After we hung up, I glanced out the window. The snow hadn't stuck to the ground, so I was safe from a footprint trail. I tugged on clothes from the hamper, mind racing. My first instinct was to arrange pillows as my sleeping form, like they always do in the movies. Instead, I left a note on the end of my bed just in case. *Mom—had to help a friend out of a bad situation. I promise I'll be back soon. Call me if you read this.*

I extracted my key ring from my purse as quietly as I could, clamping down so the metal couldn't jingle. I held my breath, turning my doorknob as slowly as possible. I used to sneak downstairs for midnight snacks in the weeks after Aaron died, when I was barely sleeping. My mom never knew.

I stepped lightly into the hallway, and every rustle of carpet—a sound I'd never even noticed before—made my heart race faster. I didn't exhale until my feet found the foyer's hardwood floors. It was a wonder I didn't pass out.

With nerves short-circuiting, I made it out the back door. Only there, in the cold stillness of the night, did it sink in that I was really doing this. I locked the door behind me and took off running for Tessa's house, through the back of my neighborhood. The stream water was freezing against my shoes, but I kept going, up the hill. Nothing moved but me.

Breathing hard outside the McMahons' garage, I cringed as I entered the password. The garage door lurched open, far too loud.

I stood there, at the mouth of the garage, and waited for a neighbor to appear, screeching about burglary. It remained quiet.

Even the sound of the car starting made me wince— like my mom could hear it somehow—but I backed out. I closed the garage door behind me.

My hands shook on the steering wheel as I made my way out of Tessa's neighborhood.

One half of my brain took action, doing what needed to be done. The other half was flipping out and screaming, *What the hell are you thinking? You snuck out and stole your best friend's car? You're going to be in so much trouble!*

But I pushed my focus to Kayleigh, scared and cold and alone. My right leg quivered as I braked at stop signs, following as my phone spoke the directions. I tried to control my breathing, but all I could think was that my mom would call any second, panicked and furious.

When my phone announced that I'd arrived at Kayleigh's location, it felt like an hour had passed instead of only twelve minutes.

Around me was a suburban neighborhood like mine, dark but for the moon and porch lights.

I pulled the car over, scanning for any sign of life. My finger touched the brights, nearly flashing them twice in case Kayleigh was watching. Before I could, a figure darted out from the trees, in a coat I recognized. Kayleigh flew into the passenger's seat and slammed the door. She threw her arms around me, hugging me across the car's center console.

"You came!" she cried. "Oh my God, I was so freaked out, Paige. I've never been so relieved in my life."

I hugged her back, the familiar scent of her hair product undercut by beer and the woodsy smell of cold earth. Her presence made me fully believe it: I did the right thing. Even if my mom found out and grounded me, I wouldn't take it back.

"Are you okay?" I asked.

"Yeah. I guess. I mean, now I am. Eric's okay, too. He was just hiding in the basement so he couldn't answer my calls until just a minute ago. And like, it wasn't even that big of a party. The cops are so dramatic." She sat back, taking in the space between us. Her brows furrowed. "You took Tessa's car."

"Yeah," I said.

She gawked at me as I directed us out of the neighborhood.

I didn't ask any more about the party. Kayleigh didn't need me to tell her that this whole night was probably a series of unsafe choices. She couldn't have known that going in. She just wanted to spend time with her boyfriend and his friends. And running from the cops and hiding in the cold woods was a more lasting educational experience than anything I could say.

Besides, sneaking out with a senior boyfriend to a party seemed so foreign to me, especially a party with drinking and cops. It wasn't that I wanted to be invited, exactly. I just didn't want to feel like such an outsider to Kayleigh's new life. Morgan's recent mood made a lot more sense to me in that moment.

"It's different from what I thought it would be," Kayleigh said quietly.

"What is?" I asked.

"Being in love." When I glanced over, she was looking out the passenger's-side window. "The highs are so high. But the lows are even lower. It's like he can make or break my entire day."

I frowned. That didn't quite sound right. Handing

someone else the only set of keys to your happiness—it seemed like too much to part with, even for love. A little voice in my head whispered: *That's not how it should be.* Maybe it was my intuition talking, but the voice sounded an awful lot like Morgan's.

A part of me resented Eric—that he would put Kayleigh in a position to run from the cops. I'd only met him once, and he was subdued. Not like I thought he'd be. Kayleigh chattered extra, prodding him with questions like, "Tell them about that night," and he'd give us a halfhearted explanation.

I didn't say anything, though. Because what did I know? My expertise on romance included grieving your first real boyfriend and desperately crushing on someone from afar. And I wasn't even doing either of those things very well.

When I pulled onto Kayleigh's street, every nerve in my body coiled up all over again. I had to return Tessa's car and sneak back into my house.

She reached over, clutching my arm. "You're the best, you know that?"

"I just did what Morgan or Tessa would have done."

"No." She smiled in an almost sad way. "I mean, they might have picked me up. But Morgan would have lectured me about making safer choices, and Tessa would have judged me in silence for being, like, immature or something."

That was probably true.

"Anyway," she said, "I owe you one."

"No, you don't," I said, and she blew me a kiss as she went around the back of her house.

I thought about that on my hurried walk home, after I'd put the car back in its place and shut the garage. In friendship, we are all debtors. We all owe each other for a thousand small kindnesses, for little moments of grace in the chaos. How many times had Kayleigh laced her fingers through mine when people were pity-gawking at me? *They're only staring because they're jealous of our love*, she'd say, and I couldn't help but smile.

I slipped back into my quiet house and crumpled the note I'd left on my bed. Huddling under my covers, I felt a little bit proud.

Because with true friends, no one is keeping score. But it still feels good to repay them—even in the tiniest increments.

Chapter Fifteen

As winter forged on, the doldrums found me. School was back in full force after break, and it seemed like I was the only one who wasn't busy. Kayleigh was with Eric, Tessa was racking up yoga hours for her certification, and Morgan was in overdrive with her many school activities.

A few weeks after break ended, I decided to venture out in the snow on a Friday night so I could spend a gift card I'd been hoarding since Christmas.

My parents were cuddling on the couch when I asked my mom if I could take the car.

"To where?" She hit Pause on the romantic comedy they were watching.

"Just Alcott's."

"With whom?"

"No one," I said. "I want to pick something out with the gift card you guys got me."

She frowned, glancing over at my dad. "I don't know. Is it still snowing?"

"Nope."

"Well, there could be black ice," she said. "We can just take you."

I hung my head. As I often did when my mom imposed psychotic restrictions, I tried to remember her expression at Aaron's funeral. She looked physically ill, watching the Rosenthals' pale faces after losing their son. It was an image that wouldn't leave me, and I knew it wouldn't leave her either.

"Your car has all-wheel drive," my dad said. "It's only a few miles."

"I suppose that's true." My mom looked at me intently. "Drive slowly and text us when you get there and when you're leaving. Understood?"

"Sure," I said, trying to sound nonchalant. The more excited I got about something, the more skeptical my mom became about allowing me to do it.

She reached for the remote, and I mouthed *thank you* to my dad as she hit Play. He nodded, giving me a wink.

I drove as carefully as I'd promised, staying a bit under the speed limit and braking evenly. But I did blast the radio, singing along with whatever lite-rock radio station my mom had set as the default. The parking lot was more crowded than I'd expected—other people with cabin fever finally braving the weather.

Alcott's looked warm, the front window glowing with soft light. Inside, there was a line at the coffee counter, curling around the pastry display case. I hurried in, the cold nipping at my face. When I pulled the door open, the smell of fresh coffee and cured paper hit me. As it often did, Alcott's Books and Beans felt like coming home.

I sent the obligatory text to my parents, then started scouring the fiction shelves. Using book lover's math, I quickly calculated that the gift card could get me five paperbacks, three hardcovers, or one hardcover and three paperbacks. In half an hour, I selected eight contenders. I stacked them in my arms, balancing the unwieldy pile as I made my way to the seats in the coffee shop. There, I could take my time reviewing them, maybe reading first chapters to see which most compelled me.

People were packed into every table—couples leaning over their hot chocolates to talk in quiet tones, older folks with their noses buried in autobiographies. I stood in the center of the seating area, pressing my chin into the top book to keep the stack upright. Then, in a near booth, I saw a familiar face half buried in a book.

"Max!" I said, gripping my books as I made my way

toward him. He looked up, a smile springing to his face. "Hey!"

"Hey, girl," he said, standing up from the booth. He relieved me of a few books in my pile and set them on the table. "Sit."

Max wore a green knit sweater over a white collared shirt, and I smiled at the idea that he got kind of dressed up for a date with a pile of books.

"Thanks." I slid into the seat. "I guess a lot of people had the same idea. I thought I'd be the only loser here on a Friday night."

"I'm often a loser here on a Friday night."

"Yeah, me too," I said, unraveling the scarf from my neck.

"I know. I've actually seen you here once or twice before."

I frowned. "Why didn't you say hi?"

"Oh, it was when I was at Coventry. Last year. I was here hanging out with a friend. I just remember because a nearby couple was having the nastiest, loudest breakup. Right over there." He gestured toward the table a few over from ours. "Everyone in the store was gaping at them, including me. But then I saw you, sitting in the corner booth."

"I was here?"

"Yeah," he said, with a laugh. "I remember because you were reading a book with Lucille Ball on the cover, and you didn't even notice them."

"Really?" I laughed, too. "I don't remember that."

He shook his head. "Of course you don't. You were in another world, completely occupied with whatever you were reading. And you just had this *look* . . ."

"I had a look?"

"Yeah. Totally."

"What look?"

Max thought hard, his eyes moving away from me. He blinked and then returned his gaze to mine. "Like you had been drowning, and the book was air."

I was quiet, caught in the surreal moment of having my feelings described so exactly. That was how it felt to me, to live in other worlds—books or TV—like breathing became second nature again within their safety.

"Oh my God," he said, covering his mouth. His expression warped until he looked as though he was about to get sick. "Paige, I'm sorry. I didn't even think about what I just said."

"What?" I clearly hadn't thought of it either. The realization hit me like a hardcover book to the chest. "Oh."

Drowning. Maybe Ryan told him because it came up at the lunch table. Maybe he overheard at school. Before that moment, I wanted to believe Max didn't know about Aaron. It made things so simple. "I didn't know that you knew."

"I—um. Yeah."

"Oh." I wondered how long he had known, but it didn't matter. I wasn't going to lose my candor with Max just because I felt a little vulnerable. Clearing my throat, I pushed my bangs out of my face. "You don't have to apologize or tiptoe around me. I never even notice until people stop themselves. They'll start to say something like 'I'd rather die than . . .' and then look at me like I'm going to cry. They're almost *too* considerate, out of pity."

"I don't pity—"

"I know you don't," I said, cutting him off. "Really. It's okay."

"Okay." He looked down at his hands. Glancing up at me, he added, "But you can talk to me about it, you know. If you ever want to."

"Thanks. But I've talked about it a lot. To my friends, my grandma, to a therapist," I said, smiling. Then I pulled the top book from my pile and set it in front of me, ready for review. "Okay, I'm going up for coffee."

By the time I returned with my latte, Ryan Chase was sitting in our booth, red-faced in his Oakhurst track sweatshirt. I commanded myself to play it cool, even though my mouth wanted to form a slap-happy grin.

"Hey, Ryan," I said, settling into my side of the booth.

Ryan looked between me and Max. "Seriously? You're both just sitting here reading? I thought you were joking when I texted you."

He glanced at Max, who just shrugged.

"Ugh," Ryan said. "Maybe I'll just go back to the Y and work out more. Sounds more fun that whatever it is you're doing here."

This time, it was me who shrugged. I mean, it wasn't my coolest moment, but there was no hiding it. Max and I were sitting at a table with no less than a dozen books.

"Hey," Ryan said suddenly, looking at me. "You wanna hang out two weekends from now?"

"Sure," I said, and I swallowed back the urge to say, *If by "hang out," you mean "make out."* I tried not to stare at his lips.

"Sweet," he said. "Since this loser and Tessa will be off seeing the Whatever Brothers."

"The Baxter Brothers," Max corrected. I barely heard him, as I realized that Ryan meant it would only be the two of us hanging out.

"Whatever," Ryan replied.

"Are they a band?" I asked.

Max nodded. "Tessa got me tickets."

"Oh yeah. She told me that." I'd been surprised when Tessa told me she was taking Max to the Carmichael—her spot. When I pointed out to her that he'd need a fake ID, she rolled her eyes and told me not to worry about it. Her life was, in some ways, a mystery to me. "For your birthday, right?"

"Yeah. It's not till early March, but the concert is before then, and we're both dying to see them live."

"Cool," I said.

"We'll do something cooler," Ryan said, nodding assuredly at me. I grinned like a deranged idiot, fluttering my eyelashes so fast that they could have taken flight off my face.

Max rolled his eyes. "You're just jealous because Tessa thought of an awesome gift, and you don't know if you can compete with it."

"Am not," Ryan said, indignant.

Max looked at me, ignoring Ryan. "He takes serious pride in his gift-giving abilities."

"Hey." Ryan held up his hands in mock arrogance. "When you got it, you got it."

~

"I've got it," Ryan announced nearly two weeks later. It was February 14th, which is why my heart completely stopped. I stood frozen at my locker, staring into those baby blues.

"Got what?" I said when I finally found words. I didn't actually believe that he had come over to confess his love. But on Valentine's Day, it's easy to give in to the stupid hope that life will become a romantic comedy.

"Okay," he said, leaning closer to me. "I have a proposition for you."

Dear God, let it be marriage, I thought. My heart sputtered along, waiting for his next words.

"A surprise party." He glanced around to make sure no one was listening. "For Max."

I should have known this would be about Max: the one thing that Ryan Chase and I had in common. I nodded. If my life had TV sound effects, a sad trombone would have *womp-womp*ed overhead. "Oh. Okay. Yeah."

"My parents are going to visit my sister at college two weekends from now," he continued. "But they said I could have people over, as long as it's just our friends."

Our friends. I smiled at the idea that I belonged to a group of friends that included Ryan Chase. Even though we'd been hanging out for a few months, I was still getting used to it.

"So you'll help me plan it?"

"Of course."

"Sweet," he said. "Okay, we can plan everything while Max and Tessa are at the concert on Friday. He already knows we're hanging out then, so he'll never suspect anything."

"Great. It's a plan." *And so,* I thought, *are you.*

~

The next weekend, I attached my sample script and clicked Submit on my summer program application. Ms. Pepper had mailed her recommendation, I'd asked the school to send a transcript, and I'd winced as I typed in my account number, thereby parting with the one-hundred-dollar application fee.

Congratulations! the next page said. *Your application has been received!*

I printed the confirmation page.

I couldn't wait to tell my grandmother during our Sunday visit. My mind buzzed as I drove my mom's car over, chest tight with anticipation.

My grandmother and I talked about TV and screen writing all the time, but she never remembered what I'd told her a few months before: that I was trying my hand at writing.

After she told me about Madelyn Pugh and *I Love Lucy,* I watched more and more shows—especially in the quiet days after my parents' divorce. But, freshman year, I took it a step further. Whether I loved an episode or hated it, I analyzed: What worked? What didn't? What were the most powerful character moments? Where did the conflict come from? I watched classic sitcoms from my parents' generation; I kept up with all the shows my friends were watching. I found a website where original TV scripts were archived, and I read through all the dialogue and cues.

It wasn't until after Aaron died that I bought *Screen Writing for Beginners.* I learned that aspiring screen writers often draft episodes of currently running TV shows, called "spec scripts"—like a writing audition. I figured I understood *The Mission District* well enough to emulate it. So I started writing late at night, and it wasn't very good at first. But I knew it wasn't good because I knew what good writing sounded like. So I fixed it, little by little.

My friends teased me about my intent viewing of so many shows, joking that I should be writing columns for *TV Guide*. Most people think watching a lot of TV is just lazy, that TV is a lowbrow form of entertainment. It seemed like a weird thing to be truly passionate about. But my grandmother understood, and I knew she'd understand about the screen-writing program, too.

I let myself into her apartment and called out my hello. She stayed in bed for most of our visits, no longer bothering to "put on her face" beforehand. I did it for her last time, smiling as I applied red lipstick on her now-lopsided mouth. She laughed when I put the mirror up and accused me of making her look "saucy."

"Hi, Grammy," I said.

"There's my girl." She sat up, and I cozied on the bed beside her.

I'd printed out the program page, detailing the basics, and I placed it in her good hand. Her eyes moved left to right, left to right, slower than usual. She turned to me. "Oh, honey, how fabulous. You're thinking about it?"

I handed her the page confirming my application, and she gasped, delighted.

"I doubt I'll get in, though. And there's no way Mom will let me go. Especially because of how expensive it is."

"I couldn't be happier, sweet girl. This is exactly what I needed today."

We sat in her bed and talked about everything—the details of my application, the classes offered. She told me about her trips to New York, about all the places I could see. I held her paralyzed left hand as we daydreamed out loud together, and for once I didn't stop myself with how unlikely it was that my dreams would ever come true.

Chapter Sixteen

I never expected that my first almost-date with Ryan Chase would end at the grocery store. We started the evening at his favorite pizza joint, conspiring over a medium-size deep-dish pie. Ryan laughed a lot, draining several sodas as we mapped out the party plans. We decided we'd lure Max to Ryan's house under the guise of picking him up for a movie. We texted everyone the details, including where they should park so Max wouldn't suspect anything. By the time the check came, we'd spent two hours talking about things Max would like and laughing over the idio-syncrasies that were familiar to both of us.

After dinner, we roamed the aisles of the grocery store together like an old married couple, if old married couples bought lots of party decorations and soda. I smiled as we passed the cereal aisle, feeling our relationship had come full circle. It would be perfect, if only he actually *knew* about said relationship.

"Streamers," he said, pitching two more packages into the cart. "Check."

I put a check mark on the list, which Ryan had written down on a napkin. He had even, left-slanted handwriting, much neater than I'd expect from a guy. If Morgan only knew.

Ryan's idea was to make Max's birthday like when they were younger, with cheesy decorations—streamers and noisemakers and enough balloons to inundate the house. Pushing the cart forward, I caught up with Ryan, who was scanning the racks for trick candles. He leaned closer to one of the packages, studying the label.

"They don't sell them here," I said. "My dad tried to buy them for my sister's birthday last year."

He selected number candles—a one and a seven—and a pack of the standard-issue colored candles. "These will work. I think that's everything. Decorations: check. Candles: check. Cake order: check."

The cake was a specialty design, and it took Ryan five full minutes of his best flirting game to sweet-talk the bakery department into it. I nodded. "Looks good."

On our way to the checkout, we walked past the floral

department. I paused in front of the lines of bouquets, from simple red roses to wildly purple irises. I thought of the fancy pink peonies in my eighth-grade collage.

"You wanna get Max flowers, too?" Ryan teased.

"Nah. I'm just trying to decide which one is my favorite."

My eyes passed over white lilies and fuchsia Gerbera daisies, Morgan and Kayleigh's respective favorites. But not mine. No, my gaze caught on the tulips: beautiful but not showy, in white and yellow and pale pink. They looked like they belonged in a bicycle basket on the streets of Paris.

"Can I guess?" Ryan asked.

I laughed a little. "Okay . . ."

He moved down the line of flowers with his hand out, like he was searching for gold with a metal detector. He paused at the daisies, turning to glance at me. I shook my head.

"Yeah," he said. "A little too simple."

His feet stopped at the tulips next, and he turned to gauge my reaction. When he pointed to the orange ones, I wrinkled my nose, and he switched to pale purple.

"How'd you guess?" I asked as we moved toward the self-checkout lanes.

"Everything else seemed too fussy or too bright. Tulips are sweet, but unassuming."

I felt my face turning tulip pink. This wasn't a date—I knew that. So why did it feel like a date? There, in the same grocery store where Ryan Chase first snagged my heart, I promised myself: if the moment happened, I'd kiss him tonight. Checking off item number three on my list felt so close. Maybe he just needed a little nudge.

After we'd scanned everything, my heart pulsing faster every time he looked at me, I heard a peal of laughter from behind us.

I glanced back to see Leanne Woods in tight jeans and spike heels, hanging on the arm of a tall guy in a leather jacket. He looked older, but not old enough to be buying the case of beer in his hands.

I turned away just in time to watch Ryan's face fall. It was almost a wince, as he concentrated on the payment screen. In another minute, I heard Leanne's heels clacking toward the exit. My eyes followed her, that long, dark ponytail swishing across her back. With the clopping of her shoes, she reminded me of a show pony, beautiful and meant to be seen.

When she was gone, I asked, "You okay?"

Ryan nodded, loading the final bag back into the cart.

"Orchids," he said quietly, "if you were wondering. Those are her favorite."

I pushed my bangs off my face, puzzling over what I could possibly say to him. He had been downright gleeful all night. Now he looked like one of the deflated balloons that we'd purchased by the dozen.

We were quiet the whole way back to my house, and I

wished bad things on Leanne for hurting this sweet boy and ruining our night. Not really bad things, of course—just, like, split ends and a few zits that even concealer couldn't disguise.

When he pulled into my driveway, I glanced over. "Max is going to love this party."

"I hope so." He slid the car into park and leaned back in his seat. I took this to mean that he didn't want me to leave quite yet, so I waited for him to continue. "You know, I feel kind of responsible for Max, since I convinced him to come back to Oakhurst. He liked Coventry, and I literally begged him to transfer so I'd have, like . . . one good friend here. What a loser, right?"

He gave a bitter laugh, running his hand through his hair. Seeing him with his cool-guy facade down only made me like him more.

"When Leanne broke up with me, it was like . . . ," he trailed off. "It wasn't just her that bailed on me. It was everyone, trailing along behind Leanne like they were her royal subjects. Well, everyone but Connor and Ty."

Tessa had mentioned this before, in so many words. It seemed much worse coming from Ryan, seeing the betrayal creased in the lines of his face. "That's pretty cold."

"Yeah." He snorted. "Which is, ironically, one of the things I liked about Leanne. She does what she wants and says what she thinks: really mean, really nice, doesn't matter. She has no filter, and I always thought that was so cool. No bullshit, no guessing."

He could have been describing Tessa, too. No wonder he always seemed taken by her. She shared a quality with Leanne that he'd loved—a quality I was markedly lacking.

"You're not over her, are you?" I asked, and he shrugged.

"My parents are high school sweethearts, so I thought that's how it might go for Leanne and me." He gave a self-deprecating laugh. "That's so lame, right? I'd probably get kicked off the track team for saying crap like that."

"It's not lame." In fact, I knew all too well how it felt to have your expectations flipped upside down. Anytime something you're sure of changes in an instant—even when it's your own parents' divorce—it feels like a carnival ride: sudden and off balance and nausea inducing.

Ryan turned, staring straight into my eyes. "Hey, Paige?"

Heat broke out across my skin. "Yeah?"

"Thanks for being so cool to Max," he said. "Really. It means a lot to me."

Of course it would be about Max, our common denominator. "You don't have to thank me. It's not a favor."

"I know it's not," he said, shaking his head. "I'm just glad that he's found people that he clicks with. He's awesome, and not everyone sees it."

Max was the human equivalent of a cult-classic TV

show. Most people didn't get it. But the people who did? They loved it for all of its quirks.

"You're a good guy, Ryan," I said, coiling up all my nervous energy and trying to convert it to braveness. "If Leanne doesn't see it, then she's an idiot."

He smiled a little, looking down at his lap. "Yeah, well."

And with the gusto of a much more confident girl, I leaned over and kissed him on the cheek. "See you Monday."

Okay, so it wasn't quite the actual kiss I had planned. But, as I made my way up the driveway, I felt a swagger in my walk. I was inching toward the edge of something big, stepping closer to being Paige Hancock again.

In my room, I searched my mom's collection of Martha Stewart magazines until I found a picture of tulips, bundled into a blue vase. They filled a blank space in my new collage, next to a picture of an open planner and a nail polish ad that looked like a row of Easter eggs—all the pastel colors Morgan used to paint on as a reminder. All the colors I'd loved ever since.

Tessa texted me as I was gluing on an ad for *The Mission District*, asking if she could stay the night at my house after the concert. I let my mom know she might hear Tessa come in late, and she nodded without looking up from her book. It had been my mom, after all, who bought Tessa a toothbrush to keep in my bathroom.

I nodded off but woke up when I heard my bedroom door close.

"Hey," I said, turning over.

"Hey." Tessa opened my bottom drawer, where I kept T-shirts and sweats.

When she climbed into bed, I asked, "How was the concert?"

"Amazing. Just . . . completely beyond." I could smell the Carmichael on her—not bad, but hints of spilled beer and other girls' perfume.

"So everything's okay?" I was so tired, my mouth barely opening.

"Everything's okay. It's just that my parents haven't been home in two weeks. Going home to a quiet house after such a great night sounded lonely."

"Tell me about the concert," I said. "It'll be my bedtime story."

She laughed, and I fell asleep to her descriptions of dancing and banjos, the long draws of cello strings and how being there made her feel like the world might be way more beautiful than anyone has been giving it credit for.

Chapter Seventeen

"Do you have any exciting plans for the weekend?"

"I'm going to a surprise birthday party tonight," I told my grandmother, snuggling into the floral pillows on her couch. I tried to say these words with nonchalance, even as my nerves did tiny pirouettes under my skin.

Ryan himself had dropped me off for my visit with my grandmother. He was picking up our special-ordered cake, and he'd be back to get me in an hour. We would head straight back to his house to set up for the party and wait for everyone to arrive.

"Who's the guest of honor?" my grandma asked.

"A friend of mine." I talked about Max a lot, but of course she didn't remember.

She smiled. "So, how was your QuizBowl match?"

"Oh, it was good." Then I thought for a moment. I was sure she didn't remember me mentioning it a week before. My mother must have told her earlier today. "We won."

"Wonderful. Who is Max?"

I blinked. "What?"

She'd heard stories about Max—about QuizBowl and other silly anecdotes. But there had never been an indication that she retained this information.

"Max. Who is he?"

"How do you know about him?"

"You told me." She produced a little notebook from her purse on the floor. "I've been feeling forgetful lately. Your mother said that could happen after a stroke, and I should jot things down."

My mom tried to protect her from the confusion and fear of Alzheimer's, so it made sense that she would blame its effects on the stroke—never mind that my grandmother had to be reminded every morning that she'd had a stroke in the first place.

"Here," she said, opening the notebook. On a page dated a week before, she had written: *Paige here today. School is good. Ask about "QuizBowl." Ask about Max.*

"It's funny," she said, smiling. "I don't remember talking about him. Is he a friend of yours?"

"Yes," I said, too quickly. On legal TV shows, the jumpy witnesses always had something to hide. "It's actually his surprise party tonight."

240

"What's he like?" she asked.

My grandmother would forget later anyway, but how could I box Max into a few sentences? The airplane obsession, the babysitting, the self-imposed uniform of button-down shirts and Converse.

"Um," I said. "He's in all honors classes. He's the captain of the QuizBowl team. He actually, uh, took me to the hospital the night you had your stroke."

She peered down at her nails, trying to seem casual. "Is he cute?"

Then she studied my face intently. Subtlety is lost on the elderly.

"Maybe," I said, shrugging. "To girls who are into the dorky-cute look."

"What did you get him? For his birthday?"

"Oh. Just a book that I know he hasn't read, but I think he should. And, um . . . an IOU for a TV-show marathon. With me. Only because there's this show he really likes, and I've never seen it. He keeps trying to get me to watch it. I'm kind of curious, so . . . ," I trailed off, all too aware that I'd overexplained.

This was, based on her expression, the exact response she'd been hoping for. "Sounds like this Max fellow might be more than a friend."

"No, it's not like that. He's great. He's just . . . I mean, he's on the robotics team at school. Like, he builds robots. For fun. And is routinely sent to the nurse's office because he's so clumsy in gym class." I heard my own words—and they sounded snobby. But not as mean as the flat-out truth: that I just wasn't attracted to Max like that. There was no zing, no confetti cannon, no tickle of butterfly wings in my stomach. "I guess he's just not my type."

My grandmother smiled. "That's what I said about your father, Katie."

"Paige."

She closed her eyes for a moment. "Paige. Yes."

When she opened her eyes, they seemed bleary and far-off. "I'm Gloria."

"Right," I said, reaching over to pat her hand. Sometimes physical touch brought her into the present, reminding her of the where and when.

She shook her head. "Silly me! I don't know what made me say that. What were we talking about?"

"Max."

"Yes. And what were you saying about him?"

"That he's a nice guy. But not my type."

Despite the confusion that preceded this comment, my grandmother's mind seemed perfectly lucid as she smirked. "Oh, right. And I was not believing you."

~

As I set out drinks for Max's party, my grandmother's cheeky commentary bubbled inside me like carbonation. I was already nervous about pulling off the surprise part of the surprise party. But now I kept thinking about Max. If a septuagenarian with Alzheimer's saw a spark there, was I missing something? Did Max like *me*? If so, I sensed major awkwardness in the making. I replayed clips of him in my mind, and yes, we had fun hanging out. But the same could be said for him and Tessa.

I'd seen my friends exchange looks once or twice when I mentioned Max—Morgan pressing her lips together to lock a gossipy comment inside of her mouth. But I never thought anything of it. Morgan could read relationship chemistry into me and a bag of potato chips.

Nearly everyone had arrived, now busying themselves with the superfluous amount of streamers and balloons. Ryan and I were in the kitchen, setting out the food and drinks.

"Hey," a guy's voice said. "Sorry I'm late. I parked all the way down the street."

Connor was one of Ryan's track friends whom I hadn't officially met. I'd always thought of him as a frat-boy-in-training type, but up close, he looked nicer—dark eyes and an easy smile. In addition to Connor, Ryan had invited our usual group, plus Malcolm and Lauren.

"It's cool," Ryan said. "Max won't be here for another few minutes. He thinks we're going to a seven-twenty movie."

"I brought bottled root beer," Connor said, heaving

two six-packs onto the counter, "since you said no real beer."

"That's awesome," Ryan said. "Max will think that's funny."

I nodded, smiling at Connor.

"You want one?" Ryan asked me, pulling a bottle out of the pack.

"Sure."

"There you go, ma'am." He twisted the cap off and slid it to me, winking like a flirty bartender in a sitcom. My mind went blurry with swooning. "Can you get everyone together? I'm going to start watching for him."

"Max is always on time," I told Connor before calling for everyone to assemble.

"Everyone, quiet!" Ryan yelled as he hurried back into the kitchen. "He just pulled up!"

All nine of us crouched behind the kitchen island. From outside, Max beeped his horn twice.

"He'll come in," Ryan assured us. "Give him a second."

We waited a few beats, an excited silence buzzing through the room.

"Ry?" Max's voice carried in from the front door. I ran my fingers against my palms, stomach tight. "You ready to go?"

I could hear Max's footsteps, getting closer to the kitchen.

"Ry?" he yelled louder.

"Now!" Ryan stage whispered.

"SURPRISE!" It was loud, collective, and excited, as we all sprung up from behind the island.

Max jumped backward, wide-eyed, as he took in our sudden appearance and the ridiculous decorations strewn around. Tessa held up her phone, capturing Max's genuine surprise. Everyone clapped and cheered as Max's mouth slid into a slightly embarrassed grin. I exhaled in relief, half because we'd really surprised him and half because he was still just Max—no matter what insinuations my grand-mother made.

"You *guys*," he said, sheepish.

"Happy birthday, bud," Ryan said, putting his arm around Max.

In the basement, streamers were taped at every angle around the walls and ceiling. Ryan set up video games on the big screen, and I settled into a corner of the L-shaped sofa to take in the festivities. Tessa cranked up the play-list she'd made for the party as Tyler and Connor broke off to play pool. I sat back and watched everyone settle into comfortable conversations. "Our friends" Ryan had said, and that's exactly what this group of people had become.

The energy died down after a little while. I kept one eye on Kayleigh, who wasn't quite herself. She was leaning against the pool table, locked into whatever Connor was saying. Her laugh rang out—forced and overdone—and it triggered a gut feeling that something was wrong. Her body language bordered on flirty, like she'd get this attention from the other guys if she couldn't get it from Eric. I flashed back to the night I'd snuck out to get her and the wistful way she'd said love wasn't what she thought it would be.

"Is she okay?" I whispered to Morgan.

"Who knows?" Morgan gave me an eye roll that was so drawn out that I momentarily feared for her ocular health. "Why does he never come to stuff like this? It's like he thinks he's too good for us."

We'd been around Eric only three times. He was cute— wide in a football-player way—but still distracted, constantly texting. I figured he was shy, overwhelmed by meeting lots of new people at once. That I could certainly understand.

"We should play a game or something," Tyler said.

"Well, if it's up to the birthday boy," Ryan said, "we'd be playing a rousing game of Scrabble."

"Shut up," Max said, smiling good-naturedly. "You're still mad about *aliquot*."

"It's *not* a word!" Ryan said.

"It is," Tessa interjected. "It's a math term."

"Traitor," Ryan said, but he grinned at her like a fool.

"I have a game," Kayleigh announced, smirking as she downed the final sip of her root beer. She then held up the empty glass bottle and jiggled it back and forth.

Tyler, the first one of us to process what she meant, made a whooping noise as everyone else caught up.

"Kayleigh," Morgan said sternly. "No."

Tessa looked disgusted. "What are we, in fifth grade?"

Morgan's head shot toward her. "You played spin the bottle in *fifth grade*?"

"No," Tessa said. "Because *nobody* actually plays it."

"False," Kayleigh said. "I played at camp."

"I want to go to that camp!" Tyler said.

Everyone laughed, easing the tension.

"In popular culture," Lauren said, "spin the bottle is played after the participants have been imbibing alcohol. I don't imbibe alcohol. So."

Connor muffled a laugh with his hand, and I felt a surge of protectiveness toward Lauren. Yes, she sat with ramrod-straight posture and spoke like we were in a formal debate at all times, but there was more to her than that. Malcolm patted her leg. "No one's drinking tonight, Laur."

"I'm in," Ryan said. Cold sweat broke out across my back. This couldn't really happen. It was too awkward, too public. Tessa was right: no one really did this—and certainly not us.

Tessa sighed, shrugging. "All right. Why not?"

There was clapping and laughing as everyone agreed. My stomach already felt sort of jittery, but now it was grumbling inside of me. I looked over at Morgan, hoping she would call the game to a stop. She didn't, probably owing to the chance of kissing Tyler or even Malcolm, whom she'd been eyeing all night.

Kayleigh centered the empty bottle as everyone positioned themselves into a circle.

"Now," she said. "We're playing with one little modification."

"The 'camp way'?" Tess asked, making air quotes as she rolled her eyes.

Kayleigh ignored her.

"So, same rules as spin the bottle only every seventh spin, those two people have to go in there," she said, pointing to what seemed to be a closet door, "for seven minutes in heaven."

Max groaned. "So we're combining the two most clichéd kissing games in history."

"Yep!" Kayleigh looked around at everyone. There were no protests as the music switched to the next song. I thought about ways to get out of playing, but the possibility of actually kissing Ryan Chase kept me anchored to the ground, silent.

"I'm not sure I'm comfortable with that," Lauren announced. I wanted to throw my arms around her neck and bear-hug her.

"You could think of it as a sociocultural rite of passage," Malcolm suggested. "Plus, statistically speaking, the odds that it lands on you after any given spin are relatively slim."

"A fair point," she agreed.

"Oh, what the heck," Morgan said, sighing. "Just spin."

The way that Tessa and I looked at her, she might as well have announced that she was dropping out of high school to become a stripper.

"All right, Morgan!" Connor said, laughing. "Spin, Kay-leigh."

I sat cross-legged and relaxed my arms, trying not to look as tense as I felt. For a moment, I considered excusing myself to the bathroom and staying there until the game concluded. But, as I glanced around, no one else seemed to be defecting or even making a big deal about it. For once in my life, I wished my friends would think of Aaron and realize that I hadn't really kissed anyone since him. Sure, I'd given Ryan Chase a peck on the cheek, and while it was sweet, it wasn't the same as kissing someone on the lips.

But maybe it was as good a time as any—get it over with, less buildup for later. There didn't have to be a right reason, or even any reason at all. Besides, I didn't want to be seen as the only girl who wasn't fun. I took a deep breath as Tyler gave the bottle a decisive spin that landed on Kayleigh.

Everyone clapped as Tyler laid a chaste but dramatic kiss on Kayleigh. I took a sip of my soda as Kayleigh's spin landed on Malcolm, whose spin pointed to Max. We agreed that spin would count for the nearest girl: Tessa.

These were just little pecks, but still the blood thumped in my ears. Tessa steadied herself for her turn. She spun the bottle and it loped around, finally landing on Ryan.

I wrinkled my nose, blurring my vision as Tessa leaned in to kiss the love of my life. He wrapped a hand around the back of her neck. She jerked back and smacked his arm. "Ryan! Honestly!"

He grinned. "I knew you loved me, Tessa."

Tessa's cheeks reddened. "One more word, and I *will* have Morgan give you the consent lecture."

This was it. Ryan Chase's spin. I didn't breathe as it spun around, slowing and slowing. *Come on, a few more degrees in my direction,* I begged. But the open bottle pointed directly at Morgan. It was the first time in my life that I actually hated Morgan.

The group—except for me, horrorstruck—hooted as Morgan squirmed.

"I'm not going to embarrass you," Ryan said. "That was just for Tessa."

Tessa made a face, and I averted my eyes. Watching two of my best friends kiss my ultimate crush was not my idea of a fun evening.

Morgan took a deep breath and spun, watching the bottle land on Max.

"Whoo!" Connor yelled. "Both cousins in one night!"

Kayleigh made a *tsk*-ing noise. "Promiscuous!"

We all giggled as Morgan gave her a death look, blushing furiously. Max looked down at Morgan.

"Are you going to freak out on me, Morgan?" Max asked.

"No," she mumbled, smiling as Max kissed her. It was sweet and quick, and Morgan giggled as he sat back.

In truth, Morgan looked pretty pleased with herself. And, in more truth, I was now a little peeved that the bottle hadn't landed on me yet. Even Morgan was kissing people, and I was sitting there like an idiot.

"By my count," Kayleigh called, "this is spin seven!"

"Ooh, pressure!" Connor yelled as Max's hand hovered over the bottle.

He really put his wrist into the spin, and the bottle went wild, veering sideways as it lost momentum. I can't explain why I knew in my bones what would happen one second before it did. The bottle circled back, slowly now, as it stopped so closely that the top almost touched my knee.

It was pointing, irrefutably, at me.

There was uproarious cheering as I looked up at Max and shrugged, an embarrassed smile creeping onto my face. I mean, we didn't actually have to do anything in the closet. This was the ideal compromise: I would participate, but I didn't actually have to kiss anybody.

"Rules are rules!" Kayleigh called over the cheering.

Max stood up calmly, smoothing his shirt.

"Janie," he said, formal as he offered his hand to help me up.

I took it, much to the delight of everyone else in the circle. Max seemed to be playing along, so I did, too. I turned around and winked at them as Max shut the door behind us. This set them off into a frenzy of catcalls.

"Seven minutes," Kayleigh yelled through the cheers. "And counting."

In the dark silence, a shiver shuddered down my neck and spine. I reminded myself that I was alone with Max all the time. But the expectations radiated from the other side of the door, altering our dynamic before we'd even spoken.

"Hold on, there's a side light," he whispered. I brushed my bangs out of my face, just for something to do with my hands, as the light popped on overhead. It wasn't a closet, but a small, unfinished space with cement floors and shelves of Christmas decorations. The water heater hummed in the corner. I pressed myself against a shelf behind me, looking over at him.

"We obviously don't . . . ," Max started.

"I know." I crossed my arms.

"Right." He nodded decisively. "Definitely not."

I tried to laugh, but it sounded shrill and uneven.

"Yeah, obviously that would . . . you know, mess up our friendship." I made the laugh noise again.

"Right. It's lame that we're playing this game anyway."

There were a few beats of quiet. In reality, it was probably five seconds, but it felt like five minutes. Five excruciating minutes of throbbing, hot-faced awkwardness. Outside, I could hear people exchanging stories about worst kisses. I strained to hear Tessa launch into her lizard-tongue story.

"So," Max said. "Who was your first kiss?"

I thought for a moment. "Brian Marburg, sixth grade. We went out for two days. Ah, true love."

Max laughed, eyebrows shooting up. That was all it took for me to relax. It was just us.

"What about you?"

"Technically, Lauren," he said, gesturing to the closed door. "In fifth grade. She was in sixth grade, that cradle robber."

"No *way*."

"Yep. Of course, it was exploring a scientific theory more than a kiss. Very clinical."

I smiled, but neither of us said anything more, and I pulled my arms in tighter without really meaning to.

"It's okay." He pushed up one of his cuffed shirtsleeves. "Don't be embarrassed."

Blood rushed to my face all over again, even though I wasn't sure why.

"Embarrassed about what?" I asked. But he was right. I was embarrassed, and Max pointing it out made it worse.

"How badly you want me."

"Ha-ha." I rolled my eyes as I stepped forward to push his shoulder lightly.

"You have a thing for nerds, and that's fine."

"I do *not*!" I laughed. "No offense or anything."

He held his hands up dismissively. "No offense taken, since you're lying."

"I'm not lying."

"You *think* you're not lying." He tapped his forehead knowingly. "But you're lying to yourself."

"Sorry to break it to you on your birthday," I said, "but you're not my type."

"Oh?" He grinned, raising his eyebrows. "You have a type now?"

I shrugged. "Possibly."

"Yeah." He thought for a moment. "Your type is nerd."

"Maybe *your* type is nerd."

"Oh, it absolutely is."

My eyebrows pulled together, thinking of Nicolette from Coventry—pretty and smart, with a kind of avant-garde cool I envied. "Nicolette doesn't really seem like a nerd."

"She is. But maybe not nerdy enough. Maybe that's why it didn't work out."

"Alas, I'm not your type either, I guess." I meant this to sound overdramatized, like it was all a big joke to me. But Max looked smug—like he was smirking *at* me.

"You're very defensive about this," he observed, leaning

a little closer to me. "So, you're telling me that if it weren't for the 'ruining-our-friendship' issue, you would never, ever want to be in here with me?"

"Um. Pretty much." I believed this as I said it, though it pained me to be unkind to someone who had become such a good friend. "Sorry."

"It's fine, Janie," he said, with a wave of his hand. "You're in denial."

"Okay, Max," I said sarcastically.

He stepped closer to me, so that his body was nearly up against mine. Before I could react, he put one hand around my waist and his other behind my neck. He didn't hesitate, didn't pause. He tilted my head up toward him, his thumb on my chin. Oh God, he was seriously going to kiss me. And in that moment, I seriously wanted him to kiss me. My heart gave a surge like a confetti cannon, so loud that I was sure he must have heard it as his lips moved toward mine. My eyes closed instinctively.

"Denial," he whispered, close to my mouth. He backed away immediately, moving a few steps from me. I opened my eyes instantly, and he grinned like this was a hilarious joke. It stopped being funny to me, as jokes often do when they wind up being true. My brain tried to recover while my body tried to melt into a puddle on the floor. Never in a million years would I have guessed that Max Watson had moves. Moves that worked.

He was giddy with laughter, head tilted back. "Oh my God, I freaked you out so badly. Wow, Janie. Your face. Total panic."

I exhaled and placed my hands on my hips. He misread my reaction completely, to my relief. "Seriously. God, Max."

"Okay," he said, still oblivious. "I have a plan."

"For what?" My hand found a shelf ledge, and I steadied myself against it.

"Our audience."

I narrowed my eyes at him. "Okay . . ."

He reached his arms over toward me again, only this time he ruffled my hair.

"Hey!" I cried, swatting him off before he could mess up my bangs.

But Max was now mussing his own hair, beyond even its normal mussed state.

"Ten!" voices called from the outside. "Nine!"

I looked over at Max and grinned slyly. I undid the top button of my shirt.

"Good thinking," he said.

The countdown continued, a mounting chant. "Six! Five!"

Max undid his belt so that both ends swayed against his jeans.

"Two! One!"

The door flew open, and I pretended to look panicked. I

rebuttoned my shirt, and I heard Max's belt jangling as he redid the buckle.

We were met with hoots and laughter. We walked out of the room feigning sheepishness, and I attempted to fix my hair.

"You all think you're so funny." Morgan shook her head.

Max gave her a wily smile. "Whatever do you mean?"

"You guys are dorks," Kayleigh added, laughing.

We sat back down in the circle, where Max was met with a slap on the back from Tyler.

"I knew you had it in you, cuz," Ryan called from the other side of the circle.

"Oh, please," Morgan said. "Nothing happened."

Everyone knew that already, of course, and the game died off in favor of video games. But while I was still breathing, and participating in the conversation, I felt stunned. The movement of the room seemed to slow down around me as I replayed what had just happened. I could barely look at Max, who was laughing, his disheveled hair falling in his face. I doubted that he actually liked me because, if he did, the moves he pulled would have been pretty gutsy. Plus, he seemed to be joking around. But I couldn't undo it now, the feeling of his hand on my waist and the way my heart had bungeed to the floor and back.

Ryan was more of an idea in my mind, and Max was a person—my person. Sure, I daydreamed about Ryan, imagined being his girlfriend and what that would be like. But it was Max who remembered everything I ever told him, Max who looked perpetually delighted when I made him laugh, Max who watched me from the driver's seat as we talked, hour after hour in his car. I could pick up the sound of his laugh in the busiest hallway. When had I learned him so completely? His rolled shirtsleeves and his jaunty walk and the way he chewed at his thumbnail when something was really perplexing him. It all played like a montage in my mind; Max by my side all these months.

I had seen myself reflected back in his glasses a hundred times—my own face smiling, interested, at ease in his presence. How had I not seen *him*?

Maybe my feelings for Max had been there the whole time, obscured by the rubble of the Ryan Chase crush that I'd somehow outgrown. I'd been focused on rebuilding with the debris of my former life when instead I should have been clearing myself a path out. And that path led straight to Max.

For the rest of the night, I found myself watching Max, his smiles and reactions and the way his face was illuminated when he leaned forward to blow out the candles on his cake. He looked flushed with excitement, his friends' voices echoing against the walls in a sugar-fueled rendition of "Happy Birthday." He laughed heartily as he made out the *Firefly* ship in icing form, and he glanced up at Ryan and me. My lips formed a smile as we launched into the final verse of the song.

"Make a wish!" Morgan said as Max took a deep breath.

The flames sizzled out.

"What did you wish for?" Kayleigh teased.

Through the trails of candle smoke, I searched his face for tells, for any sign of what Max Watson's wish would be. He didn't give Kayleigh an answer, or even look at her, but his mouth turned up into a content smile. And in that moment, I found myself hoping that he had wished for me.

Chapter Eighteen

In the weeks that followed, I wasn't sure how to act around Max. Sentences tied themselves into knots in my brain, and I kept stuttering when I spoke to him. We watched *Indiana Jones* at his house—and . . . fine, it was awesome—but my heart beat double time for two straight hours. Even when his mom sat down with us to watch the end.

He cashed in the *Firefly* marathon I'd promised him, and Tessa watched it with us out of genuine interest. We were all parked on the couch at Max's house when we heard a voice.

"Hey, hey," someone said from the door leading in from the garage. Ryan walked in, looking relaxed and purposeful until he saw Tessa and me. With *Firefly* still blaring on the TV.

"Oh, hey ladies," he said. His eyes found the TV. "Okay, *what* is happening here?"

"Sci-fi education at its finest," Max said. I had to admit—the show's world-building was impressive, with well-drawn characters and masterful banter.

"Oh my God," Ryan said, his gaze moving between me and Tessa. "Are you being held here against your will? Blink twice if you're hostages."

Ryan nodded off in a recliner as we continued our marathon. After three episodes, Max paused the show and turned to me. "Okay. Early verdict from the TV buff."

"Well," I said. "It has scrappy underdogs, a large-scale setting, subtle character moments, and great pithy humor."

"In other words," Max said, "you *love* it. *Firefly* is your *life* now."

I threw a pillow at him as Tessa laughed. "Just hit Play."

As the days wore on, I spun possible scenarios in my mind, time and time again, when I was lying in bed at night or daydreaming in class. But I knew the truth deep down in my gut: I couldn't do a thing about it, even though I suspected he might feel the same. Max was just so intimidatingly real. I already knew him better than I'd ever known Aaron. If we did go out, there wouldn't be any hesitant, getting-to-know-you dates. He'd seen me upset, seen me in sweatpants during the weekends. He already knew so many of my secrets. So us together? It would be intense immediately. Serious, even.

Still, I edited my plan for the third time: 3. Date (R̶E̶).

The whole idea seemed silly and shallow now. I'd liked Ryan the way I liked fashion magazine editorials—girls in full skirts, with doe legs and tall heels—the ones that make you think: *How beautiful. I wish that could be my life.* Ryan Chase was my eighth-grade collage, aspirational and wide-eyed. But Max was the first bite of grilled cheese on a snowy day, the easy fit of my favorite jeans, that one old song that made it onto every playlist. Peanut-butter Girl Scout cookies instead of an ornate cake. Not glamorous or idealized or complicated. Just me.

Besides, Max had never given me any concrete reason to think we were more than friends. Maybe that's all I was to him, and I was extrapolating us into totally fictional territory. I read into every comment, every glance, every paper airplane note in class. I honestly couldn't remember what I thought about before I met Max Watson.

"So," Max said. We were walking down the hall together after school, heading to his car for an away QuizBowl match. "Tessa and I are getting tickets for another concert at the Carmichael. It's not till June, but I think you'd really like the band. I mean, if you're not at NYU, which I still think you will be."

"I'd have to ask Tessa," I said. "She's particular about who can go to concerts with her. She hates when the other person isn't as into the music—says it distracts her. The Carmichael is like her fort, and I'm not always allowed."

"I could get you in with her," he said, with a half-joking confidence. "I know the secret knock."

I turned my head to grin at him, but I was distracted by the sound of plastic hitting the floor by my left foot—a pen with a chewed-up cap.

"Hey," I said to the guy in front of me, shuddering as I picked up the mangled pen. "You dropped this."

The boy turned around. It was Stoner Josh in a baggy black sweatshirt, blinking at me with bloodshot eyes.

"*Whew*," he said, taking the pen from me. "That's my only one. Thanks, Grammar Girl."

"Hey," Max snapped, turning toward Josh. "Her name is not Grammar Girl."

My face flushed, caught between embarrassment and affection. Max looked down at Josh, who was clearly startled by the confrontation.

"Uh," he said, glancing over at me before he took off down the hall. "Sorry."

"Her name is Janie," Max called after him. "JAY-NEE."

"Thanks, Janie!" Stoner Josh said over his shoulder.

"I hate you," I muttered to Max.

"Sure you do."

I crossed my arms. He stood there, a few steps ahead of me, waiting for me to catch up. I weighed it in my mind for the thousandth time: the fluttering in my chest versus the shattering possibility of destroying our friendship.

And even though I rolled my eyes, I made my way toward him.

~

"This was actually good," Cameron proclaimed, scraping at her plate. "I'm stuffed."

"*Grazie*," my dad said, affecting a heavy Italian accent as he took a bow. As usual, he was already hunched over the sink, scrubbing dishes.

I shook my head at his dramatics, savoring the last bite of his chicken tetrazzini.

"Why didn't Mom come over?" Cameron bit into another bread stick, apparently not as stuffed as she claimed.

"Can't I still have an evening with just my girls sometimes?" he asked.

"Of course you can," I said.

"You know what I mean," Cameron said. "I'm, like, used to you being over there most of the time. It seems weird to come here without her."

"Well," he said. "Some alone time is good for her."

There was a pause as I handed off my plate to my dad. I dropped my silverware into the dishwasher.

"So, like," Cameron said through a mouthful of bread stick. "Do you think you and her will get married again?"

I cringed at both her pronoun usage and her bluntness.

264

"Cameron!" I said, shooting her the most contemptuous look in my repertoire.

"What?" She sneered at me. "It's a legitimate question."

I did appreciate the four-syllable word, rare as it was for her.

"Dad, you don't have to answer that," I said, making my way back to the table to clear the glasses. I swatted my sister's arm as I walked by. I didn't want my dad to feel on the spot, but more important, I wasn't ready to hear his answer.

"No—it's fine," my dad said. His voice sounded relaxed, but he kept his eyes fixed on the pan in front of him, scrubbing vigorously. "The answer is that I have no idea."

I sighed in relief because that was the only answer I could handle. If he'd said no, I would worry that he was leading my mom on. But I wasn't ready to hear him say yes either, unwilling to imagine that another signed marriage certificate could end in a second set of divorce papers.

"I think you should," Cameron said.

"Cameron, seriously," I hissed.

"What? I'm just letting him know that I don't have a problem with it, even if *someone else* does." She glared at me, in case there was any doubt that I was the *someone else*.

"Cami," my dad said. "Cool it. Your sister was there for some stuff that you're too young to remember. She's earned her skepticism."

Cameron looked stunned, like this was new information. She must not have believed me when I'd told her the same thing months before, and she huffed at her seat. "It's, like, so unfair that everyone in this family knows what happened, and I apparently don't or something."

"Well, the divorce was mostly my fault," my dad said. It was like he'd been waiting to say this the whole time, like he knew Cameron would ask. "You should know that much."

"Dad, that's not true." I turned to Cameron. "It's not."

"No—it's okay, Paiger. She should know," he said, waving me off with a soapy hand. He placed a glass upside down in the dishwasher, wiping his brow against his sleeve. "I was young and immature. It was before my column, and I was jealous of your mother's success in journalism. I felt inadequate because she was making more money and because she was a better parent than I was. I shut her out."

"Dad, c'mon," I said. I hated to see him like this, the most gregarious person I knew waxing introspective. Sure, he was introspective in his column, but in a jokey, self-deprecating way. "You don't mean that."

"I'm afraid I do, kiddos." My dad smiled up at us, looking surprisingly at ease. "I'm not proud of it, but there's a reason why I've always been 'good cop.'"

"You're a great dad, though. A fun dad," Cameron said.

He smiled. "Thanks, kid. But I shouldn't have stuck your mom with all the rules and discipline of parenting."

"Hey, Dad?" I began. After Cameron's inquisition, I felt guilty continuing to grill him. But I'd always wondered, especially now that he'd found self-awareness.

"Yeah?"

"Did you guys ever go to marriage counseling?" I asked.

"Your mom wanted to, but I wouldn't go," he admitted. I wasn't expecting what he said next. "But I've been seeing a therapist for the past couple months."

Cameron's eyes widened. "Are you okay?"

"Of course I'm okay," he said. The dishwasher whirred to life, adding some much-needed background noise to this conversation. "I just wanted to take every possible precaution so that I wouldn't mess things up with your mom again."

"Really?" I asked.

"Yep," he said, winking at me. "You think I figured out all that 'jealous of her success' and 'good cop' stuff on my own?"

I sat completely still, stunned by my dad's revelation: the person who was most worried about their relationship failing was my *dad*—not me. All this time, I thought I was the only one who saw this as the danger zone, a dizzying ledge between the past and future.

"Listen, girls," he said, finally. "Nothing is more important to me than doing right by you and your mom. But relationships aren't perfect, not a single one of them, and that includes your mom and me. The difference is that I'm fighting for us this time."

I wasn't sure what to expect next. Maybe the instrumental music they play at the end of family sitcoms, where the moral of the story is revealed. Maybe a group hug. Instead, my phone gave a shrill sequence of beeps, announcing a text message.

"Sorry," I muttered, reaching into my bag on the floor.

K + E broke up it said in Tessa's cell phone shorthand. *My house. Now.*

"Everything okay?" my dad asked.

"Um. Kind of. Kayleigh's having a breakup meltdown at Tessa's."

"Ouch," my dad said. "You need to head over there?"

"I mean . . . I don't want to interrupt family time."

"Hey," he said. "Kayleigh's family, too. If she needs you, you need to go."

I couldn't help but smile at my dad, thinking that there's a difference between "good cop" and "good heart." I knew exactly which he was.

~

By the time I made it to Tessa's house, Kayleigh's face was already puffy from crying. Her hair was in a sloppy ponytail, with wild flyaways framing her head. Even more distressing, she wore a white T-shirt and black yoga pants. Kayleigh, in all the years I'd known her, had never looked so underdone. She even wore makeup during gym class, with sneakers that matched her sports bra.

"*Finally*," Kayleigh said when I walked in the side door. "Here's the CliffsNotes to a book called *Kayleigh's Life Sucks*: we broke up."

There were two reasons to hold crisis meetings at Tessa's house. The first: Tessa stocked junk food like she was preparing for a sugar apocalypse. The second was that, with no parents around and Gran McMahon fast asleep sans hearing aids, we could swear up a storm.

Tessa had pulled out the emotional-eating big guns: a package of Oreos, two open rolls of raw cookie dough, three types of ice cream, and a buffet of toppings. Kayleigh held a big spoon, gesturing with it like a metal scepter as she held court over her relationship postmortem.

"I know you always hear about how awful heartbreak is," she said through a mouthful of ice cream. "But seriously, it physically hurts."

None of my friends had ever experienced a big breakup before, and I wasn't sure what I was supposed to say. In the meantime, I concentrated on not giving her That Look. She deserved better than that. I ventured a question. "Did he tell you why?"

"Why what?" Kayleigh asked, sniffling.

It sounded cruel, spelled out. "Why he broke up with you."

"He didn't. I broke up with him."

I glanced at the others to see if they could fill in the gaps. Morgan bit down on her lip, and Tessa popped a chunk of cookie dough into her mouth, chewing thoughtfully. "*You* broke up with *him*? Why?"

"Because . . ." Her eyes filled with tears. She let her spoon drop back into the bowl with a clank. "Because he's a jerk. Which you wouldn't know because you barely met him. Because he always wanted to hang out alone or with his friends. He wanted everything on his terms. Because he's a *jerk*."

"He was an asshole to Morgan tonight," Tessa added.

"Oh yeah." Kayleigh glanced over at Morgan, who became very invested in pushing her ice cream around. "I planned this whole thing—like, hey, we should all go to dinner so you can get to know Morgan. And he brought one of his friends and spent the whole time talking to him. I had a freaking epiphany in the middle of the restaurant, like . . . he doesn't really care about me. If he cared about me, he'd also care about the people *I* care about. He'd want to know them! I can't believe I didn't put it together before. It was like I went along with whatever he wanted to do because he's older and kind of out of my league."

"*No one* is out of your league," Morgan said fiercely.

Kayleigh shoveled more ice cream into her mouth as I fumbled with my next lines. Tessa shot me a look—eyebrows up—but I had no idea what she was trying to tell me. I kept searching, finally landing on another touchy question. "So, shouldn't we be kind of . . . happy? About the breakup? If he was such a jerk?"

"We *are* happy," Kayleigh said miserably. "But I'm also upset that I wasted my time on him. And I'm, like, embarrassed that I made him out to be this awesome guy when he so isn't."

"Overcompensating," Tessa commented. She meant it as a paraphrase, not a condemnation, but Morgan gave her a warning look all the same. "Wait. Did you break up with him at the restaurant tonight? Like, immediately following your revelation?"

"Yeah." Kayleigh sniffed. "Because, like, once I realized he treated Morgan that way, I realized he treated *me* that way half the time, unless we were alone."

"It was awesome," Morgan said. "She walked out to the car with him, talked to him for a minute, kissed him on the cheek and walked away. Oh my gosh, the look on her face, strutting away. Awesome."

"It *was* kind of awesome." Kayleigh dabbed her eyes. "But I'm still bummed. All right. I need to eat more cookie dough and watch a movie or something."

"TV guru?" Morgan asked, turning to me. "What do you prescribe?"

"*Sex and the City*," I said. "No question."

Kayleigh fell asleep on the couch within fifteen minutes, exhausted from grieving her expectations. While it hurt me to watch one of my best friends feel so low, I was glad to have her back. It felt right, the four of us—like balance restored.

Chapter Nineteen

Considering my drowning phobia, Whitewater Lodge was my worst nightmare. Add in the necessity of a swimsuit, and Whitewater Lodge was my personal hell.

Every April, on the last Friday before spring break, the Oakhurst School Board funded a field trip. Honor roll students got to miss a day of school for a semieducational outing known as Honors Excursion. The name sounded official, but the event itself really was not.

We went to Kings Island my first two years of high school. Mr. Varp gave us a fifteen-minute, halfhearted lecture on the physics of roller coasters before setting us free for the whole day. Honors Excursion was the sole reason why Kayleigh dragged herself to math study group every week since freshman year.

272

This year, because of budget cuts, Honors Excursion would take place at Whitewater Lodge, an indoor water park in the next town over. I considered going; I really did. But I thought of all the eyes on me, watching my face as people plunged from the slide's drop-off to the water. I thought about how many times I would receive That Look, while in my bathing suit. I thought about the water that used to look clean and relaxing, now oily and threatening in my mind. My mom wrote me an excuse note and even offered to let me stay home from school for the day.

Though I was embarrassed that people might notice my absence, it was nice to have a day off. I slept in, ate a big breakfast, and took a long shower. The house was quiet, free of Cameron's incessant cell phone noise. It wasn't even two when the doorbell rang, and I nearly jumped out of my reading chair.

My mind raced through non-serial-killer examples of who might be at the door in the middle of a weekday. I decided it was probably UPS or door-to-door evangelists— harmless. I peeked out the lens and saw Max, hands in his pockets. I pulled the door open.

"Hey!" I was too surprised to hide my excitement, even if I did sound a little overeager.

"Hey, girl." The wind tossed his hair, and his hand made a futile swipe to tame it. His button-down shirt fluttered against his chest.

"What are you doing here?"

"I skipped Honors Excursion because I'm sick. Cough-cough." He gave me a wry smile. "I don't like to be seen next to Ryan in a bathing suit."

Smiling, I leaned against the door frame and the fresh air hit my face. I took a deep breath in. "It's *warm*."

"I know." Max closed his eyes for a moment. "It smells like spring."

"It *is* spring. Spring break."

"Exactly." He looked down at me. "Do you want to go somewhere?"

My heart hammered. "Sure."

I didn't bother to ask if he had someplace in mind. I ducked back into the house to leave my mom a note, scribbling a generic "Be back soon." This was the same note I left anytime I walked over to Tessa's, and I hoped she'd assume that's where I went. She was driving a few hours away to interview someone for the magazine, so I had some time. If she found out I left without her permission, I would be grounded until graduation. Before I could talk myself out of leaving, I grabbed my purse, locked the door, and followed Max to his car.

He drove with the windows down, and my hair whipped all around me. It did smell like spring, like soil and rainstorms, and he took the back roads at full speed. I breathed in, possibility tingling in my lungs. In that moment, I was free of worry about my parents, my sister, my grandmother, everything. I wanted to spread my arms wide out of the sunroof, like flying.

"Are we going somewhere specific?" The wind ripped through the windows, and I yelled so he could hear me. "Or are we just driving?"

"Somewhere specific," he called back.

I wondered where somewhere was. I wondered if this was a date. I wondered if he had planned all of this and what it meant. But most of all, I wondered if a person could actually burst from so many feelings at once.

We were still on country roads, past any area that I recognized. Finally, Max turned onto a gravel drive and put the car in park.

"We're here," he announced. Here seemed to be a field of wild grass, rising above a rickety wooden fence. I climbed out of the car, glancing around for any reason we might be here.

Max pulled a blanket out of the backseat and gestured for me to follow him.

"Are you going to murder me?" I said with a straight face, hoping to make him laugh.

He did laugh as he shook his head. "Come on."

Pulling himself onto the fence, Max swung his leg over and landed on the other side. I followed him over through the tall grass until we emerged in a clearing—a wide circle where all the grass was matted down.

"Okay," I said. "What is this about?"

"This," he said, "is about airplanes."

"Airplanes."

"Yep."

Max fanned the blanket out on the ground and lay down before the breeze could lift it away. I lay down next to him and took a deep breath. I could almost hear words rustling between the trees—*summer, summer, summer.* And then, I was acutely aware that I was lying down, inches from Max. It was enough to push my heart rate into a jumpy staccato.

"What are we waiting for?" The words hung in the air for a moment, and I wondered if he knew what I meant. I was still tiptoeing, not daring to cross the friendship line.

"Magic," he said. "Any second now."

The wind stirred through the grass, and when it settled, the whole world was quiet. I stared up at the gauzy clouds obscuring most of the blue sky. My stomach tensed with anticipation. And then I heard it, in the distance—a low rumble, building and building. Above us, an airplane tore through the sky, the sound near-deafening into my ears.

I gasped, staring up at the plane's metal underside, which seemed to be hovering right above our bodies. Almost as soon as I'd processed what was happening, the tail of the plane was out of sight, and the sound was fading and then distant and then gone. Neither of us moved. My hearing fuzzed over, readjusting to the relative silence.

"You know," Max said, "a Boeing 747 can weigh up to eight hundred thousand pounds at takeoff."

Max Watson, king of romance. Comments like these solidified it: he saw me as a friend. I glanced over at him, hoping his facial expression would explain why he'd said that. It didn't. He was still staring up at the sky with an incredulous look on his face.

"But it flies," he continued. He turned to look at me, as if he was teaching me brand-new information. "It's pretty improbable, when you think about it. We're so used to seeing planes, but there's something about them that defies reason. You wouldn't think it could happen."

"I guess," I said, sitting up. I had to admit, seeing a takeoff close-up made it seem surreal.

Max rolled onto his side. "I thought you might want to see it. Because of . . . you know . . . how you are."

"Excuse me?" I raised an eyebrow at him.

"Skeptical," he said. "A realist."

I couldn't hide my frown. "You say that like it's a bad thing."

"You know what I mean."

"Nope."

He sighed. "I mean you're always preparing yourself for the thing that is most likely to happen, instead of hoping for the thing that you most want to happen."

When you've been blindsided by grief, you tend to

imagine the worst in all things. It seemed easier to prepare for bad news in a way that I couldn't with Aaron. I just hadn't realized I'd been doing it with everything. Max didn't seem to notice my dumbfounded self-reflection.

"Anyway, we'll have to come back in the summer, when the fireflies are out," Max said, stretching his arms behind his head as he lay back down. "Looking up, you can barely tell the difference between the fireflies and the airplane lights and the stars. Tiny flecks of light everywhere. It's unreal."

So Max saw us hanging out, just the two of us, this summer. One point in the "more than friends" column. See? I could hope for what I most wanted to happen.

"Hey," I said. "Question. Why didn't you go today?"

"Um, honestly?" He moved back to his side, facing me again. My heart spun in circles, frantic with the idea that maybe he'd ditched Honors Excursion just to be here with me. "Because my dad got in touch with me yesterday. Wants to see me, et cetera."

My heart came to a halt. "Oh my God."

He rolled his eyes. "He does it almost every year, a few weeks after my birthday. Gets to feeling guilty, maybe. Who knows. But this year, it's under my skin because . . ."

I stayed quiet and still, just watching him as he paused to bite at his thumbnail. ". . . because I'm seventeen now. And he was nineteen when I was born. It's getting harder to deny that he was basically a kid. Anyway, I drove to school, but I just couldn't get on the bus to the water park. I needed a quiet day."

I felt relieved that I was no longer lying down on the blanket. It was too tempting to press myself close to him. To be so connected but not touching felt incongruous. And he looked so lost and lonely, in that moment. "So, do you think you'll see him? Your dad?"

"Nope. I'm not there yet," he said. We sat there for a few moments in the silence because, really, what could I say to that? Max gave me an almost self-deprecating smile. "All right. Enough of my drama. So why didn't *you* go today?"

I pushed my bangs off my face. Of course I'd tell him after what he just told me. "Because of That Look."

"What look?"

"The face people would have made when they saw Aaron Rosenthal's girlfriend at a pool, where drowning opportunities abound."

Max nodded, processing this.

"It's lose-lose," I continued. "Either I sit out of the pool, like I would have, and everyone feels sorry for me. Or I get brave and get in, and then everyone stares at me, wondering if I'm thinking of Aaron."

"No one would think that," Max said, as if he could have possibly known that. "You wouldn't have gotten in?"

I hadn't exactly meant to admit that part. "No. I don't . . . can't . . . swim anymore."

Max sat up now, cross-legged on the blanket. "I didn't know that."

I shrugged. "I have a recurring nightmare about drowning. Apparently it's pretty normal, a posttraumatic kind of thing."

I could feel him looking at me, working through something for a few moments. "Is that how you think of yourself? As Aaron Rosenthal's girlfriend? That's what you said, before."

"Ha," I said. "No. But to everyone at school, I am."

"Not to me."

"Well, you weren't in school when it happened."

He dodged that one. "Why don't you ever talk about him?"

His eyes read mine like the lines of a book—left to right and back, searching—and I had to glance away. "You're full of questions today."

"I brought you to my secret spot," he said, gesturing around us. "I feel I'm owed a secret or two."

"I didn't know Aaron that well," I admitted. This was a phrase I said in my head all the time but almost never out loud. "More of my life has been affected by his absence than his presence, and that's a strange thing to deal with."

Max nodded, the wind ruffling his hair. "You knew him

for a few months, but you've dealt with his death for much longer."

"Right," I said. "He, um . . . he changed me, completely. But it was his death that did that, not his life. It'll be two years in July—two years of grappling with all this gray area. One-half of high school. Nearly one-eighth of my entire life."

He glanced over at me, and I pushed a few strands of tousled hair behind my ear.

"You think about it a lot," he said. "Enough to do the math."

I nodded.

"When do you think you'll be okay?"

"What makes you think I'm not?" I was so careful to seem okay to the rest of the world, carefully disguised by my *I'm fine* mask. But Max saw more than that, saw the cracks beneath the surface.

"You didn't go today. You still fear drowning, still dream of it."

He wasn't wrong, but I felt the need to defend my efforts. Because I *was* making efforts. "Yeah, well. It's on my list. I'm going to try to swim again. Eventually."

"You have a list?"

"It's just some things I've been trying, to help me move on." I pressed my lips together. There was one fear that trumped drowning, the only fear I'd never spoken out loud.

"I mean, I've moved on from him, as, like, a boyfriend. But I'm not over his death. He was fifteen. It'll never be okay. And so maybe I'll never be okay, either."

Without looking up at Max, I knew that his eyes were on me. I stared down into my lap, waiting for him to say something. There was a part of me that wanted to look up, to hope for what I most wanted to happen, but it wasn't the time. I couldn't let a conversation about Aaron lead to something with Max. I needed them to be separate.

We sat in silence for a moment more, my hands clammy. But I knew it was time to say it out loud—one last, dark truth about the day Aaron died.

"The part I can't get past," I said, "is that the people who were there—they said Aaron was messing around at the edge of the ravine. And they said he jumped. But what if he didn't? What if he was joking around and fell?"

Max frowned. "Does it matter? I mean, wouldn't it have . . ."

"Ended the same? Yes." I stared at the grass, still avoiding Max's eyes. "But that matters to me—whether it was a jump or a fall."

"The difference being . . . ?"

"Choice," I said. "Falling implies that it's involuntary. A jump is intentional. I just wish I knew for sure that it was the latter. I want to believe that he felt happy as he hit the water. Not shocked or afraid."

There was nothing Max, or anyone, could say to assure me either way. It was something I'd discussed in therapy, at length. I had accepted that this question would sit inside me, maybe forever, and that would have to be okay. But still, like everything else, it felt better to tell Max.

"Okay," he said, standing up. "Let's go. We've gotta make one more stop."

Chapter Twenty

I expected Max to take us to a restaurant for a late lunch or maybe drive to Alcott's to spend the rest of the afternoon reading and drinking coffee. I did *not* expect him to pull into the parking lot of the YMCA.

"What are we doing here?" I asked, climbing out of the car.

Max spun his keys around his finger. "You'll see."

"I haven't been here since I was little," I rambled as we walked into the building. "For swim lessons."

That's when I realized what we were doing there.

"Max," I hissed, grabbing his arm before he could open the door. "Why are we here?"

"I just want you to see the pool," he said. "Maybe dip your legs in."

That seemed reasonable enough, but I didn't like it. In Max's glasses, I could see my pulled-together eyebrows, trying to trust him. He must have known my decision because he pushed the door open, and I followed him in.

"I'm not a member," I said as my final effort.

"I am," Max said, waving at the guy at the front desk.

"Hey, Max," the guy said.

"Hey, Gus," Max said. "Pool open?"

"You betcha," he replied. "But no lifeguard this time of day, so be careful, eh?"

At this, I smacked Max's arm. Hard. He ignored me, giving a nod to Gus before heading toward the pool. I remembered it, vaguely—the high ceilings and walls painted to look like blue waves.

The indoor pool was deserted, and the water lay so still that I could see the perfect lines painted onto the bottom, marking swim lanes. Humid air and the thick scent of chlorine filled my nose and lungs.

"No way." I planted my feet just beyond the door. "I don't even have a bathing suit."

"That's okay." From the lifeguard station, Max grabbed a big beach towel with YMCA stamped on its corner.

He sat down by the deep end of the pool. He pulled off his sneakers, rolled up his jeans and slipped his legs in the water. From behind him, I crossed my arms, trying to grow roots into the cement floor.

"See?" he said, turning to look at me. "We don't have to miss out on all the pool festivities. Plus, it's the first warm day of the year. What could be better than dipping your feet in the water?"

"*Not* dipping my feet in the water."

Max patted the tile next to him, and I stepped closer. Putting my feet in the water was no big deal. It was the idea of putting my *head* underwater that stoked a fire in my chest, the burn of phobia deep inside me.

I popped my shoes off before I could change my mind. Shoving my jeans up, I sank my legs in the water. It was warmer than I thought it would be, and it felt almost soothing, the way it did before I associated water with death.

"You good?" Max asked.

I nodded. Our legs were nearly touching, and he kept quiet, as if he knew I needed a minute.

Finally, I said, "It's weird. You're supposed to associate water with cleansing. And I guess I always did, before Aaron. I used to love to swim."

I swirled my legs in circles in front of me. "It's still so weird to me that it was *water* that killed Aaron. Somehow, I think coming to terms with the idea of death somehow got linked to water. Like it had betrayed me, or something." I heard my words as they were spoken and how crazy I sounded. "I guess that's weird."

"No, it's not," Max said. "I was *pissed* at cancer after

my grandpa died—it was Cancer, with a capital *C*. Like it was a person who I could punch in the face, if I could only find him."

In my peripheral vision, I saw Max turn to look at me. I glanced over at him, our shoulders just an inch apart.

"You should jump in," he said.

"No," I said hotly. "No way."

I retracted my feet from the water, spooked at the very idea. I scrambled up, taking a few steps back from the pool. I hadn't expected Max to spring this on me, to ambush me into overcoming a fear after I'd stayed home from Honors Excursion specifically to avoid it. He stood up, too, turning to me.

"I just . . . I know you, Paige." At the sound of my real name, I knew he meant business. That one word—more persuasive than anything else he could have said. "This is something you can do. You don't have to miss out on things like you did today."

I jerked my head back. "That's not fair. I just didn't want to deal with what people would think of me."

"I get that," he said. "But you're already here."

I wanted to be the girl he thought I was. And, even as my palms began to sweat, even as my heart rate galloped in my chest, I wanted to be the girl I used to be.

"What if something happens? There's no lifeguard and—"

"I'm a babysitter, Janie. CPR certified."

We stood there, yards apart, and I bounced on my toes. If I did it, I could check this off. Get it over with, here and now, in the company of someone who made me want to be brave.

"Okay," I said. "I'll stand on the low dive. But . . . I don't know if I can jump in."

Max nodded encouragingly. "That's a really big step."

I moved toward the diving boards. Max stayed put, as if he might startle me. The board was colder than I expected, and it felt coarse against the bottoms of my feet. Grasping the metal bars with both hands, I took two steps, and then one more. Muscle memory kicked in, beneath the fear. My body knew this sensation, and I could almost smell the sunscreen and drippy popsicles of my pool days.

When I was about halfway to the edge, the board gave a little, bending at my weight. I froze, my whole body tensing. Max stayed quiet, but I could feel his eyes on me. I took one more hesitant step, staring down into the water.

My hands balled into fists. I stood still, not daring to make that last step forward. It was only a foot or two drop into the water, but pieces of my nightmare flashed through my mind. Instinctively, I squeezed my eyes shut, and clips of an underwater struggle screened on the back of my eyelids.

"I'm right here," Max reminded me. I opened my eyes.

He stood off to the right side, waiting with the white towel in his hands. "I'm not going to let anything bad happen."

"I know," I said, my pulse ticking higher and higher. "But I don't think I can."

"You can. Stop looking down."

I shook my head, eyes locked on clear water. I imagined being deep within it, trapped like I always was in my nightmare. The heavy smell of chlorine hung in the air, and my stomach flipped inside of me.

"Paige, don't look down. Look up at me."

I tilted my chin up, enough to rest my eyes on Max. His eyes were locked on mine, as he drew out his words, slowly so I would understand. "Hey. You're already there."

My chest tightened so much that my lungs ached. The pool fanned out around me in every direction, and the broad scope made me feel dizzy, like the reflections were in a kaleidoscope. My breathing became ragged, almost gasping.

"I can't," I said, moving my left foot to step back. But as I tried to turn around on the board, my foot slipped.

Before I even realized what was happening, my body struck the water. The sting hit my skin as water closed over my head. I tried to react, to push my arms out, but my body was paralyzed by the shock of going in. Aaron's face flashed into my mind, the panic he must have felt. I felt the ache that must have filled his lungs, the burn against his open eyes.

I thrashed, struggling against walls of water closing in all around me. The weight from the water above me was pushing me down—I could feel it. Underwater, I screamed, too panicked to think about losing the very last of my air supply.

An arm wrapped around my waist, pulling me upward, and I gasped for air when my mouth met the surface. Max propelled me toward the ladder and hoisted me up to the first rung. Grasping the handles, I stepped up, and my feet shakily found the cement. Max was out of the pool right behind me. In a blurred moment, he guided me to a lounge chair and wrapped the plush towel around my shoulders.

Crouching in front of me, he asked, "You okay?"

"I'm fine," I lied, out of reflex. But my body wouldn't ease from its adrenaline rush, chest heaving with gasps instead of breaths. I felt every prickling sensation in my body, and I felt totally numb, all at once. I pulled the towel closer, but my clothes were soaked and stuck to my body. And then the past minute's events passed through my mind, and I changed my answer.

"No." I labored to inhale enough to speak. "No, I am *not okay*."

I stood up, jerking away from him. I stumbled, still wobbly, and Max caught me by the elbow. Pulling from his grasp, I turned to face him. His glasses were off, his hair dripping, and his clothes were at least five shades darker, shirt matted against his chest.

"Just because I tell you things," I yelled, "doesn't mean you know everything about me!"

The blood was rushing through my veins faster than the water rushing out of the jets, and I couldn't think straight.

"I'm sorry, Paige. I'm so sorry." Max stared at me, completely stricken. My pulse thumped in my ears, too loud and too hot.

"I could have *died*!" I heard how loud my voice was, but I felt helpless to it. The tears came, hot on my wet face, but I didn't feel embarrassed. Just angry. Max stepped toward me, his hands out in surrender, and I took a step back.

"You can't try to *fix* me like I'm a project." My words bounced off the tiled floor, echoing through the room. "You don't even have your own life figured out, so I don't need you trying to figure out mine."

"Hey," Max said sharply, pulling away from me. "I was just trying to help."

I'd hit a sore spot—all of his anxiety—and I knew it. But I couldn't stop. "This is not how you *help*. How would you feel if I pushed you into seeing your dad?"

"That is *not* the same." His voice was hushed.

"It *is* the same, Max," I yelled. "You're not brave enough to see him, and that's your problem. I'm not brave enough to swim or go out with someone new or jet off to some place by myself, but those are *my* problems."

The tears that fell from my eyes cleared my view of him. His forehead was creased in anger, his eyes squinted at me.

"Well," he said, with a measured bitterness. "It's nice that you realize you're not the only person in the world who has problems."

My jaw dropped, and I made the guttural noise of someone who was kicked in the stomach while already in a fetal position on the ground.

As I sat there, slack jawed and aching to my core, he pressed his face into his hands. "Shit. I didn't mean that, Paige."

Too late. Way, way, way too late. "Just *go*."

I buried my face in my towel and sobbed into the nubby terrycloth. I heard Max's footsteps padding toward the edge of the pool, and I looked up as the sound moved back toward me.

He plopped my shoes down beside me. "I'm not leaving you here."

"I'll call someone to pick me up." With all my friends at stupid Whitewater Lodge and my mom at an interview, my dad would be my only shot. But I'd take it. I'd rather wait, shaking and soaked beneath this towel, than ride home with him in the tense, contained silence.

"Paige," Max said. "Please. Just let me take you home."

We had derailed so quickly and so irreparably. I tried to

hear his voice the way I'd heard earlier, reverent and excited over something as silly as airplanes. Through blurred vision, I pulled my shoes back on.

I followed behind him to the car. We were silent on the ride home, while I seethed. My clothes were cold, plastered to my skin. I felt trapped by them, trapped by the towel, trapped by the car and by Max and by my own past.

When he pulled into the driveway, I was relieved to see that my mom wasn't home yet. I could dry off and clean up with no explanation. I had nothing left to say to Max, and my hand went immediately to the door handle. I slammed the door behind me so hard that it reverberated over the whole car.

It struck me as I hurried inside: I'd never left Max's car so quickly. I'd divulged dozens of secrets from the passenger's seat, laughing and listening. His car was safe harbor, but now, with my trust fractured so completely, I shuddered at the thought of spending one more second in that enclosed space with him.

I went straight into the laundry room. Grabbing a clean towel, I peeled off my wet clothes and tossed them into the dryer. I couldn't put drenched clothes in the laundry hamper, and I needed to shower before my mom got home. I didn't want her to know that I was out by myself with Max without permission or that we had gone to a pool, where I had almost died from being such a complete therapy case.

Before I stomped upstairs to the shower, I looked out the front window. I wanted Max to be there still, his head bowed against the steering wheel in helpless regret. He was gone.

I turned the shower on, and as the hot water hit me, tears formed again. This was something that I used to do in the months after Aaron died. I didn't want my mom to know how upset I was, so I'd sob in the shower, masked by the sounds of running water and the bathroom fan.

With my back leaned against the shower wall, I slid down into a seated position. I pulled my knees to my chest and wrapped my arms around my legs. The smell of chlorine released from my skin as steam filled the shower. If only it were so easy to release everything else I had pent up inside of me.

Because I felt the truth, pelting me like water: I wasn't just mad at Max. I was mad at myself.

I was mad that I was still so vulnerable after all this time. Mad that I let myself be defined by one tragic accident. Mad that I slipped into the water, that my reentry had been hapless flailing. It was a fall, not a jump. It should have been a jump. I owed myself that.

At that moment, I felt like I had just thrown a stick of dynamite at whatever chance I had with Max, burning and crackling and exploding as I slammed the car door in his face. The steam in the shower wafted like smoke, clearing after I set fire to what could have been.

I was standing up when a knock at the door nearly startled me out of my bare skin.

"Paige!" my mom called. "Just letting you know that I'm home."

"Okay!" I yelled back, scrambling to my feet. I needed a fast lie, as my mom would surely notice a single outfit—right down to my bra, panties, and socks—rotating in the dryer.

It came to me as I patted my hair dry. I would say I spilled coffee on myself. That was simple and easy enough to believe since half of my clothes had coffee stains from Alcott's to-go cups.

When I came downstairs, my mom was standing at the kitchen island, sifting through the day's mail.

"How was your day off?" she asked, glancing up at me.

"It was fine," I lied.

I opened the refrigerator, turning my back to my mother. This gave me a purpose for being in the kitchen and would hopefully show nonchalance.

"Doing laundry?" my mom said.

"Uh-huh," I said, pretending to survey the contents of the refrigerator.

"Just one outfit?"

Crap. She had looked in the dryer. I never did my own laundry, so of course she would have noticed right away.

"I spilled coffee." I didn't turn around for fear that she would see the lie on my face.

"Huh," she said from behind me. "That's weird. It smelled more like chlorine than coffee."

My body froze in place as my thoughts bounced around, searching anywhere for a lie. I scanned the refrigerator shelves, as if a believable story would materialize next to the yogurt.

"Paige," she said.

As I turned around, I knew the exact expression that would be on her face—her jaw tense, her eyes unblinking. Instead, I found a soft expression of understanding. Almost That Look.

"Why don't we go out to dinner?"

I wanted to decline, so I could stay home and continue fuming at Max and myself. But, considering that I had left without her permission, almost drowned, and then lied about it, I had no bargaining chips.

"Sure."

"I have to finish writing up my notes from the interview," she said. "Then we'll go."

~

Over a hearty portion of lasagna, I confessed to my mom in a corner booth at Arpeggio's Italiano. She was mostly quiet, nodding along as I described the incident at the pool. I skipped our trip to see the airplanes, because those moments with Max were still mine. When I told her that I couldn't get into the water, she didn't look surprised. Here

I thought it was a big secret, but of course my own mother would have noticed that I stopped taking baths, that I didn't come home wet from Tessa's pool once last summer.

"Honey," my mom said when I was finished. "I'm not excusing the fact that you lied to me today, but I do understand why you went with Max."

"You do?"

"Of course," she said, resting her fork against her salad plate. "Of course I do. And moreover, I think Max had a point in taking you there."

My eyebrows creased in reaction to this betrayal. My mom had taken a liking to Max over the past few months—a "nice young man," she called him. But I wanted her to validate my anger. "Even though I could have died?"

"I'll admit—I don't love the fact that there wasn't a lifeguard there, but I do think it's an important step. I don't want you to be held back by fear."

"It's not holding me back," I grumbled, staring down at the red-and-white checked tablecloth.

"Grief is slow," my mother said, ducking her head to get a better view of my face. "It's like wringing out a washcloth. Even after you think it's dry, a few more drops will form."

I wondered if she was thinking about her dad or about the divorce, if she had grieved that.

"It's okay to still be upset sometimes, but I'd like to see you move forward." She paused for a moment as the waitress returned the bill with her receipt and credit card. "Even if that means I have to loosen up a bit about where you go and when."

"Seriously?" The last thing I expected out of this dinner was for my mom to admit that she'd been too strict with me.

"I don't want you to be scared anymore." She signed the receipt with a flourish of cursive letters and looked back up at me. "So I guess that means giving up a few of my fears, too."

Before I could even smile, she cleared her throat. "Your grandmother told me you applied to a TV screen-writing program."

My eyes widened, guilty. "I, uh. What?"

"Don't be upset with her. She put the printouts from the website in her notebook and didn't remember it was a secret." My mom looked right into my eyes. "What I can't figure out is why you wouldn't tell me."

"I won't get in," I said. "It just seemed . . . I don't know. Silly to mention."

I waited for her to reprimand me, but she studied me with interest, not frustration. "I know you've always watched a wide variety of TV shows, but I had no idea you'd want to try your hand at writing. Your dad was thrilled. He's always hoped you'd be interested in 'the family business' someday, although journalism is much different, of course."

"You told Dad?"

"Yes, I talked to him about it. We both think that exploring an interest before you have to make college decisions is a wise choice. So, if you're accepted, we want you to go."

So apparently her "loosen up" philosophy was effective immediately. "Are you . . . are you serious?"

"Yes. We think it's a positive step for you."

"It's really expensive, Mom."

"I'm aware of the cost. You'll get a job to pay us back for part of it."

"It's in Manhattan, though."

"I know. That's my least favorite part, but your dad talked me into it. You'll be in dorms, and we'll help you move in and get settled. Good practice for college, he says."

I sat openmouthed for what felt like a full minute. "I . . . can't believe it. Thank you. I don't even know what to say."

"You're welcome," she said simply. "I hope you'll feel that you can trust me with things like this in the future."

On the way home, I felt grateful for my mom in a way that I never had before. She made an honest effort to hear me and to understand where I was coming from. There was something else I needed to tell her, something I'd been carrying around since the night of Max's birthday. Before then, I didn't know how it felt, the thrill of clicking into place with someone. My mom must have felt that way with my dad all those months ago, and I had no idea how truly involuntary it was—exactly as my dad had said.

"Mom?" I said, glancing over at her.

"Eyes on the road," she snapped. There was the mom I knew.

"Look." I sighed loudly, without meaning to. "I'm sorry about, you know, getting upset about you and dad and everything."

"Oh," she said, looking over at me. "You don't need to apologize for that."

"I know." I clasped the steering wheel. "But I still feel bad. You and Dad were the last thing that I expected, and I didn't handle it very well."

She kept quiet, allowing me my confession.

"That doesn't mean I'm totally comfortable with it," I said, eyeing her for a reaction. "It just means that I'm sorry if I made you feel bad."

She nodded, solemn. "Apology accepted."

I nodded back as I braked at a stoplight.

"I do understand why you feel the way you do." She pushed a mass of curls behind her ear. "Of course I do."

She closed her eyes for a moment, thinking, I was sure, of the past she shared with my father. The past that they shared with Cameron and me. "I know it's complicated, but your dad makes me happy."

"Yeah." I smiled. "I know."

Once home, I turned my phone back on, hands trembling. Not a single message from Max. I clicked my pictures, expecting to feel angrier at the sight of him. Instead, I found a photo I'd taken at Alcott's—Max laughing across the table from me after coffee mug steam had clouded his glasses. The memory of the total happiness I'd felt with him splintered and broke inside of me. And it didn't feel a thing like anger. It felt like heartache.

And why would I expect him to apologize? I'd hurled his nonrelationship with his dad—a secret he'd trusted me with—in his face the first chance I got. He'd thrown my pain right back at me.

I opened my planner to the list. It had become humiliatingly clear that "5. Swim" was an unrealistic goal. And how foolish, to think that going out with someone would ever help. I couldn't survive losing someone again—not to death, not to awkwardness or rejection or cruelty exchanged in a moment of weakness. Not to anything.

A tear plopped onto the page as I stared down at it, giving up.

It had taken so long to glue the shards of my heart back together, and I just couldn't afford to give any pieces away.

Chapter Twenty-One

The next night, Tessa was the last one to arrive at Alcott's. We were cramming in one last hangout before her morning flight and Morgan's family road trip to see cousins in Virginia. Kayleigh and I would both be spending spring break in scenic Oakhurst, where my only plan was to marathon *Gilmore Girls* in my bed. Yesterday's fight with Max consumed my mind, burning the edges of rational thought. I'd spent half my day bitterly waiting for him to call or show up, full of apologies, and the other half working up the nerve to apologize first.

"Sorry," Tessa said, sliding into the booth. The sloppy bun on top of her head meant she'd been at yoga earlier. "I had to at least *start* packing before my mom would let me leave."

"Where are you going again? St. Barts?" Kayleigh asked.

"Saint-Tropez."

"What's the difference?"

"One is in the South of France, and one of them is South of the Dominican Republic."

"Potato, poh-TAH-toe," Kayleigh said. "You'll come back tan, and we'll hate you."

"How was yesterday?" I cut in, my voice strained.

None of them had called or texted about how things went at Whitewater Lodge. They mumbled over each other— "Fine" and "Oh, okay" and "Pretty good."

"We couldn't help but notice," Morgan said slyly, "that Max was also absent. Would you happen to know anything about that?"

The tears sprang forward in an instant, like they'd just been waiting for the magic words. I covered my face with my hands, though it didn't matter. I couldn't hide this from them anymore.

"Oh my gosh," Morgan said. "I'm sorry! I didn't . . . I mean . . ."

"Paige, what is it?" Kayleigh asked, and I felt Tessa's arm around my shoulder. When I just shook my head from behind my hands, Tessa said, "See, Morgan? *This* is why I told you guys not to bring it up."

At this, I uncovered my eyes. "You told them *what*?"

Morgan bit her lip. "Tessa put a Max gag order on us."

"Meaning . . . ?" I looked at Tessa, but it was Kayleigh who answered.

"We're not supposed to mention Max in any way that suggests the two of you are obsessed with each other."

Of course they knew. They probably knew before *I* knew, and I felt like a complete jackass. Tessa looked right back at me—unrepentant. "I wanted you to be able to tell us when you were ready."

"So you all know?" I glanced around at each of them.

"That you're in love with him?" Morgan asked. "Yes."

"I'm not in *love* with him," I said. "God."

"Of course we know." Kayleigh snorted.

Morgan smiled. "And, duh, he likes you back."

"He didn't . . . ," I stammered, directing the question at Tessa. "He hasn't said—"

"Anything about it?" she asked. "No."

"But, to quote Morgan," Kayleigh said, "Duh."

"I'm really not so sure." My voice cracked, and the words poured out like a burst-open dam. I told them all about the plan I made at the beginning of the year, which I'd never even fully told Tessa, and the drowning nightmare.

"I kind of figured," Morgan admitted gently. "You didn't get in the pool once last summer."

I almost smiled. "You mean you didn't believe me that I was working on my tan?"

Kayleigh laughed. "You wear SPF 100 even in the winter."

I glanced over at Tessa, who was notably quiet. Several times, I'd woken up at her house in the middle of the night, tears on my face and gasping. "You probably knew, huh?"

One of her shoulders lifted. "I didn't know your nightmares were *always* about drowning. But I figured they had something to do with Aaron, yeah."

They were equally unsurprised when I told them about screen writing and my application to NYU.

"Girl, you're weirdly into TV," Kayleigh said. "But it's like you're not just watching it—you're dissecting it. And that's coming from me: obsessive, number-one fan of *Toil and Trouble*."

Tessa turned to her. "Is that your witches-at-boarding-school show?"

"With the hot warlock boys' school across the pond? Yes."

"Anyway," Morgan said, settling her eyes back on me.

They cringed as I told them about the pool—about how I'd fallen in, terrified. How Max and I had fought. I covered my eyes with one hand again. "I said something awful to him, you guys. And he said something really mean back."

The three of them exchanged looks, silently deciding that Tessa would be the spokesperson. "What could you have said that was so bad? You were *traumatized*. He had to understand that."

"I can't . . . ," I said. "I can't repeat what I said. It's personal stuff. But it was bad."

"I'm sure you guys will sort it out," Tessa said. "Even if you don't wind up together—"

"Tessa!" Morgan gasped, as if that was a sacrilege.

"No, listen. Even if you don't wind up together, neither of you are the kind of people who would let this ruin a friendship."

"I guess that's true," I said meekly. I repeated Max's words in my head, wondering if I could ever forget them. "But he said, basically, that I act like I'm the only one with problems. And . . . I think he might be right."

"He did *not* mean that," Tessa said firmly. "He knows exactly how often you deal with my problems because I talk to him about it."

"I mean, hello," Kayleigh said. "You snuck out of your house and stole a car for me!"

"Excuse me, *what?*" Morgan cried.

"I'll tell you later," Kayleigh said.

"But, I mean, look at me now," I said. "Blubbering all my problems to you *again*."

Tessa jabbed my leg with her finger, prodding me to look over at her. "Your problems are our problems."

"They better be," Kayleigh said. "Because *my* problems are sure as heck *your* problems. You all are going to hear me whine about Eric for at *least* a few more weeks. I'm going to max out the friendship punch card!"

"No such thing," Morgan said.

Max out. I almost laughed. It felt like I'd Max'd out my feelings punch card. But Morgan was right. If you're lucky, relationships—with family or friends or boyfriends—are limitless. There's no maximum on how much you can love each other. The problem is, there's also no limit to how much you can hurt each other.

I glanced at my phone for any word from Max, but still I came up empty.

~

Kayleigh and I spent the week together, indulging in manicures and the TV marathon I'd been hoping for. She confiscated my phone on two different occasions, claiming I was "compulsively" checking for any word from Max.

But the phone was back in my possession on Saturday morning, with only two days left of break. I was picking up my room, blaring *M*A*S*H* on DVD to keep my mind quiet. Still keeping a hawk's eye on my phone, I noticed right away when it lit up with a local number.

I pitched a sweater into my hamper and muted the TV. "Hello?"

"Hi, is this Paige?" a guy's voice asked.

"Yeah?"

"It's Clark. Driscoll." He hesitated. "You . . . gave me your number, after the funeral. I wasn't sure if—"

"Yeah, I remember." I sat down on my bed and tried to

sound as if this call wasn't bafflingly unexpected. What if he needed to *talk* talk? Like, about feelings? "Hey, Clark."

"I know this is out of the blue, but . . . some of the guys and me . . . ," he paused, and I locked my mouth closed so I wouldn't say: Some of the guys and *I*. "We're, uh . . . going to play trampoline dodgeball this afternoon. In honor of—"

"His birthday," I finished, remembering in an instant. Aaron would have been seventeen. I cohosted a party for Max's seventeenth birthday, and yet I *forgot* Aaron's? It's not like we'd ever celebrated it together, but I pressed my face into my hand all the same.

"Yeah," Clark said. "Anyway, that probably sounds dumb to you . . . it's just that, you know, Aaron went there every birthday. We, uh . . . wanted to invite you."

"Really?" I'd figured Aaron's longtime friends thought of me as an outsider—someone who didn't have any right to be devastated.

"No pressure," he said quickly. "I just tried to think about what Aaron would want, and I know he would have wanted me to call you."

It wasn't quite the same as *I'd like for you to come*, but it was close enough. "I'd love to."

He told me the details, offered to pick me up, and after the conversation was over, I stared at my phone. Clark Driscoll reaching out to me—including me in a group of people who cared about Aaron so much—became just another thing I never would have guessed at the start of the year.

~

Clark and I were quiet until we hit the first stoplight. The lack of both sound and movement was too grating, and I had to speak. "So, um, did you do this last year?"

He shook his head, not meeting my eyes. "I couldn't. You know how it is."

"Yeah. I guess I do," I said. I'd experienced only a fraction of his loss, but I *did* know that feeling. Our strange camaraderie made me bolder. "Man, the first time I went back to Snyder's Diner, I kept expecting him to walk in. But being there, I remembered details that I couldn't before. I remembered exactly what we both ordered on that first date. I know it's weird, but the taste of the French fries . . . it's like I could close my eyes and see him so clearly in my mind."

He nodded, jaw stiff, as he steered us onto the highway. "Thanks."

I brushed my bangs to the side. "For what?"

"For telling me that. Hearing people talk about him makes me feel like . . . like I'm not the only one who remembers, or something."

I wanted to reach over to him, to put my hand on his arm. But we barely knew each other, so I took a different angle. "Well, then, you *have* to hear this one . . ."

I told him, with as much animation as I could, about Aaron's epic showdown with the claw machine cat. Clark laughed along, especially at the part where Aaron announced to everyone that he'd gotten it on his first try.

He ran his hands over the steering wheel. "That sounds just like him."

At the trampoline center, called FlyHigh, I met—or re-met—a few of Aaron's other friends. There were a couple guys from school and a few from his Boy Scout troop, whom I could barely look in the eyes—afraid they'd sense all the questions I'd never be cruel enough to ask.

"Everyone, this is Paige," Clark said. "Paige, everyone."

This wasn't the beginning of a new friend-group, and we all knew it. But I was grateful to be allowed in the treehouse, even if our togetherness came only from a shared absence.

We stashed our shoes and cell phones in lockers and listened as a FlyHigh employee explained the many rules. I stared into the arena, which had dozens of black trampolines built into the floor, complete with side trampolines built to lean against the walls.

On my little rectangle of trampoline, I pressed down, barely bending my knees—a hesitant bounce to feel it out. The trampoline gave way and pushed back up under my feet. I steadied myself, arms out. I jumped down this time, and I sprang right back up. As my hair lifted from my shoulders, I grinned like an idiot, already eager to be weightless again.

I leaped from one launchpad to another, hardly noticing how out of breath I was.

The guys bounced all around me, whipping dodgeballs at each other—without a single one sent in my direction. I wondered if Morgan would call it sexism or chivalry. But I wanted to participate fully, the way I would have if Aaron were here.

I scooped up a nearby ball and, focusing all my meager hand-eye coordination, I sprang down on the trampoline. Midair, I launched the ball, pegging Clark right in the stomach.

He made an *oof* sound, looking to see where the hit had come from. I waved to him, still grinning. This made me fair play, even if the throws seemed to be gentler in my direction.

We bounced until my forehead sweated beneath my bangs, but I still didn't want to stop. I took a running start toward Clark, who leaped away from me as I retracted my arm. My ball missed him, but his swerve cost him his balance.

"Oh, shit," he said as he stumbled, but an angled wall trampoline caught his fall. He bounced off it, on his side, and landed on another trampoline, shaking with laughter.

I bounded toward him, dropping down.

"Are you," I said through gasps of laughter, "okay?"

He was laughing so hard that there were tears in his eyes. He bonked me lightly on the head with the ball in his hand. "Yeah. Totally."

I sat there, legs folded beneath me, as Clark's shoulders slowed from the laughter. Rosiness pooled in his cheeks— the way it used to before he thinned out.

"He'd be happy," I said. "Knowing we were doing this."

"Yeah. He would be."

"Hey!" an authoritative voice yelled from the platform, "You two! No sitting!"

Clark scrambled up and offered me his hand. "I think we have to keep jumping."

"Yeah," I said, letting him pull me up. "I think we do."

Later that night, I reexamined my plan, now tearstained in two different places. My progress was no different than it had been at the beginning of the year.

1. ~~Parties/social events~~
2. ~~New group~~
3. Date (RE)
4. Travel
5. Swim

But so much more had happened—things that didn't exactly fit on the list. So I wrote everything out, just to see it all together. *Kissed Ryan Chase (kind of), came to terms with my parents dating (kind of), applied for screen-writing program, sneaked out of my house for Kayleigh, planned a party, tried new ice creams and TV shows and movies, made new friends, played trampoline dodgeball.*

The smaller steps mattered, and I could finally feel the distance they'd put between me and the past. I never could have had a day like this last year. I never could have let my heart feel as buoyant as my body, midair. Sadness still fell—the soft pitter-patter of spring rain—but each small joy opened like an umbrella right above me.

And so as I closed my planner, I opened my heart another inch.

Chapter Twenty-Two

Sunday night, I barely slept, knowing I'd see Max at school. I clicked his name on my phone—the only light in my dark room—at midnight, at 1:00 a.m. What would I even say? Since that first day at his house in the fall, Max and I had never gone this long without talking.

I awoke with shadows beneath my eyes, and my first three classes couldn't hold my attention at all. As I took my seat in Honors English, my palms went clammy, and I told myself it would be fine. I heard him sit down as the bell rang, and I glanced over my shoulder. He was staring down at his desk.

"Hey," I said.

"Hey." His eyes didn't move.

That was it. I couldn't process a word Ms. Pepper said throughout class. When the dismissal bell rang, I turned around again. Max was already ducking out the door. My mouth opened to call out his name, but for what? To talk it out in front of everybody?

"Do you want me to talk to him?" Morgan asked as we walked out together. "I will."

"No," I said. "I need to do it. I just . . . need to figure out what I want to say."

On Tuesday, I caught Max at his locker before school started. I strode over confidently, even though my lower lip quivered, giving me away.

"Hey," I said.

His eyes flicked to me. "Hey."

"Listen. Are you . . . are we okay? It was so messed up, what happened, but—"

"I'm fine," he said. "I'm just really busy. I have robotics stuff and everything. Sorry."

"Oh. Okay."

The locker door shut with a clang, and he said, "See ya."

I was left standing there, gaping. Morgan appeared at my side within seconds, her gossip radar flashing red.

"Hey," she said. "What was *that*?"

"That," I said, "was Max blowing me off."

"The pool thing still?"

"Yeah." Heat pushed at my eyes, but I blinked it away.

"He has no business being mad at you!" Morgan said.

"He does, though, Morgan. We both screwed up."

"Will you see him any other time, outside of school? Where it might be easier to talk? QuizBowl maybe?"

I shook my head. "Not until the QuizBowl semifinals. And that's two weeks away."

"It'll be fine," Morgan said. "He just needs to cool off. I'm sure you guys will make up by then."

~

We didn't. In the eight school days that followed, Max disappeared with the finesse of an actual ghost. He sneaked in as class started, bailed out right as it ended. His avoidance confused me the first week but pissed me off the second. I had a right to be mad, too, but I wasn't dodging *him*. Still, I couldn't work up the nerve to corner him again or stop by his house. I replayed the situation over and over in my mind, trying to figure out how I'd hurt him more than he hurt me. I told myself I was giving him some space to collect himself, but really, I was just terrified that I'd get weepy and confess my real feelings at the exact wrong moment.

In the evenings, I started a new spec script on my laptop. I wrote mainly fight scenes, characters passionately yelling about how they really felt. At least Max's freezeout was good for my dialogue. I refreshed my inbox, hoping to see NYU pop up. Radio silence from them, too.

As I got ready for the QuizBowl semifinals, I felt sweaty just thinking about sitting next to Max, facing an audience of parents and other teams. The tension between us shrilled like a dog whistle—not everyone could hear it, but, for those of us who could, it was grating and impossible to ignore. I feared, once we sat down, the auditorium windows would crack from our awkwardness.

"Can you put the flash cards down, please?" Kayleigh asked, wrapping the curling iron around a lock of my hair. "You keep moving your head, and I'm almost done. You already look much cuter than Lindsay Lohan when she went to the Mathlete finals in *Mean Girls*."

"Ha-ha," I said, but I set the flash cards down.

Kayleigh's dark eyes examined the newest curl, giving it the lightest mist of hairspray.

"So, what are you guys doing tonight?"

"I thought we told you," Kayleigh said. "Tessa's parents got us tickets for some art gallery thing. I dunno. Sounds kind of boring, but Morgan's excited."

"Cool," I said. I knew that already, and I also knew how bored they'd be at the semifinals—it was a bit of a drive to Anderson, Indiana, and they'd have to sit through two other matches before our team went onstage. But I wished they were coming anyway.

"There! Cutest nerd I ever saw," Kayleigh proclaimed, and I had to smile. I'd borrowed lilac nail polish from Morgan and a blazer from Tessa, which I wore over a cute dress. All in all, I hoped I looked put together and academic, but not too serious. Only my dress and flats were my own, but I felt like myself. And I felt like I was taking all three of my best friends with me.

Kayleigh wished me luck and called good-bye to my parents as she left.

"You look nice, honey. You ready to go?" my mom asked, reaching for her purse. I nodded, holding my flash cards so tightly that the paper edges pressed lines into my hands.

My dad practically danced his way to the driver's seat. "This is so cool! Can't wait to see you up there, kiddo."

My nerves quivered like tiny live wires right below my skin. The semifinals were different from regular matches in a few ways: parents attended, the location was at a neutral away school with a neutral moderator, and we would actually be seated at a table on the stage. With lights beating down on us. Also, there were two other matches tonight between different schools. We were third, so I'd have to sit through other wins and defeats, imagining which ours would work out to be. I chugged my entire bottle of water and asked my dad to blast the air-conditioning. Neither helped.

Normally, knowing I'd see Max there would have calmed me a little. But it only made me more nervous.

When I'd texted him to say I wouldn't need a ride, he'd replied with an empty "OK." I didn't know what I'd expected him to say, but tears itched at my eyes. *I'm a basket case*, I thought. *Who gets emotional over two letters?*

But then I remembered that "no" also has only two letters. Almost everyone in the world has cried over those.

~

It was clear from the first five minutes onstage: we were going to lose. My brain couldn't even fully process the questions before Noblesville answered them correctly.

"Instituted by the Clinton administration in 1994, this policy—"

Noblesville buzzed. "Don't ask, don't tell!"

Correct.

Their speed, compared to our openmouthed lagging, was absurd. At one point, Malcolm actually started laughing to himself, taking Max and me right with him. Lauren's cheeks flushed pink with frustration. My parents were in the audience, so I should have been mortified, but there was nothing to do but laugh.

The inevitability of defeat was oddly freeing. There was nothing to lose, only to gain, and each question we answered became cause for celebration. Everyone else got a few in, including me. I was shell-shocked during the first round, but I recovered in the second. I buzzed before the moderator had finished his sentence: "A onetime employee of Thomas Edison—"

"Paige, for Oakhurst," the moderator said, acknowledging me by my name card. I knew in my gut that I was right. I'd once read a book that fictionalized a friendship between a young maid and . . . "Nikola Tesla!"

"Correct," the moderator said.

"Yeah!" my dad called from the audience, leaping to his feet. "That's my girl!"

My mom tugged him down, and the other parents laughed. I wasn't even embarrassed.

A few minutes into our cataclysmic loss, a small crowd filed into the back of the auditorium. They were trying to be quiet, but the chairs squeaked as they sat down—maybe four or five people.

My people. Tessa, Morgan, Kayleigh, and Ryan. I was sure of it by their heights and the silhouettes of their hair.

If I'd had any doubt, it would have been alleviated when Noblesville flubbed with Krakatoa, and Max responded correctly with Mount Tambora. There was a chorus of girlish whoops from the last row of the auditorium, and Ryan Chase's bro-iest voice calling: "YEAH, SON!"

I dared a look at Max. He shook his head, smiling. The Noblesville captain scowled at us. They were winning, but we were having more fun.

And when Noblesville was announced the winner, I had a feeling that most of the cheers were from the losing side supporters.

Malcolm offered me his hand as I stepped down from the stage. Max trotted down to talk to his mom, who waved to me. I waved back, cringing against the ache in my sternum. I pushed away thoughts of her watching the end of *Indiana Jones* with us, of her making snacks for me and Morgan as we studied for an English test with Max. Of her always, always hugging me when I left. I looked away. Max had been sitting right next to me for the past hour, but he'd never been so distant.

"Well, we may have lost tonight, but, overall, this is farther than we got last year," Lauren announced. "I'm pleased."

"We're going to miss you next year," I said. She was off to Johns Hopkins, where she'd be splitting her time between the conservatory and an applied mathematics major.

She blinked at me. "I'm very much looking forward to an academically rigorous college curriculum. So. I probably won't miss this."

"Yeah," I said, laughing. "I know. But I had fun this year."

I leaned forward to give her a quick hug. To my surprise, she squeezed me back. "Me, too."

The moment Lauren walked away, hands wrapped around me from behind, my dad nearly lifting me off the ground. "I'm so proud of you, kid."

I grinned. "I wish you could have seen us win."

"It was fun to see you up there," my mom said, squeezing my hand.

I didn't have a chance to respond before Tessa, Morgan, and Kayleigh surrounded me, all talking at once. They smelled like hairspray and perfume, and I could have burst from love for them. "What happened to the art gallery thing?"

"We made that up!" Morgan said. "Duh."

"You lied?"

"Not exactly," Kayleigh said. "It was just a secret."

"Sorry we were a little late. We got lost," Tessa added.

"Because *somebody* had to make an 'emergency pit stop,'" Kayleigh said.

"Hey, I *needed* that milkshake," Tessa said. She turned to my mom. "Can Paige spend the night?"

My mom smiled at this age-old question. "Sure."

"I can still drive home with you guys," I said.

"Nah," my dad said, winking. "Go with your friends."

I did. As we left the auditorium, Max looked up from a conversation with his mom, Ryan, and Ms. Pepper. He put his hand up in a wave, eyes trained away from me. Tessa waved back, and so did Kayleigh, but Morgan just looped her arm through mine.

Ryan held up one finger, then pointed toward the exit.

"He drove," Tessa said. "I guess he'll meet us out there in a few."

"Is Max freaking kidding me with the moping?" Morgan demanded as we bustled out into the spring air. "He is being such a baby. So you guys had a fight. Big deal."

"Seriously," Kayleigh said. "Morgan and I fight all the time. You get over it."

Tessa gnawed at her lip, gazed fixed on the asphalt in front of us.

"I know," I said quietly. "I don't get it either."

"Has he said anything to you?" Morgan asked, looking at Tessa.

She shook her head. "No. He's just been kind of quiet, I guess. I asked him if he was okay at lunch, and he just said he was 'in a funk.' But I could talk to him if—"

"No," I said. "I don't want to put you in the middle. He's your friend, too."

"Funk *that*," Kayleigh said. We'd reached Ryan's Jeep, and we leaned against the bumper. "We need more information. Has he said *anything* to you, Paige?"

"Not really. I get zero eye contact and one-word text messages. It's brutal."

Morgan held out her hand, palm up. "Give me your phone. We need to do text analysis."

"Definitely," Kayleigh added. "Dig for textual innuendo."

"Be my guest," I said, pulling my phone out of my bag. "You'll see for yourselves that he's giving me *nothin'*."

I punched in my phone's password, but as I went to click into messages, I saw that my e-mail icon had changed since I'd last checked.

"Hold on," I said.

From NYU. Subject line: *Congratulations!* My heart's rhythm became less of a beat and more a repeated collision with my rib cage. I opened the e-mail.

"Oh my God," I whispered.

"What?" Tessa stepped closer.

"The screen-writing program. I'm in."

"Oh my God," Tessa said, echoing me.

"That is the best news!" Morgan said, and Kayleigh woo-hooed into the quiet parking lot.

I kept staring at the e-mail. It was real. They'd read my *Mission District* spec script. I'd move to Manhattan for an entire month. Assuming my parents really would let me go.

"I mean, it's still not for sure," I said. "My parents said they'd pay for it, but who knows if—"

"Hey," Tessa said. "Cease and desist order on the negativity."

"It's not negativity! I'm being realistic."

"And realistically," Kayleigh said, "we are super excited for you."

I smiled tentatively. "Thanks."

"Are *you* excited for you?" Kayleigh prodded.

"Well, obviously, I'm excited."

"I think she's in shock," Morgan said, tilting her head to study me.

Kayleigh got to her feet, standing in front of me. "C'mon. Get up. We gotta dance it out."

She pumped her arms, rocking back and forth. "Victory dance. Do it."

Morgan joined in with the same goofy dance. "Yep. C'mon."

I shook my head, laughing, as a voice called out near us.

"What did I miss?" Ryan jogged toward us.

"Paige got into a summer writing program!" Morgan said.

"Nice!" he said, holding up his hand. I high-fived him, grinning. "But it seems you're missing something. Be right back."

He ducked into the Jeep, and music blasted out of the now-open windows.

"There we go!" Kayleigh said, right back to dancing. Morgan bumped me with her hip, and I laughed as even Tessa raised her hands up, totally into it.

The beat of the song pulsed through the evening air, and Ryan Chase stood before me. I could hardly believe I'd been so overcome by a crush on him. I actually knew him now, and he was just as great as I'd always thought. But his traits were academic facts to me now: Ryan Chase was handsome, charming, and kind. I didn't feel those things in my chest, sizzling like neon light. He cocked his chin. "Aren't you gonna dance?"

"Yeah." I stood a little taller, feeling the swell of happiness through me. "I am."

"Yeah, you are." Without warning, Ryan scooped me up, my feet leaving the ground. I gasped, hands clutching for something—anything—until I regained equilibrium from higher up. Once I realized I was secure, I laughed, and he spun around. I didn't even have time to be self-conscious that he was holding me by my bare legs, his arms wrapped around my thighs.

I held my arms out wide and tilted my head up to the night sky. I felt like I could lift right out of his arms, spinning to the ground like a maple seed.

Ryan slid me down, and we pulled apart as the song hit the fast-paced chorus, and there was really nothing to lose. So I put my hands up, I swayed my hips, I shook my shoulders. I was dancing—really dancing—for the first time in almost two years.

Morgan's laughter pealed through the air as the three of them performed some kind of do-si-do, Tessa's blond waves shimmying with every swing. I could make out their grins in the yellow streetlights. My crazy, dancing friends. Mine.

And I didn't feel like I'd lost a thing that night. Not a single thing.

Chapter Twenty-Three

I knew Max would dart out of English the second the bell rang on Monday. But the reality that I'd be gone for almost half the summer gave me courage: I had to fix this soon. I psyched myself up all morning, mentally scripting a conversation. *Nothing could be worse than the tense silence*, I told myself. Even talking it out had to be easier. So when the first tone of the bell sounded, I swiveled around to take my chance. I gripped Max's arm even though he was already sliding out of his seat.

"Will you stay for a minute? Please?" Everyone was filing out of the classroom. Morgan shot me a wide-eyed look as she passed through the door.

"I have class," Max said, not meeting my eyes.

"I know that," I said. "Please?"

He didn't respond, but he didn't leave either. We stayed this way, in silence, and I fought the desire to cringe.

"I have to go make some copies. See you two tomorrow," Ms. Pepper said, heading out the door. She wasn't carrying any papers to copy.

"So," I said. I moved my hand from Max's arm. The room was too quiet, the faint hum of air-conditioning and the wall-mounted clock. "I'm truly sorry for what I said at the pool. I shouldn't have brought those things up no matter how—"

"—traumatized you were?" He rubbed at his forehead with both hands. "Paige, I triggered some kind of PTSD for you, then acted like an asshole, after everything you've been through. You can be mad at me. *I'm* mad at me."

"Well, you sort of had a point," I said. "And I did, too. So, can we just . . . not be mad at each other anymore?"

"I'm not *mad* at you, Paige. I'm just—"

"Hurt?" I guessed, and the next words came out in a frustrated jumble. "Me, too, Max. But you're not the only nonconfrontational introvert here, and I'm *trying*, so can you just look at me?"

Finally, his eyes pulled up to mine. "I'm sorry about what I said."

"I know." I balled my hands into fists, pressing my fingers into swampy hands. The worst was over—it had to be—and my next question would be the turning point. "So, can we just be okay now?"

He chewed at his thumbnail, and I wondered what,

exactly, he needed to consider so torturously. I was giving him a clean slate, and all I wanted was the same in return. "I think I just need . . . some time. And space."

I collapsed inside myself, smaller and smaller until I wished I could disappear from my seat. What did that even *mean*? We were equal offenders in that ridiculous, poolside fight, and if anything, *I* had more cause to push him away. Now I come to him, palms up in surrender, and he backs away farther?

"Fine," I said, picking up my things. "Well, just so you know, I got into my screen-writing program."

"That's great," he said. "I got into my Italy program, too."

The whole summer whooshed away, right there. First I'd be gone, then him.

"Well," I managed, even though my lungs shrank inside my chest. "There's your time and space. Maybe you should transfer back to Coventry while you're at it."

"I've thought about it," he said quietly.

I recoiled, jaw dropping. My pulse quickened, pushing the mortification and confusion and anger through my veins.

"Great," I said, standing in a huff. "Just great. See you around."

"Wait," he said.

My hair flew around me as I spun back—still pathetically hopeful.

"At the beginning of the year, why did you even become friends with me?"

My eyes went squinty with confusion. "I . . . I mean, we had QuizBowl together, we sat next to each other in this class . . . I don't know."

"That's the reason, then? Circumstance?"

"Yeah. Why?" Okay, technically, I'd thought that being friends with Max would be my ticket to Ryan Chase. But that was before I knew Max. It stopped being about that a long time ago. And it's not like he could have known that.

"No reason." His head still sagged, defeated in a way I couldn't understand. "I really am sorry."

"Yeah," I said. "Me, too."

And I was. Sorry that we burned each other, sorry that he'd pulled up a drawbridge—shutting me out so completely. But not sorry that I'd tried to talk it out. Not sorry that I'd tried to fight for our friendship even when I felt awkward and confused.

I darted down the hallway in the opposite direction of our usual path, just to spite him. Still, I waited to hear my name called out over the hallway bustle. It never came.

~

I went over to my grandmother's after school, even though I'd seen her on Sunday to tell her about my New York news. Of course, she'd forgotten that I applied in the first place, so it was a huge surprise. She cried happy tears, kissed the top of my head and kept saying, "my little Madelyn Pugh." If there ever came a day that she couldn't remember that part of our history, I'd remember it for her. I'd remember it all for us both.

After such a good day Sunday, I felt terrible dragging my misery to her on Monday. But I didn't know what else to do. I sat down in the chair next to her bed—my new usual spot.

"What's on your mind, sweet girl?" she asked. Her voice had become quiet in recent weeks, with a soft rasp to it.

I leaned over so that my head was on the bed. I felt my shoulders twitch, trying to absorb the restrained sobs from my stomach. I didn't want to cry, but my body insisted.

"Honey," she said, running her hand over my hair. "Oh, honey."

My tears slipped onto the quilt, and I let them. I didn't wipe my eyes or cover my face. After a few minutes, the tears made space for words to fill. I explained as best I could without confusing her, but it came out in rambles and sniffs.

"Everything is so messed up," I choked out. "I was doing so much better about Aaron. But then I met Max. And it just got so real, so fast. I lost someone again, in a completely different way, but it still hurts, and I just feel so stupid."

She brushed my bangs out of my eyes. "I know it's difficult to bare your heart, sweet girl, but it's the least stupid thing in the world."

I sighed, wiping my face. "I really was trying to move on. But I don't know why I bothered."

When she was quiet for a moment, I looked up. Her bleary eyes became fierce. "Paige Elizabeth, you are allowed to be sad, but you are not allowed to be a defeatist. The fact that you are hurting means that you let someone truly matter to you, and that is exactly—exactly—what your friend Aaron would have wanted for you."

I paused, blinking, and more tears leaked out. "Yeah?"

"Of course. You've had your cry, but now you'll pick yourself up and keep living your life. Doubly, for that sweet boy. Love extra, even if it means you hurt extra, too. That's how we honor them."

"But everything else with . . . ," I began, but she raised her hand to stop me.

"Everything else will fall into place," she said. "Just live your life."

"But . . . ," I tried again.

"No buts." It was there, in her insistence, that she reminded me of my mom.

"Live my life," I repeated, and the mantra stuck in my mind even after I left my grandmother's bedside.

Chapter Twenty-Four

In other circumstances, I probably would have worked up the nerve to talk to Max again the next day. Instead, the words I might have said were gone, replaced by my grandmother's: *Everything else will fall into place. Just live your life.*

I'm not sure if those words would have mattered to me as much if they hadn't been some of the last words she ever said to me.

My grandmother died that night, after another stroke that came out of nowhere. I had been there just a few hours before.

After getting the call, we slid into that blur of sobbing and numbness. "Mom, no," I kept repeating as I cried. "I'm so sorry, baby," she said, and tears dripped off her chin. She held Cameron and me against her on the couch, and we sobbed in a little pile until my dad got there. Cameron climbed onto his lap like a little kid, and he clutched my mother's hand between us.

Eventually we broke it up to deal with the notifications. It took the last of my energy to call Tessa and tell her. She sniffled into her end of the phone line, one of the few times I'd ever known her to cry. When she asked if I wanted her to come over, I told her I was too tired, too sad, too much of everything.

When I slumped upstairs, I could hear, faintly, my mother's voice from her room, calling relatives and making arrangements. Her bedroom door was closed for the first time I could remember. The open door meant she was always available to us—if we got sick in the middle of the night or rushed in after a terrible dream. But no matter how much it felt like a nightmare, this night was not a bad dream. And even if it had been, the door was closed. I was used to her being a mother to her daughters. Now, she grieved in private, a daughter with no mother.

I begged my mind to turn off as I climbed into bed. At the beginning of the school year, I thought nothing could be worse than returning to That Look at school. But I would have given anything to go back there: when my grandmother was around, before I messed up everything with

Max. I cried all over again, muffling the sounds against the pillow until, at the edge of sleep, a creaking sound pierced into my consciousness. I sat up, blinking. There was a small figure in my doorway, its arms crossed in the darkness.

"Cam?" I mumbled. I blinked again. It was definitely my sister. "What are you doing?"

"Can I sleep in here?" she whispered.

"Yeah," I told her. "Sure."

I adjusted myself, leaving plenty of room on the side where Tessa slept when she stayed over. Cameron hurried toward my bed, as though she thought I might change my mind. Climbing under the covers, she clutched the stuffed rabbit she'd had since infancy.

"Are you okay?" I whispered.

"I don't know." Her voice cracked in the darkness.

I laid my head on my pillow, facing her.

"Me either." Maybe as the older sister, I should have lied and said something more comforting. But she deserved to hear the truth, to be commiserated with.

"I miss her so much already," Cameron said.

I bit my lower lip, fighting against the lump in my throat. "Me, too."

"Do you think Mom will be okay?"

"Yeah." I thought of the pain after Aaron died, blistering beneath my skin. *It will not always feel this way*, Tessa had insisted. "Just not right away."

Cameron was quiet for a moment. "I don't ever want anything to happen to Mom."

"It won't."

"It might," she said, calling my bluff.

"It won't." I needed to believe that, too. "Good night, Cam."

"Good night."

When I awoke the next morning, Cameron was already up. I wondered if I had dreamed the whole thing, but there was an indentation on the pillow next to mine where her head had been. The morning light felt harsh—too real. My grandmother was really gone, and even a night's sleep didn't dream it away. I curled myself into the fetal position for another little cry. When I eventually heard footsteps on the stairs, I expected my dad. But it was Tessa, holding two to-go cups from Alcott's.

My eyes felt swollen as I propped myself up to greet her. She sat down on my bed, where Cameron had been, and handed me a coffee.

"I am so sorry," she whispered, her voice breaking. From Tessa, it was never That Look, especially not now. She loved my grandmother, too, and her sadness was her own.

I bobbed my head and bit down on both of my lips. I had a feeling that I would be doing that move a lot for the next week. The coffee tasted hot but not too hot—bitter and comforting.

We sat here for a moment. I felt my forehead creasing, my body instinctively knowing that I was going to cry again. "I didn't get to say good-bye."

"She knew." Tessa turned to me. "She knew how much you loved her."

I nodded through my tears.

"It will get easier," Tessa promised all over again, linking her arm with mine and settling back against the headboard. I believed it this time, even as I stared down the long road ahead of me.

It certainly didn't get better as the days dragged on. The funeral service was solemn, with all the expected formalities. My dad handed my mom tissues, his hand never leaving hers. Tessa sat in the pew exactly behind me, with Kayleigh and Morgan on either side of her. When the pastor launched into a diatribe about the finality of death, I felt their hands on my shoulders, assuring me that they were behind me. That they were always behind me.

I hated everything about the service. I hated the depressing music, hated how much I missed my grandmother, and hated the heartache radiating from my mother. I hated how much it reminded me of losing Aaron. I hated the graveside service, and I knew I would hate the repast at our house. I had no interest in appetizers or the people milling around, giving us That Look.

Two hours into the repast, I was long past exhaustion,

emotional and physical. I was tired of saying "thank you" to all the "I'm so sorry" speeches, tired of wearing my brave face. So when there was a knock at our front door, I escaped to answer it. The police could have been on the other side for all I cared, as long as I could leave the groups of people pooling in the living room, the family room, and even into the edges of the kitchen.

"Hi," I breathed, pulling the door open. It was Ryan and Max standing side by side, each with an armful of various containers. I recovered from my stunned silence and opened the door wider.

"Come in, come in," I stammered.

They filed into the house and made their way to the kitchen. I watched them go, suddenly very aware of my appearance. I smoothed my hair down and wiped beneath my eyes for stray mascara.

Shallow, I accused myself, but I still straightened out my dress as I walked toward the kitchen.

They set everything down on the counter. I opened my mouth to say something, but what? I wasn't sure. Now that they weren't holding a mound of stuff, I noticed they both had ties on. Something about that made me want to cry again, but before I could, I was engulfed in Ryan's chest, his arms wrapped around me.

"I'm really, really sorry, Paige," he said quietly. His chin rested on the top of my head and held me there—a real hug. Max gave me an awkward side-hug and cleared his throat.

"These are from my mom." He nodded toward a small arrangement of calla lilies in a glass vase. "She's really sorry she couldn't be here."

I wouldn't have expected her to be, but I nodded all the same. "Thanks."

"This is from my mom." Ryan tapped the top of one of the containers. "It's lasagna, double cheese. Best comfort food, I promise."

"This is so . . ." I shook my head, bewildered. "Thank you."

I had seen them a few days ago, but it was still so comforting to have them in front of me now. They showed up in nice clothes with food and flowers like . . . well, like grown-ups.

"Everyone's downstairs in the basement," I told them. "If you wanted to avoid mingling with adults."

Ryan stepped toward the basement door.

"You coming?" he asked. I wasn't sure if he meant Max or me.

Max responded. "In a minute."

Ryan nodded before he turned away, and Max set an orange cookie box on the counter. Do-Si-Dos, from his personal stash. "All yours, if you want them."

My lower lip quivered. "I do. Thank you."

He smiled hesitantly. "You're welcome."

"I can't believe . . . ," I started. "I'm glad you came."

"Of course we came. We're your friends."

He slid onto a kitchen stool—relaxed, as though personal tragedy meant a reprieve from our problems. I missed this Max, the one who looked me in the eyes and *saw* me. I wanted to throw my arms around his neck and hang on until everyone else left.

"I know this is the tritest question," he said, "but how are you doing?"

To everyone else who'd asked that night, I'd said okay. I shrugged as tears tried to form again. "Not great. I mean . . . you know."

And he *did* know, having gone through it himself. "Yeah. Losing a grandparent is really hard on its own, but it's also miserable to see your mom upset."

"Yes!" I agreed, a little too loudly. These few normal minutes with Max felt like cozying up with a fleece blanket. Not enough to shield me—just enough to feel comforted.

As if on cue, Cameron meandered into the kitchen, interrupting us.

"Mom was looking for you," she said, her voice monotone.

"I've been right here."

She shot me a look of annoyance that I wasn't sure how I had earned.

"Hey, Cameron," Max said, smiling. It was more subdued than his usual grin, but it wasn't forced either. "Good to see you."

She stood up a little straighter. "Hey, Max."

"I'm really sorry about your grandmother."

Now Cameron smiled wanly and bobbed her head but said nothing.

"We should really have a Fact-O-Mazing rematch some time. Defend our title."

"Really?" Cameron smiled more genuinely. She glanced over at me, gauging my reaction to one of my friends being nice to her. I didn't know what she was expecting, but Max trying to communicate with her was the last thing on my mind. She grinned at Max, pointing at the Do-Si-Dos. "Are you just now giving her those cookies?"

"Uh, yeah," Max said, shifting his eyes downward.

Before I could ask, Cameron turned back to me. "You should go find Mom."

I opened my mouth to excuse myself, but Max beat me to it.

"I'm heading downstairs," he said.

In a flash of desperation, I caught him by the hand. Now was not the appropriate time to talk about this, but I had to say something. We were at my grandmother's repast, where my sister was still probably close enough to hear us, but I didn't care.

341

"Don't go back to Coventry," I whispered. "Please."

His gaze met mine and held for only a moment before he said, "Okay."

Simple as that. I dropped his hand, feeling at once ridiculous and relieved, and he disappeared downstairs.

The rest of the evening was a haze of people coming and going, alternately embracing me and apologizing for my loss. Their faces, their words—it all became hard to distinguish.

My friends lingered longer than most people, watching my face for the smallest breakdown indicator. Eventually, they filtered out, too. My mom went up to her room after the last person had gone, and even Tessa and my dad left to get changes of clothes.

I settled onto a kitchen stool, propped my elbows up against the island, and closed my eyes for a moment. Max's face was the first thing to come into my mind, and I admonished myself for the hundredth time that night, for thinking about Max immediately after Grammy's funeral. But the two were tied, in my mind. Before I met Max, I was only really honest with my grandmother. But Max? Max I could tell anything to. It made a difference, telling my secrets to someone who remembered every word.

He didn't hug me when he left. Instead, he reached out for my hand. Our eyes met. We said nothing at first. He squeezed my hand and stepped away before fully letting go. But then he turned back, facing me again. "Paige, I'm really sorry. About your grandmother . . . and about everything else."

"Me, too."

He was standing on the porch step, making us eye level. "I feel like I handled everything totally wrong. Can we just start over?"

"Yes," I said. "Please."

"Okay." He exhaled, eyes briefly closing, like he was relieved. "Good. Because, I mean, it doesn't even matter how we became friends, right? It just matters that we still are. So, friendship fresh start?"

What did this have to do with how we became friends? I wondered. But he stuck his hand out—a formal agreement—and I shook it.

"Deal," I said.

I told myself it was enough, at least for now. There was hardly any room left in my body to ache for anyone but my grandmother, but Max fit right into the little sliver I had left. I began to wonder, really, how much more my heart could take.

But I'd survived grief before, so I forced myself to reframe. My grandmother lived long enough to see the first bloom of a dream she planted in me. She lived long enough to see my mom and dad happy again. She had a beautiful marriage and a beautiful life after it, too. She had Paris.

There was so much to be grateful for. How much Grammy taught me in the time that I had her. My dad, caring so ably for my mom. My friends, sticking resolutely by my side. The vase of flowers from Max's mom—the one that was for me. And the container of lasagna, and a box of Girl Scout cookies all my own. I was supported, not pitied, and I wondered if maybe that had always been true.

This thought, even in the bleakness of an unmapped life without my grandmother, put another tiny light in my jar, another breadcrumb on my trail. Darkness might keep flooding in, but I finally had just enough light to find the way back to myself.

Chapter Twenty-Five

I laid low for the rest of the weekend. Tessa and Morgan and Kayleigh each stopped by once, bringing me magazines or coffee and trying to cheer me up. I figured they were each taking turns, rotating shifts. While I appreciated it, I was happiest to stay in my pajamas in front of the TV, lost in loving Lucy and her squawky antics. I used to think rewatching and rereading were embarrassingly boring pastimes. But there is something to be said for how comforting it is to already know what happens. There is no such luxury in real life.

Soon enough, Sunday evening rolled around, and the reality of the last two weeks of school sank in around me. May, so far, had been gray and dreary, which suited me fine. The idea of putting on something other than pajamas to go out in the drizzle was enough to make me shudder. I swore to myself that I would get out of bed in an hour. I was looking up information about the NYU campus, planning a packing list.

Beyond my laptop screen, I saw my bedroom door open just an inch or two. I looked up and saw my sister, peeking in. Her eyes were buggy, her mouth forming an expression of half surprise, half glee.

"I bet I can cheer you up," she said, her voice a near whisper, before I could ask her why she was being such a creep. She opened the door a bit more.

I furrowed my eyebrows. "How?"

She pursed her lips, wanting to savor every moment of what she was about to say. "Chrissie Cohen is failing out of college."

My jaw dropped. "No."

"Yes."

I placed my hand over my mouth, hiding a barely repressed smile. "Oh my God."

Cameron nodded and bit down on both of her lips, her eyes wide.

"It's not funny; it's not funny," I chanted.

"Yes it is!" she squealed, and we both burst into uninhibited laughter.

We both took a minute to recover before I asked her, "How do you know?"

"Zach Cohen and I are friends online," she said, then turned a bit. "Oh, hey Mom."

Behind Cameron, I could see that my mom wore her robe and no makeup, crossing her arms.

"What's going on with you two?" she asked. It was only the second time I'd seen her all weekend. We had each stayed in our own rooms as my dad shuttled between us, taking food requests. He must have made tea for my mom ten times in the past two days, and I could hear them talking quietly in her room as her favorite old movies played in the background.

"Well?" my mom asked. "What's so funny?"

Cameron cleared her throat. She knew very well that our mom would not appreciate us laughing at her friend's daughter failing out of school. So she ad-libbed. "Uh. Paige . . . told me a joke."

My mom glanced at me. "I could certainly use a laugh."

I shot Cameron a look, not wanting to be caught in a lie. Miraculously, a joke Max told me weeks before popped into my head.

"So, the past, present, and future walk into a bar," I said. "It was tense."

"Ha!" my mom said.

Cameron laughed, too, since it was the first time she'd heard the joke.

"That's a good one," my mom said, smiling as she pulled her robe tightly around her and headed down the stairs.

When she was gone, Cameron gave me a conspiratorial smile. "Nice going."

"Thanks."

"Where'd you even hear that joke?"

"Max," I said, and a thought occurred to me. "Oh, hey, I meant to ask you. At the repast, you said something to Max about those Girl Scout cookies. What was that about?"

She shrugged. "He came over here to drop them off one day."

Now she had my full attention. "He what? When? Where was I?"

"Over spring break. I think you were out to dinner with mom."

Right after our fight at the pool? Not possible. Right? I would have known that. "What? Why didn't you tell me?"

"Because he told me they were a surprise!" Cameron crossed her arms.

I closed my eyes, trying to breathe evenly. My pulse thumped in my neck. Getting my sister worked up was not the way to handle this. "Okay. Could you tell me exactly what happened? Please? It's important."

"I answered the door, and he had this box of Girl Scout cookies. He asked me if I could leave them in your room for you, but I told him I wasn't allowed in your room." She looked at me pointedly, making sure I'd noticed her adherence to my rule, and I nodded. "I said *he* could leave them for you, but I couldn't go in there."

I shot up. "You let him in my room?"

She gave me her are-you-crazy face. "What was I

supposed to do? I was the only one home! You always yell at me for going in there!"

My mouth hung open, my throat too dry to swallow. My planner. I had it open on my desk. I was sure of it. No. No, no, no.

Cameron sighed. "It was not a big deal. He went in for, like, a *second*. And I stood right by the door and waited! But he said he changed his mind and that he'd surprise you with the cookies later."

Why did you even become friends with me? he'd asked. I was too stunned—too sickened with embarrassment—to cry. He changed his mind because he saw that list. He saw that Ryan Chase was a part of my stupid plan. My stomach clenched, almost heaving in horror.

He knew. This whole time, his avoidance of me, those glances full of hurt—it wasn't about our fight. It was because he thought I'd used him to get to Ryan. And I had, hadn't I? At least at first.

"Did I do something wrong?" Cameron asked, her voice quiet now.

"No." My voice shook, even over that one syllable. I wanted to blink, like in *I Dream of Jeannie*, and magically change everything back. But it was so undoable. Heat spread across me like a fever. "No, you didn't. I did."

I pressed a pillow against my face. Could I apologize? The words seemed too mortifying to think, let alone speak out loud. No wonder he said he needed some time. If I found out he'd been using me to get to Tessa, I wouldn't have been able to even look at him.

And yet, he came to Grammy's wake. He said he wanted to start again. Even after that.

"Hey, Paige?"

"What?" I asked miserably. The pillow muffled the word.

"Do you kind of love Max?"

I pulled my face away from my pillow, so Cameron could see whatever tortured expression was on my face. "Why would you ask that?"

"No reason." She stood from my bed, giving me a half smile. "I just think you should, is all."

~

"You're sure you're up to this?" Morgan asked. We were sitting in the parking lot of the high school track with Kayleigh, all wearing identical red shirts. "Warrior Track," they read on the front. On the back, thick letters spelled "Chase." Ryan's mom had ordered them for all of our friends. In other words: I was actually such good friends with Ryan Chase that his mom ordered me a shirt with his name on it. If someone would have told me that at the beginning of the school year, I would have passed out in delight.

"I'm sure," I said. Instead of shutting down, I was

forcing myself out into the world, to see Ryan run in one of his last track meets of the year.

It was Tuesday, and I had just finished my second day of school since my grandmother died. Max walked with me after English both days. Our conversations were tentative— two wounded people trying to trust that the other was unarmed. But that was okay, for now—especially with how the tremors of losing my grandmother shook me. I needed to have my feet on solid ground before I could move forward.

Still, I hated the idea of being apart from Max without having time to spackle over the fractures in our friendship. I would leave for New York in June, and he would be in Italy for July and some of August. Maybe I'd e-mail him from New York, telling him everything—like I had all year. Maybe we could start from there.

Morgan, Kayleigh, and I walked toward the bleachers where Tessa was already sitting, her hair in two braids. She even had eye black smeared across her cheeks, making her look like an official fan. She and Malcolm were too busy clapping and cheering to see us at first. A few rows behind them, I spotted Clark sitting with one of his friends. Our eyes met, and I gave him a little wave. It would always be there—our quiet connection.

"Hey!" Tessa said.

"Well, look at you," I said, smiling at her. "Sports fan. Is Ryan up soon?"

"Yeah, you're just in time for the relay."

There was a pause, and I added, quietly, "Is he here?"

She knew exactly who I meant. "No. He's babysitting today."

Tessa shielded her eyes from the sun, searching for Ryan in the group of runners taking their places.

"Get 'em, Chase!" she yelled, and the gun fired.

I smiled over at Tessa. At the start of the year, I never would have guessed she'd let new people in—let alone make real friends out of Max and Ryan. But here she was, fan getup and all. Caring. When the baton made it to Ryan, we screamed and clapped until he crossed the finish line in first place. He slowed to a jog, catching his breath. After a moment, he looked up to the stands and gave us a wave.

We all waved back. And standing there with my friends, I felt a kind of contentment beneath the twinges of loss—a steadiness that I'd fought for.

"I'm gonna grab a drink," I told Tessa. "I'll be back before Tyler's race."

I trotted down the bleachers and ducked underneath them, taking a shortcut to the concessions. As I popped out on the other side, I bumped into someone. I didn't even see her until our shoulders connected: tall, athletic, brunette.

"Oh gosh, sorry," I said. I was looking at Leanne Woods, hidden in the shadow of the looming bleachers. Only, she didn't look quite like Leanne Woods, ex-girlfriend of Ryan Chase. She was as pretty as ever, and even up close, she didn't seem to have pores. But her eyes were glassy as she glanced over in Ryan's direction and wiped a finger under each lower lid. Once she did, she straightened up.

In fact, she looked me right in the eyes and said, "Hey, Paige."

I couldn't remember if I'd ever talked to Leanne before, and I was surprised that she knew my name. We weren't on bad terms, but we ran in completely different circles and even had different classes. I shoved my hands in my pockets. "Hey, Leanne."

She shifted, clutching her purse close to her side. "How are you?"

"I'm okay. How are you?"

She shrugged, her eyes wandering off in the distance again. I wasn't sure if our conversation was over, so I stood stupidly until she focused on me again. "I've seen you around with Max Watson a lot this year."

That I wasn't expecting. "Oh. Uh . . . yeah."

"You guys are cute together. We haven't always gotten along, but that's only because he's protective of Ryan. And I could be a real bitch to him." Leanne laughed ruefully, smoothing her makeup again.

"Max and I are actually just friends," I said. Or trying to be, these days.

"Too bad. Everyone would love to see you happy with someone, after everything with Aaron."

"Oh," I repeated, flustered. "That's, um. That's really nice, Leanne. Thanks."

She shrugged again. "It's true. Everyone wants good things for you."

At that point, I was completely dumbstruck. Ryan talked about this—how Leanne would say whatever she actually thought. I'd always assumed everyone in school felt nothing but pity. Leanne seemed to think I had a whole "everyone" of well-wishers.

Leanne's eyes found Ryan again and then slid over to Tessa. "He really likes her, doesn't he?"

I bit down on my lip. After how nice Leanne had just been to me, I hated to admit how unwavering Ryan had been in his pursuit of Tessa. Leanne read my silence as a 'yes,' and she sighed. "Of course he does. She's smart and gorgeous."

Because Leanne was being so open with me and because I had always wondered, the question jumped out of my mouth. "Why'd you end it with him anyway?"

"Ha," she said, her voice bitter. "I don't know. I felt trapped. I wanted to shake things up, take a risk. It was like life was too perfect, you know?"

"Not really," I said flatly.

"Well, it's not now. So great job, me." With one final

wipe of her eyes, she turned away. But she glanced back, over her shoulder. "Don't tell anyone, okay?"

Before I had a chance to agree, she walked away, headed toward the parking lot. Even though she was the one who broke up with Ryan, I felt for Leanne. Brokenheartedness is a sisterhood with involuntary membership. I'd keep her secret like I kept all the rest.

~

The last week of school felt like sleepwalking. I moved from class to class, taking pages full of notes to keep me sane. Teachers handed out final assignments, and I tried to pay attention. When thoughts of my grandmother sneaked in over class lectures, I focused on screen-writing school, which made me feel so connected to her. Or I added to my packing plan, even though one suitcase was already full.

Max slid me one note in class that week, and, even more than the sunshine bending through classroom windows, it felt like summer. New starts, warmer days—even if we were in different cities. At home, I glued the tiny paper airplane to the edge of my collage. Max's hopefulness and wonder had become a little piece of me, somehow. He belonged there, among all my other favorite things.

When I sat down to write thank-you notes, the ones for Mrs. Chase and Max's mom were easy enough. I expressed how grateful I was for their kindness—for the lasagna and flowers, respectively—and how much it meant, to be thought of. But I wrestled with how to thank Max for everything he had done for me. In the end, I chickened out and wrote a note almost identical to the others. I meant to pen the same sign-off—"Sincerely"—on Max's card, too, but my hand tried to write an *L*. An *L* and three other letters. It was true whether I wrote it or not. That's the confusing part of falling for a friend: I loved him the way I loved Tessa, Morgan, and Kayleigh—protectively and completely. There were just so many feelings layered over that foundation.

I stared over at my collage. *Love extra*, my grandmother had said. *Even if it means you hurt extra, too.* Fine, then. I threw my first note to Max in the trash and began again—truthfully this time. This was it: the one way I could say what I needed to.

Dear Max,

I made a plan at the start of this year, and I thought everything would be fine if I just stuck to it. There were some good ideas on there—ones that led me to QuizBowl and to screen-writing school. But other parts of my plan were misguided—things that I wasn't ready for or that just weren't right for me.

I realize now that I could never have planned
some of the best things that have happened
to me this year. One of them is you. I'll
always be grateful, for the cookies and
everything else.

Your friend,
Janie

Chapter Twenty-Six

With only a few minutes left in Thursday's class, Ms. Pepper dropped a bomb.

"As you all know," she said, pacing across the front of the room. "I have tried this year to force you all to get to know both literature and each other. So, your last project is a little unusual. Has anyone heard of PostSecret?"

There was a collective, indiscernible muttering from the class.

"For those of you who don't know," she explained, "PostSecret is a community art project. People anonymously send their deepest secrets, on postcards, to the man who runs the site, and he posts new ones online every week."

The class was abuzz, speculating what this had to do with our project.

"PostSecret epitomizes Keats's principle of truth and beauty for me," she continued over the noise of the class. "That's what I wanted for you this year: to see literature as a way to understand your fellow man, to find kernels of truth and the scopes of beauty. So, as a final effort on the behalf of that cause, you will each be creating an anonymous postcard for tomorrow. For display purposes."

The class became outright noisy, everyone protesting the idea of publicly disclosing their secrets. I was glad Max couldn't see my expression—the panic that accompanied the idea of confessing my one last secret.

"Now, before you freak out," Ms. Pepper said, raising her voice over the commotion. "Hear me out. There are four rules. First, the secret must be something that you have never told anyone. Secondly, so I don't get fired, please keep the secret reasonably school appropriate. I'll be screening them. Third, the secret can be about anything, as long as it is true. It doesn't have to be a dark or serious secret."

The release of tension from the class was audible, sighs and *whew*s.

"For example," Ms. Pepper offered. "I actually, genuinely wish that my dog, Grendel, could talk to me."

The class chuckled.

"Or . . ." She stood before us, her face solemn. "I could

write that I believe teenagers have much more to offer the world than most adults would have them think."

The class stayed silent. I think we all knew how truly she believed that.

"And, as for the last rule," she said, "turn them in to me tomorrow when you get to school. In the morning, people, okay? I'll mark you with a pass grade, and I'll put them up around the classroom after I screen them."

The bell went off overhead, and everyone scurried to collect their things.

"Sounds cool," I said to Max as I scooped up my binder and book from my desk. We walked into the flow of people in the hallway.

"Yeah," he agreed. "I'm kind of bummed that I might miss it."

"Oh?" I asked, tensing up. Was this the last time I would see him in English class? The last time I'd see him before he left for the summer? I thought I'd have more time.

"My mom and I are leaving for Florida tomorrow, so she's picking me up sometime after third period so we can go straight to the airport without leaving my car here."

"Ditching the last day of school, huh?" I tried to joke but I somehow managed to sound as disappointed as I felt.

"Yeah. She really wanted to get a vacation in before I leave for the summer." He used his free hand to push his glasses up, and I caught myself smiling at the familiar tic.

"Well . . . that sounds fun," I said. We were almost at the point where our paths diverged. *Now or never,* I thought. And, somehow, I felt the same surge of confidence that I had in our QuizBowl semifinal match. When you accept that you'll lose sometimes—and how freeing it is to keep trying anyway.

I stood in front of him, heart beating in my chest and throat and cheeks. "Last walk from class, I guess."

"I guess so," he said.

"Oh," I said, as if I'd forgotten. "Here. Thank-you notes. For . . . funeral stuff. I mailed Mrs. Chase's, but I figured I'd just hand off yours and your mom's in person."

"Oh," he repeated, taking the two white envelopes from me. "Okay. My mom makes me write these, too. Every Christmas and birthday since I could hold a pen."

We stopped at the spot where our directions split.

"Well," I said, "I'm really glad you had to switch seats with Ryan."

He smiled a little, staring down at his Chuck Taylors. "Yeah. Me, too."

"Otherwise I never would have known," I said, pausing to swallow, "that I'm such a Jane after all."

He looked down at me now, green eyes searching mine. *Come on, Max,* I wanted to scream. *I'm the Bennet sister who was too shy to admit her feelings.* Nothing registered on his face.

"Okay," I said, before embarrassment could creep in. "See you tomorrow, maybe."

"See ya," Max said.

∼

I came home that afternoon to a note from my mom, asking me to pick Cameron up at dance. My mom trusted me to drive her car, and she was on a date with my dad. Somehow, since the previous fall, this had become almost normal to me.

I picked Cameron up from dance at seven, and we drove in silence. Cameron turned the radio on after a few minutes, and I drummed my hands against the steering wheel, trying to think of a secret I could submit to Ms. Pepper. I'd opened up to so many people that I had no real secrets left. Sure, I hid my feelings for Max from him, but I'd made my peace with that. I'd had the guts to get us on the same page, and that was enough. Same page. Same Paige.

And suddenly, I knew what I had to do, what would inspire my secret. I thought of my face in the mirror at the beginning of the school year, the one that was so desperate for change. And it had changed. *I* had changed, and it was more than bangs and more than my parents' reconciliation or my grandmother's death. It was a new group of friends, it was freedom, learning, failing, grieving. It was getting back to my old self and defining a new self at the same time. There was only one thing waiting for me, standing between who I was and who I wanted to be. It had been here this whole time, but only now was I ready.

I turned the car into a sharp right.

Cameron glanced over at me. "Where are you going?"

I kept my focus on the road ahead of me. "There's something I have to do."

After a few more turns, I stopped the car at the Oakhurst Community Pool. The pool had opened for summer just a few days before, but the parking lot was nearly empty.

Cameron peered at me. "What the heck are you doing?"

I turned and looked at my sister, my eyes on hers. I didn't say anything. I didn't intentionally make an expression. I just let her read on my face that this was something that I needed to do.

When I opened my car door, she followed. I pulled our family pass out of my wallet and held it out as the lady at the desk reminded me they were about to close. There was only one person in the pool—an old man doing laps in the shallow end. The lifeguard wasn't even in his chair, just leaning against the snack bar with the occasional glance at the water. Cameron trailed behind me as I grabbed a towel that someone had left draped over a lounge chair, a cheap striped one with PROPERTY OF OAKHUST COMMUNITY POOL stamped onto it.

"Do you have your phone?" I looked at Cameron, who

363

still seemed to be game for whatever I was doing here. She nodded. "Can you take a picture?"

I didn't wait for an answer. I slipped off my shoes at the base of the high dive and steadied my hands against the railings. Before I could change my mind, I pressed my bare feet against the first rung, then the second, climbing higher. I was about halfway up when I paused, noticing how the cement framed the edges of the pool beneath me.

No, I told myself. I heard Max's voice, a chant in my mind: *Don't look down.*

When I reached the top, I wanted to crawl, to stay as near to the ground as possible. But I stood tall and put one foot in front of the other. The board gave a little, and I held my arms out to steady myself. So many pieces of my year swirled around me—Kayleigh, brave enough to demand better, and my dad, brave enough to try harder this time, and even Clark, brave enough to start looking for happiness again. And me, in my own way: brave enough to come this far. I gathered these moments inside of myself, and I took one last step forward.

The deep end was a clear, chemical blue beneath me, as still as glass. I closed my eyes for a moment, so I could see my grandmother's smiling face in my mind. She wasn't here now, but I would find a way to be okay anyway. When I opened my eyes again, I found Cameron looking up at me, shielding her eyes from the sinking sun.

She didn't encourage me; she didn't command me to just do it already. She stood waiting because Cameron, for all of her attitude, was still younger than me, still willing to follow my lead. I wanted to do this for both of us—because the divorce didn't take us down, and losing Aaron and my grandmother didn't take us down, and this wasn't going to take me down either.

There was a part of me that wanted to swan dive, to make an elegant reentry into my deepest fear. But I was new to this, and it didn't have to happen gracefully. It just had to happen.

This is it, I told myself, taking one more deep breath. And I jumped, feetfirst.

I was only airborne for a moment, but that single moment was long enough to feel terrified and certain at once. The freezing water rose to meet me, and the cold seemed to reach my internal organs. But I relaxed, letting myself sink in farther, and then, with confidence, I curled my arms against the water. I kicked my legs and ascended until my face broke through the surface. I took a deep breath, and then another.

It was the baptism of myself, the renewal of me and by me. The water felt, finally, like it could wash away the dust of the past, cleaning off the second skin of sadness. From here, I didn't have to do laps or perform a skilled crawl stroke. The point remained no matter what: I wasn't

sinking anymore. I had been floating, however precari-
ously, on the surface of my own grief. And it was time to
get out.

I climbed out of the pool, shuddering in my drenched
clothes. Cameron held the towel out to me, and I wrapped
it around my shoulders.

"I thought you were afraid of—" she began, but I cut
her off.

"I was."

She nodded at me, a look of understanding crossing her
face. She handed me her phone so I could examine the picture. My body was a blur, halfway between the high dive
and the water, and you couldn't see my face. But sure as
the blue sky beyond us, it was me. Cameron watched my
face closely as I shook my head. "I can't believe I just did
that."

My sister gave a hesitating smile. "I can."

That night, I plucked the claw machine cat off my bookshelf. I placed it gently in a shoebox, which I slid under my
bed. I couldn't bear to remove the framed picture of Aaron
and me. After all, he would always be a part of my history,
a part of me. So I moved the snapshot of us to a higher shelf,
where I could remember without being reminded every
single day.

In that space, next to my flower crown, I set the framed
photo of my grandmother, mid-spin in front of the Eiffel

Tower. I was going to be me, but I hoped that meant being a lot like her.

I put a huge strike through my plan: ~~5. Swim.~~

I'd done three things out of the five that had felt so impossible just months before, and so many other, smaller things that filled my life back up. I smiled at my new collage—but not because it was a representation of the girl I was now. No, that girl was changing moment by moment, and no static collection of images could capture that. I smiled because it showed the loves that glued me back together. The tiny lights that, together, led me home.

Finally, I uploaded the picture of me jumping into the pool, printed it on thick paper, and cut it into postcard size. I grasped a black Sharpie and wrote my secret—my truth—in thick letters across the infinite expanse of blue sky:

I am living my life now. Period.

Chapter Twenty-Seven

After I turned my secret in the next morning, I couldn't concentrate. There was no need to, really. The last day of school bent toward chaos, as teachers granted the leniency they'd withheld all year. It was class after class of games and "free days."

I almost hoped that Max wouldn't be in English class. I wouldn't have to wonder if he'd read my thank-you note and known what it meant. Besides, we'd left things in a good place, and I could ride out the whole summer on the hope of next year. But as I walked into my last day of fourth-period English, there he was. Butcher paper hung around the perimeter of the classroom, presumably covering everyone's secrets.

"Hey, girl," Max said from behind me.

"Hey," I said, smiling.

"How are you?"

"I'm good. You?"

"Good." It was the most basic of conversations, but our easy expressions changed the entire tone. We were happy to see each other, and we weren't trying to hide it. "I didn't think you'd be here."

"Me neither. My mom was supposed to be here already."

"Well, tell her I say hi. And I hope you have fun."

"I will—thanks."

The bell rang from behind us, signaling the start of class. The intercom beeped after the bell chimed for the final time, and a secretary's bored voice cut in. *Max Watson to the office, please. Max Watson to the office.*

"Have fun, buddy," Ryan called from the front of the classroom.

Ms. Pepper smiled. "See you next year, Max."

"See ya," he said. I turned around as he swung his backpack over his shoulder. He gave a wave to the class and moved the few steps toward the door. His eyes connected with mine, with one quick smile that was specifically for me.

And then he was gone. My last sight of him for months. The familiar ache in the left side of my chest returned. This time last year, I hadn't even known Max Watson. And now my life felt so much different, just because of a seat in a shared English class.

Ms. Pepper's voice cut into my thoughts. "I hope you've learned something about yourselves and each other this year. But, in one last-ditch effort to make sure that you did, I give you . . ."

She tore off the paper from the front of the room, then the back.

". . . your classmates' secrets."

There were definitely more than thirty, so I figured the other class's postcards must be up there, too. People were peering around, squinting at the secrets around them.

"Why are you just sitting there?" Ms. Pepper asked. "Mingle!"

Everyone leaped up from their seats, chattering to each other as they dispersed. I stood up slowly, after everyone else, because something had just occurred to me: one of these postcards would be Max's secret. How had I not thought of this before? Would I recognize it? My eyes flitted desperately over a line of postcards, hoping I would know.

I took a few steps closer to Ms. Pepper's desk, gaze darting around the secrets that hung closest to the front of the classroom.

"I put it next to the door," she said quietly, not looking up from her laptop, "in case you had an Elizabeth moment."

"What?" I asked.

"An Elizabeth moment," she repeated, her lips curling into a small smile as she studied the screen in front of her.

"Elizabeth?" I repeated stupidly. I wasn't sure what she meant.

She looked up. "Sometimes we get it wrong the first time. But you only have to get it right once."

"Get what right?"

She shrugged. "Anything."

Confused, I turned away, toward the door where she had directed me. Without another word, I pushed through everyone else, nearing the classroom door.

There it was. The top half of the cover of *Pride and Prejudice* cut into postcard form. I could hear my pulse in my ears, blocking out the chatter. The cover featured two girls in dresses, presumably Elizabeth and Jane Bennet. Across the bottom, it said, in scrawled handwriting I'd come to know so well—

I think I've loved you since that first day.

That simple. I stood there, only the postcard in focus, while the rest of the room blurred. I felt Morgan walk up by my left side.

"Whoa," she breathed, staring up at the wall, then at me.

I nodded, eyes still fixed on the wall.

"I knew it," she said, laughing incredulously. "I *knew* it. What are you going to do?"

I could feel her looking at me, and even though I didn't

respond, I knew the answer. I didn't know what Elizabeth Bennet would do, but I knew what I would do. I *knew* it because it was true, and it was beautiful: I was living my life now.

I ducked through my classmates, who were still staring up at postcards. In one quick motion, I pulled my own down from the wall. Before anyone could react, I slipped out the open door and into the empty hallway. I turned the corner and began to run desperately, my legs flying beneath me. It felt like breaking free, like snapping the last cords that tethered me. I didn't have to be defined by Aaron or by my crazy family or by any character in a book. I didn't need a plan. I was just me, Paige Elizabeth Hancock, and I was making it up as I went.

There wasn't a single person in sight, all the classroom doors closed with end-of-the-year parties inside. I turned another corner of locker-lined walls and saw a tall figure at the end of the hall. I skidded to a stop, my shoes squeaking against the floor.

"Max!" I yelled into the distance. But he wasn't leaving— wasn't moving away from me. He was waiting. He stood at the base of a small flight of stairs, just three or four steps near the front doors of the school. I should have felt so crazy and vulnerable, but I didn't. I was exactly where I was supposed to be.

Still clutching my postcard, I walked toward him— because this was never about getting there fast. This was about being sure of my steps forward. They always call it falling in love, but for me? It was also a choice.

I used to think it took me so long because, on some level, I wasn't quite ready to be with Max. But now I think I wasn't quite ready to be *me*. I needed to relearn myself, to venture into new friendships and nerdy after-school activities and my own mind. I needed to realize that I was one-fourth of a family that is not normal and that no family is normal. I needed to start seeing my sister as a person, so nearly a peer, and to watch my girlfriends grow, each in her own way, together. I needed to paddle without my grandmother, despite my sadness. I needed to let go of my unknowns about Aaron, to let peace fill the empty spaces.

Max stood waiting for me, not moving closer, and maybe he had been waiting for me to take the steps for myself this whole time. I was closing in, nearly reaching the three steps down that separated us. And I jumped.

I felt my feet leave the ground, the air beneath me. If I was scared, it was in that pulsing, breathless scared you feel when what you've just done might change your life forever. When you know that there's someone to catch you, and he does.

He set me down, and, the moment my feet hit the floor, I pressed up onto my toes and kissed him for the exact right reason: because I wanted to. Not because he was a silly crush or an item on a checklist. Because he was Max, plaid shirts and robots and airplanes and all.

When I dropped back to my heels, it was only because I had to do this all the way—no more overthinking. So I looked up at him, his rumpled dark hair and a flustered smile I knew so well. I almost laughed crazily—with both nervousness and relief—but instead I said, "I think I might love you, too."

"Oh, please." He rolled his eyes. "You do."

I opened my mouth to agree, but before I could, he kissed me again. It was the second of so many—the second of not enough.

He pulled back, looking at me as if he were about to say something. Before he could, I held my postcard up, the image of me midair, nearly touching the pool water.

There was no surprise in his smile—not even the tiniest lift of his eyebrows.

I pointed to the picture. "That's the *high dive*. Aren't you shocked?"

"Nope." He reached for my hand. My face reflected back in his glasses, but I looked past to his familiar green eyes. I could see both of us completely. "I knew you'd get here."

My hand clasped in his, I could not have known what would happen in the time that followed—how much we could love and hurt each other. How much we could change each other. But even if I could have seen a glimpse of my future, Max was right. Knowing what happens is different from knowing how it happens. And the getting there is the best part.

How will Paige and Max handle
their summer apart?
Read on to find out!

Dear Max,

Greetings from New York! (Imagine a skyline postcard, okay?)
Thanks for the Florida postcard—it got to me right before I left, and
I read it on the plane.

My parents are back at their hotel now, but they're not flying out
till tomorrow. It feels like I'm supposed to be with them. My room is
tiny, and my roommate's name is Eloise. I made a joke about how
we should be staying at the Plaza, not in a dorm. She looked at me
blankly, but I wasn't sure how to explain. How can you live your
whole life being named Eloise and not understand that reference? It
doesn't bode well for us.

I can't sleep. The ceiling looks too bare, which makes no sense
because there's nothing on my ceiling at home, either.

When our plane approached Manhattan this morning, I
pressed my face against the window like a little kid. We circled to
land, and I could see the park and Brooklyn, boats in the water,
everything. I couldn't look away, couldn't even blink. The island is
crammed so full, and now I'm in it—just a little speck. It doesn't
even feel real.

My sheets still smell like home. I didn't even realize before,
how distinct a scent it is—the laundry detergent and fabric
softener combo that my mom uses, I guess. I'm dreading the
day it fades.

How is it possible that you can be so thrilled to be somewhere and homesick at the same time?

New York, New York-ly yours,

Paige

Dear Paige,

I don't know, but I've been feeling that way for a week now. It's nice to see my mom so relaxed, and I'm trying to enjoy it while I can since I have a lot of long babysitting hours ahead of me before Italy. And Florida's beautiful, of course.

But there is decidedly not enough Paige—that is my number one criticism of Florida. I think I'll leave it in the rental house's guest book comments: *Enjoyed the beach access, comfortable bed, and extensive collection of books. Did not enjoy the egregious lack of Paige. Also didn't love the sunburn.*

Call tomorrow when you can!

Lobsterly yours,

Max

Dear Max,

I'm currently missing our phone date and typing this e-mail in my Drafts folder to send once I'm off the subway.

Okay, fine. Once I'm off the *wrong* subway. I was supposed to be home half an hour ago, but I got on the wrong line somewhere. I think I'm back on track, but maybe I live here now, with the rats.

Over a week in, and sometimes New York seems almost conquerable. Sometimes I fancy myself among the ranks of Carrie Bradshaw, Rachel Green, Liz Lemon—career girls making their way in the Big Apple. Then there are the days I can't seem to get anything right. Like taking the wrong train until I feel doomed to live in the sewers. Ugh, I'm so stupid.

Teenage Mutant Ninja Turtle-ly yours,

Paige

Dear Paige,

Well, cowabunga, dude. Look, I can't even *imagine* myself getting around Italy next month. I'm good with maps, but uh—I speak beginner Italian. SCUSI, AIUTAMI. That means "excuse me, help me." I think. But I do know the root language! Latin! . . . Something tells me that won't help much.

I'm glad to be home in Oakhurst, and on full-time nanny patrol. ("Manny" is such a dumb word.) I love those kids, but wow. That early-summer-break energy is something else. Everyone was hanging out at Ryan's house last night after I got off work, and I literally just fell asleep on the couch in the basement. Kayleigh and Morgan gave me the hardest time when I woke up.

They miss you. I miss you. And you'll figure out the subway in no time. You're the furthest thing from stupid—do you think I'd really date a stupid person? That's what I thought.

Stupidly yours though,

Max

Dear Max,

I know, I know—why am I still e-mailing you back even though we talked earlier? Haha. I did wind up walking to the library, and it's gorgeous. The quiet environment is helping me focus, actually. I'm studying two original pilot scripts against the actual episodes. I have to note where tweaks were made from the script, maybe improvised by actors. In other words, I'm watching TV at the library, and I'm SUPPOSED to be. How great. If only I didn't have to also take my improv class, which continues to be mortifying.

 I ran into a girl from my program outside the library, and she invited me to MoMA tomorrow night with some people. I guess it's free on Fridays! Doesn't that sound very New York? I'm going to have to Skype Tessa about what to wear!

Gallerina-ly yours,

Paige

Dear Paige,

Good thing I'm going to Italy later this summer! Gotta stay culturally engaged or you might become too sophisticated for your Podunk boyfriend. I'll start pronouncing "vase" as vahz. Seriously though, can't wait to hear about MoMA. We should go to the Indianapolis Museum of Art this fall. Consider it on the itinerary.

Midwesternly yours,

Max

Dear Max,

I mean, I am VERY sophisticated now. I wear lots of black. (Mostly because I keep spilling coffee on myself while rushing to class.) I live in the Village! (In a tiny dorm.) I know that "Houston" Street is pronounced HOW-stun. (My friend Maeve had to tell me.)

Also, there's an *itinerary*?

Poshly yours,

Paige

Dear Paige,

Well, the itinerary isn't, like, written out. But yeah, I have a mental list of things we should do together once we're home. Do you not? Hm. Step it up, Janie. Because not to brag, but my date ideas are GOOD. This is partially what I think about while making sandwiches for three kids or sitting at the pool with all the moms. It's no art museum, but my life is also very glamorous.

Manny McPhee-ly yours,

Max

Dear Max,

Tessa coming this weekend is the BEST SURPRISE EVER. I should have figured she'd get restless in Oakhurst and visit at some point, but I'm so excited. I can't wait for her to meet everyone here. And I have to admit—I can't WAIT to stay in her parents' hotel with her.

Taking a shower without flip-flops on! A big bed! Towels that someone else is going to wash!

But it feels so strange, that she's with you now and will be with me tomorrow. Why are you so tall and incompatible with carry-on regulations??

Are you sure you can't come too? I know you have babysitting, but could you take the weekend off? I know, I know.

Worth a shot-ly yours,

Paige

Dear Paige,

Curse my height! I'm so jealous, I can barely stand to be around Tessa.

But it'll be better this way, just the two of you. Even if I want to be there so badly that I actually tried to talk my mom into letting me visit you. She said, "Very funny, young man." She cited "lack of supervision" as the reason. This is what I get for being the kid of a teen mom. (Just kidding, Mom, if you're snooping in my e-mail.)

Very funnily yours,

Max

Dear Max,

I'm typing this from my phone in our room at the hotel. Tessa is conked out on her side of the California King, but I can't sleep.

Maybe I should have guessed after what you've told me about Laurel—how often she's been hanging out with Tess, but I didn't. And I'm so, so happy for Tessa. She cried when she told me, and I cried too. Not because I care that she's dating a girl, obviously. Because she's my best friend. I should have known. I felt so guilty. I mean, sure, I kind of wondered why she's never seen Ryan as more than a friend. But it never crossed my mind that she might be interested in dating girls. She told me she never really has been before but that Laurel is a "force of nature."

I just want to come home. I feel like a crappy best friend, being gone while she experiences this huge thing in her life. Suddenly, every cool thing about being here feels silly by comparison.

But she told me what you said to her. And that's the one thing that made me feel better. As much as I wish I could be in Oakhurst, I'm so lucky you're there to be as supportive to my best friend as I would have been. I just couldn't fall asleep until I told you that. Thank you.

Yours—luckily,

Paige

Dear Paige,

You don't have to thank me. I didn't do anything except tell her the truth. She and Laurel are great together. I've been trying to come up with a way to describe it to you, and I think it's an eye contact thing. We've all been over at Tessa's pool a lot. They're in the kitchen cutting up limes to put in seltzer water, and they stand close, heads together, laughing. Or they're talking in quiet voices in the loungers while the rest of us swim. But always, their eyes are locked. It's like they rotate around each other.

When Laurel tells a story, Tessa starts smiling way before she gets to the funny parts. Like she's not really grinning at the story at all. She's just grinning at Laurel's presence, as a whole person.

I think Tessa maybe looks at Laurel the way I look at you. Like she's discovered the greatest person ever. Like everything has clicked into place.

Clickedly yours,

Max

Dear Max,

Okay, I'm walking home to Indiana, starting tonight. Gonna pack some granola bars and an audiobook. Look for me in . . . four days?
    I miss you too much. I miss everything too much.

And I would walk 500 miles-ly yours,

Paige

Dear Paige,

I know. But it's true what they say about good things being worth the wait.
    Trust me. I have almost a year of experience in this area.

Patiently yours,

Max

Dear Max,

Fine, I'll stay in Manhattan.

But I'm going to kiss you senseless the minute you get home in August.

Impatiently yours,

Paige

Dear Paige,

Forget what I said! Start walking! Pack water! Plenty of people hike across four states!

Sensibly yours,

Max

Dear Max,

Tessa gave me the box from you before she left for the airport. When I pulled the airplanes out, I thought, *Hmm. I wonder why eleven. Is that just a good number for a string of paper airplanes? Max would know*, I figured.

It wasn't until Eloise helped me hang them above my bed that I saw the letters on the bottom. Now I stare up at them, flying across in the New York City streetlight as I'm trying to fall asleep, and you don't feel so far away.

It's funny that you made them out of maps, because I made the thing I sent back with Tessa last week way before I could have known.

Great-mindedly yours,

Paige

Dear Paige,

You're welcome. And I do—miss you, girl.

I love the map you sent back with Tessa. I do wonder how the nice people of Ohio and Pennsylvania would feel about being completely blacked out, just because one red heart in Indiana and one in New York hate being separated. Let's hope the NSA doesn't read this e-mail!

Aiding and abetting-ly yours,

Max

Dear Max,

They'll get over it. I'd say the world is just lucky I made that map before your trip to Italy. I'd cross out whole nations, whole continents, if they stood in our way.

    . . . this took a really menacing turn.

Villainously yours,

Paige

PS NSA, if you're reading this, that was a JOKE.

Dear the NSA,

Please feel free to peruse my Internet doings to confirm what Paige said. Recent searches include how old you have to be for a NASA Space Program, news about the new Star Wars movie, and online Latin Scrabble. And YEP, I do, in fact, have a Pinterest board for activities to do with the kids I babysit. I'm hardly a concern. I mean, my lack of coolness is a slight concern, but that's really my problem.

My girlfriend, on the other hand, has been visiting art galleries and wearing a lot of black, by her own admission. Sounds like prime heist material, just saying.

Innocently yours,

Max Watson, concerned citizen

Dear Max,

Sorry Maeve barged in during our Skype date last night. She had been dying to meet you, so she "coincidentally" came by my room when I said I'd be talking to you. She's a tricky one. But I'm glad you got to meet, since I know I've talked your ear off about her. And vice versa.

She liked you a lot. Anyway, thanks for being so charming to a surprise guest.

Classes are killing me this week. Everything is hitting at once. We don't really have tests or anything; we're just expected to write a lot. Which is why I wanted to do the program, of course. Even when it's hard, time-consuming work, getting to study dialogue is more fun than anything I've done in high school classes.

Nerdily yours,

Paige

Dear Paige,

More fun than Pepper's name quiz? I'm insulted!

And certainly no thanks needed about Maeve! I mean, I'm always charming, so it's no particular strain on me. And I'm glad she barged in. She seems as smart and funny as you've made her out to be. Are you guys still working on a pilot together? I can see why you make good writing partners.

We're going downtown to a new restaurant Laurel heard about. Apparently Ethiopian, which none of us has ever tried. I'll send you a pic when Ryan inevitably eats the spiciest food to show off and winds up crying from the heat.

More nerdily yours, let's be honest,

Max

Dear Max,

I know we just got off the phone, but something just. *happened*. I even tried to call and wake you up! But I have to get this all out. Okay. Are you sitting down?

I just met a celebrity. I know, I know—how? I told you I was going to bed, and I was. I met her in my dorm.

Well, not my dorm. In my RA Reagan's dorm. I locked myself out while brushing my teeth before bed, and when I knocked on Reagan's door, she yelled, "Who is it?"

"Paige!" I yelled back, feeling like an idiot. "I locked myself out of my room, and Eloise sleeps with her headphones in."

"Oh," she said. "Come in."

Since Reagan's the RA, she gets a room to herself, but there's still another single bed in there. I've been in her room before, and the bed's always bare—same as the dresser and desk.

Today, though, the bed had floral sheets. And a girl sitting on the bed, in a big T-shirt and pajama pants. Her hair was in a little blond ponytail.

And it was Lilah Montgomery. Just . . . sitting there. Staying there! Having a sleepover! In our dorm! What??

"Hello," she said.

This is what I said: "Uhhh . . . I . . ."

Reagan bailed me out. "Paige, this is my best friend, Dee."

"Hey," I said. That's when it clicked. Reagan. As in, "Riding top down with Reagan."

I said, "Uhh . . ."

Lilah Montgomery just smiled at me.

"Paige is cool," Reagan said. "She won't say anything."

"I won't!" I agreed.

"I'm not worried," said LILAH FREAKING MONTGOMERY. She INHERENTLY TRUSTED ME. (I mean, I'm telling YOU, but you're not going to tell anyone.)

I was such a loser! Why did I not prepare for this moment? I would have told her how much *Middle of Nowhere* meant to me during sophomore year when everything felt impossible.

After Reagan let me into my room, I just sat on the bed staring at the wall. One of the girls down the hall SWORE she saw Matt Finch leaving our building last week, but we didn't believe her. But I bet it was him!

I can't handle this.

Starstruckedly yours,

Paige

_____

Dear Paige,

Well. I never took you for the kind to have a celeb meltdown! That was completely hilarious. And I'm glad I was asleep because now I have this entire account saved in e-mail.

If Reagan is Lilah's best friend, why don't you just tell her to pass on your compliments? I'm sure she'd love to know how much her songs have meant to you.

Call if you're around! Packing is monotonous, and I'd like to hear about the excitement for myself.

Con affetto,

Massimo
(That's Italian me. I'm cramming!)

Dear Max,

By the time you read this, you'll be in ITALY, six hours ahead of me in New York and eating pasta while riding a Vespa. Or something. Anyway, I figured if I e-mailed now, you could e-mail me back by the time I get up.

So how was your flight? What are the dorms like? Do you like the other students so far? Is Florence as beautiful as it seems in pictures? Tell me everything.

Gelosamente yours,

Paige

(Does that mean "jealously" . . . ? I Googled it.)

Dear Paige,

The dorms are old and small, which is fine, because I don't plan on spending much time here. The other students seem to love

Latin and ancient art and history as much as (or more than!) I do, so I like them very much. Florence is surreally beautiful. I wish you could see it. I'm staring out the window, and it's all right there. Yet it feels like a backdrop or a movie set. On the way in, I ran my hand across the outside of the building just so I would believe it was real.

. . . This could be partially due to delirium from being awake for 24 hours. I'm going to have to tone it down before we start seeing art. I don't think they'd love me touching it to prove it's really there in front of me.

And are you kidding? The flight was awesome. My legs are too long for nine straight hours of plane seating, but being IN THE SKY? Improbable! It doesn't matter how many times I've done it. I look down at the clouds and think, I'm in the air!

(You knew that level of enthusiasm was coming. Baiting me, Janie.)

Improbably yours,

Max

Dear Max,

I'm surprised to find that leaving New York and my friends feels like *heartbreak*. I can't believe that, just last month, I didn't know the city or Maeve or any of the things I've learned in class. Those things feel essential to me. And yet, I never stopped missing Oakhurst and everyone at home? I'm taking a break from packing up my dorm, which felt so foreign when I moved in. Now I'll miss my little desk, the walk back home, a space that has become mine. I will not miss the communal dorm bathrooms.

It's so, so weird to think that I'll be moving into a dorm again a year from now. And I have no idea what college that dorm will be in. What state, even! Part of me wants to rush through this summer so we'll all be together for senior year. Another part is slamming the brakes, not ready to be a senior so soon.

What's it called when you feel nostalgia for something that isn't gone yet?

Overdramatically yours,

Paige

Dear Paige,

I think it's called being a teenager.

You know, my godfather, Oliver—the one we go to Florida with—is my mom's best friend from high school. Ryan's parents are high school sweethearts.

The idea of moving forward is hard. But everything you really need? You can take it with you.

Sagely yours,

Max

Dear Max,

Wise you are. (Yes, my film-nerd friends here made me marathon Star Wars with them this summer.)

I'm officially home and in my own bedroom! I've already gone swimming at Tessa's, so it feels like real summer now. Bring on the

Kemper's ice cream and Alcott's iced coffee. Wish you were here. Eat some extra gelato for me! Pistachio! Or butter pecan, if they have that.

Nuts for you,

(OMG SORRY THAT WAS UNFORGIVABLE)

Paige

Dear Paige,

Your friends "MADE YOU" marathon Star Wars?! Surely you meant they SHARED with you the gift of Star Wars.

Regardless of this lexical oversight, I did in fact eat extra gelato for you. See attached picture.

May the Force be with your TERRIBLE PUNS

Max

Dear Max,

Clearly the one on the right is pistachio, but I can't tell if the other one is chocolate or maybe espresso? Or toffee?

Okay, gotta go to the grocery store now and stock up.

I like you a lato,

(This time I'm NOT SORRY)

Paige

Dear Paige,

We just got back from our weekend trip to Rome, and I'm
still kind of stunned. I saw the Colosseum, the Pantheon,
the Trevi Fountain, the Roman Forum. I stood amid history,
which I guess is always true. I've just never been so aware
of it.

How frenzied will I be when I see Pompeii? It will be like you
meeting Lilah Montgomery!

The world is so old—and yet still so new. God—Italy is
turning me philosophical.

Rome-antically yours,

(Yep, I typed that. Dear God.)

Max

HEY GIRL!

It turns out that they really like watching sports here. In pubs.
It turns out that they'll serve you without checking ID.
It turns out I like beer more than I thought!!
Unrelated, you're my favorite and I miss you and you're so
pretty but you're even smarter and funnier than you are pretty,
which is like . . . WHAT? HOW?

Soberly* yours,

Max

*Lie

Dear Max,

Good morning, sunshine! How rough do YOU feel right now? Luckily Italy is supposed to have great coffee, because, boy, are you gonna need it.

Unrelated, you're my favorite too. Even drunk, you didn't misspell a single word!

Grammatically yours,

Paige

Dear Paige,

Help, everything is crooked. Beer is a FAIR-WEATHER FRIEND, let me tell you. This is the first time I've been glad you AREN'T here, because I look like I slept in a gutter.

In fact, I slept in my own bed—inexplicably in the wrong direction. Everything's coming back to me in pieces. I now recall that, at the pub last night, I showed my mates a picture of you. Yep. I'm THAT guy.

I'll call after I have minimum two espressos. And a lot of water. And . . . for some reason, I NEED hash browns. Or home fries. Somebody in this country better fry me some potatoes.

Hungoverly yours,

Max

Happy BIRTHDAYYY,
dear Paige,

HAPPY BIRTHDAY TO YOU! Just saying hi real quick! There are plenty of Internet cafés here in cosmopolitan Milan, even though the wifi's slow as hell on my phone. Hope you're having the best time with the girls.

It's killing me not to be there. Let's celebrate every holiday this year, okay? Like, full-blown. Halloween costumes, Christmas cookies, a fancy New Year's party, the cheesiest Valentine's Day. Like, literally cheese. Because eating cheese is the realest way to celebrate love.

And many more,

Max

Dear Max,

I might as well tell you before one of my traitor friends does. Tessa gave me the present from you at dinner, and I cried. Yep. It was just so thoughtful and I miss you so much that I burst into tears, in this fancy fondue restaurant. But I was 98% crying from happiness, so they all just kind of laughed at me. And ordered more cheese.

In other news, my parents got me a CAR. Well, more like I'm getting my dad's current car. He'll get a new one. I still can't believe it because . . . well, you know how they are. That means I really can get a job. New summer plans: become a working girl ASAP. Applications start tomorrow.

Skype when you get this? I'm going to set my alarm for 2 a.m. so I'll be online when you wake up.

Seventeenly yours,

Paige

Dear Max,

Job achievement unlocked. The fools at Cinema 12 have hired me. I thought about applying to Alcott's, but I like my odds at the Cinema: free movies, ice-cold AC in the summertime, and high chance of free candy. Besides, that's as close as I get to TV writing in Oakhurst, right? Movie watching. My first day is tomorrow.

But I have to wear a tuxedo. That's the one downside.

I can hear you laughing from here. I look ridiculous. I even made Kayleigh come over to see if she could style it somehow and make it cuter. She fell down laughing on my bed for three full minutes. I just stood there like a moron in my frumpy tuxedo while she wiped tears away.

Penguinly yours,

Paige

Dear Paige,

Something must be wrong with my computer because the e-mail you sent me doesn't seem to be loading a picture of you in the tuxedo. Please resend immediately!

Actually, just wear it for our Skype date!

Delightedly yours,

Max

Dear Max,

Ha. I've never even seen you in a tuxedo before, and I'm supposed to pony up a picture of myself in one? No way.

Dream on-ly yours,

Paige

Dear Paige,

Luckily for me, this weekend's excursion was to Milan. Attached is a picture of me in a tuxedo at the Armani store. After hearing that I was trying to impress my girlfriend, a kind salesman named Gionni let me try it on. He took the picture for me. I think it was a slow day for him, and I bought some cologne to be polite.

That was the deal, right? I showed you mine. Show me yours!

Bond, James Bond-ly yours,

Max

Dear Max,

I hate you.

Begrudgingly yours,

Paige

PS If you show this picture to anyone, I WILL make a shirt that says

PHANTOM MENACE IS THE BEST STAR WARS MOVIE and wear it when I'm out with you.

Dear Paige,

Ahahahaha. That is the cutest thing I've ever seen. Ever. And I once saw a baby hedgehog. I especially like the grumpy face—really adds to the overall look.

I feel obligated to inform you that middle school nerds will be falling in love with you this summer. They'll try not to stare as you sell them a ticket for yet another Marvel movie, wondering how this girl could make a tuxedo so cute. I have . . . some experience as a middle school nerd.

Please make sure they know you're already taken. By a high school nerd who, let's be honest, can really pull off a tux of his own. Is the Armani tux photo your desktop background? Oh my God, it IS, isn't it? I knew it.

Smugly yours,

Max

Dear Max,

I'm e-mailing you from the break room at the cinema.

Everything I own smells like stale popcorn. Eight hours is a really long time to be standing up.

This afternoon, I got yelled at by a middle-aged man who wanted to buy student tickets. I asked to see the student IDs, like I'm supposed to, and he screamed at me about taking online classes. Fortunately, one of the other employees stepped in for me as I panic-cried. I do that sometimes, with confrontation—just burst into tears. It always makes me wish I was like Tessa, who can make her face an impassive mask. And when the person is done being a jerk, she says something perfectly apathetic like, "Are you finished?" or "Well, that was . . . something."

Then, of course, I calmed down and got angry and thought of all the biting ways I could have responded. My coworker has assured me that I will have another opportunity. Great. Ugh.

Anyway, I miss you.

Popcorny and corny, but yours,

Paige

Dear Paige,

Alcott's is across the street—maybe it would help to take your breaks there? You could decompress. Step out of the stress for a moment. I know this would mean wearing a tuxedo to Alcott's, but hey—a lot of those books were written in a more formal era. And honestly, everything in life is black tie optional. I mean, you always have the *option* to wear a black tie. You'll look great. And there will be coffee!

Brilliantly yours,

Max

Dear Max,

You have all the good ideas. Alcott's breaks start tomorrow. And perfect timing—I just started reading Elena Ferrante to feel in touch with your Italian summer.

I know you're already on your way to Cinque Terre, so I searched a picture to imagine where you are.

UM. SCUSI MY FRANCESE but holy shit. I can't believe you're going to be in that dreamy little creamsicle city.

We have to break up. I'm too jealous.

Formerly yours,

Paige

Dear Max,

Okay, breakup off. You're still in Cinque Terre, and this no-Internet thing while you travel is no buona.

We went to see one of Laurel's friends play in a band tonight. I never told you this, but maybe you could tell: I was a little wary of Laurel at first. Tessa is just so hesitant to open up to new people, and I worried this magnetic girl—a stranger to me—would wind up hurting the person I love the most. And they'd already been together for a few weeks by the time I got home to Oakhurst.

But Laurel brings us all right into her world. Her friends are fantastic—well, you know. You've met them. The party was a blast, and she and Tessa are so natural together. Like that couple that's been together for years instead of a summer. I don't know how I ever imagined her with anyone *but* Laurel.

Seeing Tessa with her person breaks my heart with missing you. But it fills my heart in a way I never expected. What strange dichotomy.

Wholeheartedly yours,

Paige

Dear Paige,

I felt a bit like that before meeting Laurel too, so I can't even imagine how you must have felt. We were all protective—maybe Ryan most of all. I think some guys would have been sulky after it just didn't click with someone. But one night at Tessa's house, Laurel and Ryan were upstairs getting snacks, and I came up just in time to hear Ryan announce, "I like you."

"I like you, too," Laurel said.

But then he went serious, dropping his voice. "She's special."

"I know," Laurel said. It wasn't that she said it. It was how kindly she said it—as if she liked him more for telling her that.

Anyway, we just got back from Cinque Terre, and I can't even describe it in an e-mail. But I'll try on Skype later. Magical.

Oh, and I'm officially cheating on airplanes. With TRAINS. Not as glamorous as in old movies, but you get to see the country pass you by. Incredible.

Plus, one of the guys in my program brought travel Scrabble. I am among my PEOPLE.

R Y O S U,

Max

Dear Max,

Sorry I was so whiny about work yesterday. I shouldn't be using our limited Skype time to complain about Donna. (Ugh, DONNA, though. I'm still mad. But it's already helping, what you said—it IS sad that she loves lording power over teenagers.)

Besides her, though, I really love my coworkers. I went out with them again last night after work, and it's strange to have a friend group totally separate from our usual friends. They all seem a lot older than me, but they're funny and honest. It's like being in a club, where the initiation is suffering through Donna's antics.

They call you The Boyfriend. Apparently "he's in Italy for the summer" sounds like a lie. I've shown them pictures of us, but they still like to tease me about having an imaginary boyfriend.

Come home and prove them wrong, okay?

Non-imaginarily yours,

Paige

Dear Paige,

You okay today? I didn't want to ask you on video chat in case you didn't want to talk about it. So you can ignore this e-mail if you want—I really do understand. Just know I'm thinking about you, okay?

Yours,

Max

Dear Max,

I'm okay. Clark and I went to the rose garden this afternoon, and we swapped stories about Aaron. I don't have that many, but the ones I do have are easier to remember these days. It's strange—now that the loss isn't as raw, the good memories come back. Details. Clark has a lot more stories, of course, and I love hearing them. We both cried, but it was good. He would have liked it, the two of us there together.

Tessa brought ice cream over later, and I said, "Thanks, but

I'm really okay." She snorted and said, "Oh, good. Then I'll eat both of these."

I'd never have believed it if, two years ago, someone told me that I'd eventually be okay enough to truly *celebrate* Aaron's life. That I'd say I was okay and actually mean it.

Thanks for asking. Thanks for being cool about it.

You know what helped? Knowing you'll be home in a little over a week. We've been apart for over TWO MONTHS. Whose idea was that?

Almost in-personly yours,

Paige

Dear Paige,

You know what just hit me? That we have to go back to school shortly after I get home. Seems like you and I should get an extra week off since we've been learning all summer, right?

And we're not going back to any old Oakhurst classes. It's senior year. My mom has already scheduled time off for college visits . . . I'm fine. I'm fine. I'll just have to keep my inhaler in my pocket for the next year or so.

Casually yours,

Max

Dear Max,

I meant to tell you earlier—we've all been talking about trying to schedule in-state college visits together. Since she'll be visiting Laurel in Chicago anyway this fall, Tessa said we should all tag along to tour Chicago universities. I mean, good luck to me convincing my parents of that, but . . . worth a shot! There's more—IU, Notre Dame, Purdue. We figure we might as well go together. I'll fill you in later!

Collegiately yours,

Paige

Dear Paige,

You can tell me when I get home.
    IN THREE DAYS!! TRE GIORNI!! DIAVOLO SI!
    My itinerary: plane to Sicily, final sightseeing, transatlantic flight, YOU. This is probably the last time I'll have reliable Internet, so let me just say now that being apart has been both easier and harder than I thought it would be. I'm glad to have an e-mail archive of our summer apart. Perhaps not as traditional as the letters in 19th century English novels, but romantic to me all the same, Janie.
    It was one such 19th century English novelist who wrote, "Absence makes the heart grow fonder." And he was a moron. In my experience, absence makes the heart grow desperate.

Desperately yours,

Max

(I couldn't write to you all summer without trying to one-up your grumpy pal Darcy in the romance department. And you know what? NAILED IT.)

Acknowledgments

First and forever, thanks to my brilliant critique partner Bethany Robison, who coaxed this story off the shelf years ago and had no idea what she was getting into. Thanks for being my team, friend, and for letting me be yours. Special shout-out for that twenty-four-hour turnaround critique—a Hail Mary on my part and a heck of a catch on yours.

To my agent and friend Taylor Martindale, who has understood and championed this book since the first time we spoke: Thank you for carrying my stories forward with steady hands, clear vision, and relentless positivity. I'm so grateful you became a part of this story and a part of mine.

Mary Kate Castellani, this book needed you. Thank you for every fresh read and thoughtful round of insights, for having both a keen editorial mind and a knack for *Clueless* references, and for guiding me all the way through.

To Erica Barmash, Amanda Bartlett, Mary Kate Castellani (again), Beth Eller, Cristina Gilbert, Courtney Griffin, Bridget Hartzler, Melissa Kavonic, Linette Kim, Cindy Loh, Donna Mark, Lizzy Mason, Emily Ritter, Leah Schiano, Ilana Worrell, Brett Wright, and all the incredible humans who make up Team Bloomsbury: I'm so grateful for how smart, hardworking and passionate you are, but it's an extra pleasure to adore you all (and your cat-loving, sports-fan-ing, blazer-rocking, foodie ways) as much as I do. Thank you for everything.

So much love to every writer and industry friend who has shared bourbon and donuts, long e-mails, commiseration, encouragement, adventures, wisdom, celebrations, and late-night talks. You know who you are. *Thank you* for being who you are.

I'd particularly like to thank the booksellers, bloggers, librarians, readers, and teachers I've had the joy of interacting with this year. Your generosity and passion have been bright lights in my world.

Gratitude forever to my family and friends. There's this old piece of writing advice: write what you know. I write loving, complicated families and friends because *you* are what I know. Thank you for the long (champagne) brunches and late (champagne) dinners, for always answering the phone (even/especially when I'm at peak craziness), and for always picking me back up (metaphorically and also from the airport).

Finally, but always-ly, to J: Whether it's navigating grief or the open road, getting there is better with you by my side. Thank you for all the things I won't write here—the things we know by heart.